A Short Story Anthology

I0592858

OMENS

HARBINGERS OF FUTURE DAYS

TOWNSVILLE SPECULATIVE
FICTION

OMENS

Harbingers of Future Days

Copyright © 2017 Townsville Writers and Publishers Centre

ISBN :978-0-6480462-5-7

Created and Edited by Townsville Speculative Fiction
Formatted by Michael Huddlestone
Cover Design by Michael Huddlestone

Serenade Publishing
www.serenadepublishing.com

TABLE OF CONTENTS

OMEN
(Noun)

An event regarded as a portent of good or evil.
'the ghost's appearance was an ill omen'
'a rise in imports might be an omen of recovery'

[mass noun] Prophetic significance.
'the raven seemed a bird of evil omen'

(English Oxford Living Dictionaries, 2017)

FOREWORD

Throughout the centuries, humanity has taken meaning from objects and natural events as warnings foretelling the future. The fate of kingdoms and empires have long been entrusted to skilled soothsayers and oracles, and their ability to interpret these Omens. Can you fight against the prophecy of your death, even when your kingdom is divided? While some seek wisdom and guidance from the Omens, others instead tempt fate, using the omen against another for their own personal gain. Then there are those who cling tightly to superstitions, becoming puppets to their foreshadowing.

We search for meaning in the heavens, asking questions like: Is a red sky a sign of the return of the Gods or of the invasion of evil? Do the answers we seek exist in the heavens or should we be asking ourselves: What are the true effects on humans by the beautiful Aurora?

Not all Omens are the harbingers of death. Instead, some may give a new purpose to one's life. They show us that anyone can start again, even an aging killer for hire. How often have we looked to end it all, only to find the path to peace lies on the rippled light of the moon? There are times when the Omen is the only thing left behind when all else is forgotten. How many times in our history have we seen things or experienced a phenomenon that is quickly erased from our memory. What really happens when the clocks stop ticking?

We all have superstitions, things we believe passed down through time. Could we simply be wrong in their meaning? Does a broken mirror really mean seven years of bad luck, or are we meant to see what is on the other side? We no longer ask ourselves for whom does the Black Bell toll as traditions slowly disappear into folklore. Could it be that everything has a meaning and yet we are too oblivious to notice? Does it have to take the words "You are going to die" spelt out for us before we take heed?

As the modern world takes over, humanity has forgotten about Omens. The once revered soothsayers have since been labelled as crackpots who claim to find meaning from tea leaves and ravens. Will their time come again? Or will a day come to pass when their voices are silenced? Will it be that day, when their warnings and prophecies forgotten, when humanity misses the signs and start down the one-way road to extinction.

Join us as we explore the meanings buried deep within each of these Omens.

- Michael Huddlestone

Omens - A Poem

Lights in the sky, be they red or blue or green,
Whatever can those lights mean?
Is it the time that the fates come out to play?
The fates whom we wish would just go away.

The bright comet streaks across the sky
A light so bright that it hurts the eye.
Or is it an omen for good or ill
That seeks our attention for its will?

The black bell tolls three times in all
What does it mean, when you hear the call.
Ask not for whom the bell now tolls
For soon we see who has lost their souls.

Red sky in the morning, sailor take warning.
Red sky all day? Perhaps it is time to pray.
In a time when destiny is looking at you
You might want to remove yourself from view.

A mirror smashes to a thousand shards
Each sharp enough to leave you scarred
What will pain teach you today?
It certainly isn't enough to stay.

The path on the water created by the full moon
Stay off the path that will lead to your doom.
How many will try to lead you astray?
Enough to make it difficult to find your way.

Black cats and black birds sometimes cross your path,
They are to be avoided to keep from fate's wrath.
In general, if you see the colour black,
Perhaps it is time to take another tack.

Disturb the ancient dead
May lead to something you dread.
No babies born and some insanity
Will show up to plague humanity.

Blood stains a wedding dress,
Much to a bride's distress.
Though she may not know her fate,
Until after the vows, far too late.

Clocks all cease to move
Staying within a single groove.
What happens for the night?
It's guaranteed an ugly sight.

Red names scrawled on a wall,
Should cause a fright for one and all.
For the omens that red writing brings,
Tugs hard upon the heart strings.

The omens within, you will find,
Seldom bring with them peace of mind.
Dive in, my friend, read our tales,
Be strong and don't let your heart fail.

- Lynn Alford

The Light of the Silvery Moon
By Lynn Alford

O liver stood at the top of the beach. It was a perfect night; not a trace of breeze nor the smallest wisp of cloud blocked the sight of stars flickering in the dark heavens. Only the edges of the dark water moved, tiny waves pushing up the beach and back again. The bulk of the water was still, accurately reflecting the stars hovering above.

Oliver removed his shirt, neatly folded it, and placed it to one side of the path leading to the beach. Then he kicked off his shoes, placed a note on the shirt and his shoes on top of the note so it would not blow away.

Dearest Sally,
We met at the full moon six months ago.
You broke up with me last month when the moon was full.
With this full moon, I am gone.
Farewell with all my love.
Oliver

His preparations done, Oliver walked to the edge of the water and sat waiting. He watched as the full moon began its slow, deliberate ascent. The reflection of the moon on the water had tiny ripples marring the edges of the otherwise perfect sphere.

"Tonight, I'm going to do it," he promised himself. "Tonight, I'm going to walk into the water and keep walking until my strength fails. That will show everyone that I was serious."

He heaved a melodramatic sigh, which went unnoticed on the deserted beach. Sally had been the last decent thing in his life. He had quit school because he hated it. He couldn't keep any job, even a crappy one, for more than a couple of weeks. His 'friends' avoided him because he borrowed too much money without returning it. His father always referred to him as 'the failure of the family' which summed up their thoughts. There was nothing left.

By the time Oliver hauled himself to his feet, there was a sliver of clear sky separating the moon and the surface of the sea. Beneath the moon, there was a wide, silvery path extending from the horizon to the water lapping at his feet.

"So, the man in the moon has rolled out his special carpet for me. Well, it would be rude to ignore this invitation." He bowed toward the moon. "My dear sir, I'm coming. I'll be as quick as I can, so please be patient with me."

He checked up and down the beach but it was still deserted. There was no one to see him enter the water, so there would be no one alarmed when he failed to return.

He began wading into the water. It was slightly cooler than he'd prefer but not enough to deter him. Four steps later, Oliver tripped on a large unseen rock. He fell, hitting his head hard against a stone protruding just above the water line. His skull exploded with pain causing him to faint. He lay face down in the water for a long few moments, unable to move while his head throbbed with each heartbeat. Eventually, he pushed himself out of the sea and stood glaring at the traitorous water. Tripping on rocks was not part of the plan. He brushed his hand along his forehead where he had hit the rock, then examined his fingertips.

Well, at least it's not bleeding, he thought. *I hope that drowning is a relatively peaceful death. Being ripped apart by sharks would be far more painful. Or so I assume. Since I haven't experienced either, I can't be certain.*

Oliver started slogging toward the moon again. Each step was slow, fighting to move forward against the pressure of the knee deep water. Oliver ground his teeth as he struggled against the current trying to push him back to the shore.

Moments later, Oliver found that his steps were becoming easier, not harder as he would expect them to be. The water no longer reached his knees. In fact, the water was at ankle level again but the odd thing was that Oliver felt nothing under his feet. The sensation was like that of walking on a plush carpet, made of water instead of fibres.

Wait a minute, what on earth is going on here? Was that blow on the head worse than I thought? Oliver stopped walking when the thought occurred to him, closed his eyes and rubbed his temple with his fingers. When he opened his eyes, he was still standing on the path of moonlight. The scene ahead of him was unchanged, Oliver had to look back to prove to himself that the shoreline was well behind him.

He took another slow step further away from the shore. His foot did not sink into the cool water as far this time as it had last time. "I must be hallucinating. I definitely don't have the qualifications to walk on water. It looks like I'm in the water but I can't be. It's really weird that I can't even feel what I'm walking on."

Oliver took another step following the silvery path and then another. He was no longer even ankle deep, his feet stayed near the top of the sea. He watched his right foot as he took another slow step. His foot no longer broke the surface of the water, a small amount of fluid was displaced creating a dimple around his foot.

"This is too weird," he told himself. Talking to himself was a bad habit but at least he did not have to worry that someone would hear him. "I should be wading waist deep by now, not ankle deep. I'm going back."

With that thought, he tried to turn back. While walking forward had been perfectly easy and natural, turning around to face the shore proved impossible. No matter how he tried to turn, he could not make his feet change direction. As an experiment, he tried walking forward two steps and he had no difficulty. Next, he tried to step sideways off the silvery path. Oliver found that he could not force his feet to leave the path, he could go to either edge but no further.

"What the hell?" He shook his head. "I have to go forward, since I can't do anything else. This must be some crazy dream since I've never had trouble turning around before." Oliver heaved another sigh. "Damn, now I'm going to have to do this all again when I'm awake. Assuming that I have the courage to do this again."

Since he had little choice, Oliver continued to follow the path, wondering when the dream would end. He also began to wonder what would happen to the path when the moon was high in the sky. Would the path vanish at some point and leave him floundering in the waves? Would that be enough to wake him from this ridiculous dream?

He changed his pace along the path of moonlight with each step slightly quicker than the last. In an effort to wake himself from the dream, Oliver began jogging along the path. It was the first time he'd attempted anything faster than a walk in years. The effort only lasted a few minutes before he had to stop, lungs heaving to pull in enough air.

"What's it going to take to force myself out of this dream?" He wondering to himself as he stood still waiting for his breathing to return to normal.

The quiet of the night was shattered by loud splashing sounds coming toward the path. "Ho, traveller, why are you so slow?" Oliver turned his head to see a number of people riding dolphins, both men and women. He shook his head and blinked, positive that he was suffering another delusion but the dolphin riders were still there when he looked again. All of the people appeared quite young, with skin tones that varied from pale to dark.

The dolphins skipped through the water, leaping into the air for sheer joy. The dolphins and their riders swept past him, then leaped over the silvery path and raced back in the other direction. Oliver could not believe that the humans could ride the dolphins with such ease when the animals were jumping high out of the sea then plunging back down at great speed.

"We salute you, Walker," said one of the women. "Only a few can see and follow the path of the moon. Would you like to join us?"

Oliver blushed when he realised that he was staring at her breasts. "I'm sorry. I don't mean to be rude, but I don't understand. How can I join you?"

"It's simple." The woman smiled at Oliver then gave a piercing whistle. A dolphin swam up next to the path, only a few paces from him. "Here is your mount. You need only leave the light of the moon and climb on the dolphin. Come ride with us."

Oliver looked at the laughing people and their happy mounts. "I would love to but I can't leave the path. I tried to earlier but I couldn't."

The woman didn't answer because her mount gave a leap into the air then dived back into the sea. A moment later, a man slowed his mount by the path. "We can help you become one of us but this help is only available for a short time. When that time is gone, we must leave you to your fate."

Oliver took a small step toward the waiting dolphin. It felt like forever since he'd last had fun, and the riders appeared to enjoy their lives. "Can I stay with you for a time and leave later?"

"The magic of the path means that you may only leave it once." His dolphin leapt in the air and the man laughed as the animal returned to the water. "I am allowed to tell you that you cannot stop for long, only for brief pauses. The path only stretches forward, you will flounder and die if you turn around. Once you leave the path, you will never be able to walk along it again. There will be other places you may want to stay. But there are dangers as well, only the path can protect you from those dangers."

"If I stay with you, won't I regret never knowing what happens later on the path?"

"You would never ever care," he replied as his dolphin leapt over the path and landed on the other side with a loud splash. "We ride where we will and just enjoy."

Oliver took another small step toward the waiting dolphin. Then he stopped again, looking toward the horizon where the bright path beckoned him.

"If I stop now, perhaps I'll miss out on something even more wonderful. Though, these people are so full of happiness." Oliver looked one more time to the waiting dolphin and then to the horizon. He asked, "Are you sure that I can only choose once?"

"I am sure that once you leave the path, you will never be able to follow it again. But you will forget that you ever wanted to go further, if you stay with us." The man promised as he motioned toward the waiting dolphin.

Oliver watched the other riders laughing with joy as their dolphins played in the gentle waves. Desire to join them warred with curiosity of what else he might find. He closed his eyes and took a deep breath. "I would love to stay but I want to see what else exists. So, I will keep going." Oliver changed his path away from the waiting dolphin and back to the middle of the silver path.

"We wish you well, Walker." With a loud whistle, all the dolphin riders swam off leaving Oliver alone once again.

In a way, Oliver was glad that the dolphin riders were gone. The temptation to stay where he would be happy was immense. The last time he could remember laughing was that afternoon three months ago, he and Sally had played mini-golf. After the first two holes, they were seeing who took the most shots to sink the ball. They started laughing when it took each of them five shots to sink the par two. By the end of the course, Oliver found it hard to stop laughing long enough to hit the ball.

"Perhaps I should have stayed. Surely a life of joy would be as much as I could ever want. Then again, what other things might I see? If I stayed, I would never know." He glanced over his shoulder but the riders were no longer in sight.

There was no warning when a single lightning bolt struck a hundred metres to his left with an immediate roar of thunder. Oliver stopped, blind and deaf from the lightning strike worried if he might veer off the path if he kept moving while he couldn't see.

His ears were still ringing from the thunder when a second strike followed, a mere twenty five metres from the path. Oliver instinctively sidestepped to the right then stopped again, concerned that he might leave the path while blinded.

Lightning began striking all around him, another bolt hitting the water every few seconds. "I'm not supposed to stay still for long and I'm not supposed to leave the path. What can I do?" Oliver closed his eyes to help clear his vision, when he opened them again, he stared at the path just centimetres in front of his feet. He cupped his hands in front of his eyes to protect them from the blinding bursts of light then he resumed walking forward.

Oliver could only protect either his eyes or his ears and seeing the silver path was the only way that he could ensure that he stay on it. But the sharp cracks of thunder were causing his ears to ring, making Oliver wish he had some way to protect them as well.

As suddenly as the lightning had started, it stopped. It was some time later before Oliver let his hands drop back to his sides - he didn't want to risk having one last bolt blind him.

"Greetings, Walker." Oliver looked from left to right in puzzlement. He could see nothing nearby, certainly no people. So where was the voice coming from?

"Who are you? Where are you?" His voice quivered with anxiety as he scanned the horizon for the source of the voice. Oliver wasn't sure if his sight or hearing had returned to normal after the lightning.

"We are the ocean nymphs, I believe that your kind call us mermaids and mermen. We greet you, oh Walker. Look beneath your feet, if you wish to see us."

He looked down, and felt dizzy because the silvery path was semi-transparent under his feet. There he could see several people, well they looked like people barring the scales covering them from mid-torso to their broad flat tail. Small glowing fish swam around and between them, creating enough light for him to see beneath the water.

One part of his brain thought they were beautiful, while another part protested that he couldn't see their true features in the dim light. "Why did you speak to me? Do you want something?"

The nearest mermaid swam until she was near the surface of the water. She smiled, her lips parted to reveal her small, sharp teeth. Oliver was disturbed by the teeth, somehow that made her seem less human than either her scales or her tail. "We want you to join us. Come live with us under the sea."

He shivered. Why the hell had he thought death was a good idea? It was permanent, surely not the best way to deal with his problems. "Look, this may be a dream but even in a dream I can't live with you under the sea. I'll drown."

Oliver heard clicking noises reminiscent of dolphins which was the merfolk talking amongst themselves. "Those whom have followed the moon's path this far will not die but be transformed. You will become a merman, living under the oceans as we all do. You will never again be able to live on land, but it is a small price to pay."

Small price to pay? That idea confused Oliver. "Why would I want to live under the sea?"

The closest mermaid smiled and beckoned Oliver toward the edge of the path. "Why wouldn't you want to live as a merman? You will have forever to explore the mysteries of the deep; swim through the coral reefs, or amongst the great glaciers. There are underwater caves, cities that have been lost to the sea, and the lowest depths contain creatures the like of which you can never imagine. All that is under the sea is ours to know."

Oliver tilted his head as he remembered many a documentary of the strange creatures found under the sea. Then another memory struck him. "Can I find sunken ships? Would they still have their treasure?"

She laughed. "There are many ships at the bottom of the sea. Some have been buried under sand or coral, and many have been destroyed over time. Still some survive, you may explore those if you wish. But as for treasure, I do not understand."

"It's simple. Gold, silver, precious gems. Things that are worth a lot of money."

"Such things can be found but we only use them to decorate our homes. Money is not required by the merpeople." She motioned for Oliver to walk to edge of the path, the other merfolk waiting with her.

Oliver stayed at the centre of the path as he pondered his options. "They offer knowledge and a new life under the sea. It sounds interesting and yet is there something even better waiting for me further down the path? Will there be more danger, something worse than the lightning? If I choose to stay, I won't have to worry about that. Damn it, why can I only choose one?"

The mermaid's voice broke his train of thought. "If you wish to come, you must say so now. Our time this close to the surface draws to a close. We are creatures of the depths, not the shallows. Will you join us?"

"I'd like to but I don't think that I will join you. I don't think that I'm well suited to your life."

"We wish you well, Walker." The merfolk swam downward and were soon out of sight.

As he walked forward again, Oliver contemplated a life where money was unnecessary. He'd never had much money and when it came to Sally, what little he had was spent on dates. What jobs he could find were part time, minimum wage, and there was never much to spend. It was part of the reason that his friends avoided him, he'd never been good at returning the money he borrowed. He always intended to replay loans, but something more urgent would come up that he had to spend money on.

Time seemed to come to a halt for Oliver. The moon remained suspended at the same point in the sky. He could see nothing but the water and the silver path, leading onwards. With neither the riders nor the merpeople to talk to Oliver began to feel lonely. The infernal loneliness that he endured had always been part of his problem. Without his friends, without his girlfriend, without even co-workers, his days were too isolated. Now it was so quiet that he could hear his own breathing clearly.

As Oliver came out of his thoughts, he realised that the silvery path was much narrower than it had been. At the start, it had been wide enough for three people to walk abreast and now it was only wide enough for Oliver. The path was still obvious and straight but in the distance, a fog rose from the water obscuring both water and the path. Beyond the fog, Oliver could see nothing.

When Oliver reached the mist, he discovered that it was so thick that he could not even see his hand if he stretched his arm in front of his face. He was still trying to see his hand when he heard a new voice.

"Look, children. Tonight, we eat well. Isn't it so yummy?" The voice quavered like that of someone who had moved through old age and into ancient. The cackling laugh that followed did nothing to reassure Oliver that the crone meant well, nor did the sudden answering howls.

Even though the fog made it difficult, he looked around, trying to discover what was howling. The sounds were deep and resonate, not something that you would hear from a small creature. The beast had to be something large.

"What the hell? What can howl out here?"

A breeze tore a hole through the fog and Oliver could see burning red eyes level with his chest. Any remaining hope he was facing something small or innocuous died. He shuddered from head to foot when he heard howls from both sides.

The ancient quavering voice spoke once more. "Oh please, poppet, please run. My boys need some exercise and they will have so much fun hunting you."

Oliver took another step forward and the fog vanished. Now he could see the six huge beasts standing on either side of the path, their feet displacing the water as his did. An ancient, tiny female was riding the largest of the beasts. She licked her lips when his gaze reached her. "You do look so scrumptious, poppet. Please run." The crone cackled once more and Oliver shook from head to foot at the horrible sound.

"Who are you? What are those things?" He stared at the nearest beast. It was generally canine in shape but far larger than any dog or wolf he'd ever seen, the creature was half his height. It emitted a deep growl that thundered through Oliver's chest and made his hair stand on end. He could see drool dripping down the long sharp canines protruding from the creature's mouth. The upper canines were long enough that they would go clear through his arm if the beast bit him.

"I am Maude and these are my hellhounds. And you, dear poppet, are dinner."

Oliver's shivers deepened to massive shudders as one of the hellhounds approached. The rancid breath of the beast made him gag; he wanted to run when he heard the beast's teeth gnash together. Two things kept him giving in to his instincts: the first was that the crone wanted him to, the second was that he'd read it was a bad idea to run from canines because they instinctively hunt anything running away from them.

Oliver took three deep breaths, trying to control his shudders. "I don't think that being chased by hellhounds sounds like fun and I really don't want anyone to eat me. Why don't you go find someone else?"

"Oh poppet, it's been many years since we last had anyone come this far on the silver path, so you'll just have to do."

Three of the hellhounds rushed Oliver. He stood still, hoping that the magic of the path would protect him as long as he stayed within its bounds. The beasts ran toward him, baying and snarling but their huge paws never touched the silver path. When Oliver was positive that he was protected, he turned his back on Maude and her beasts and began walking once again.

It seemed to take hours before Oliver could no longer hear the angry howls of the hellhounds though they had not followed him along the path. Oliver was still shaken by how close the beasts could approach. If the path grew much narrower, his arms and shoulders might be outside of the protection. "If it has been years since they last had a meal, few must make it this far. I should have stayed with the merfolk or maybe the dolphin riders. That would have been a nice way to spend forever."

He sighed. If there was one thing that was clear, it was there was no going back. Besides, even if he could, he would have to pass the hellhounds and the lightning again. He had survived the encounters once, that was enough.

Oliver looked up to check where the moon might be and he noticed that a few stars seemed to be dancing in the sky. Not flashing, but an actual movement from one place to another. His pace slowed as he watched, entranced by the movement.

One of the stars flitted from the sky to just in front of him. It was not a true star, but a brilliant light about half the size of a human. "Oh, Walker, do you wish to become one of us? You too may join the great dance, burning with a bright light for as long as stars burn in the sky."

Oliver smiled as the joy of the dance filled his soul. He could not tell how near or far the lights were from him. Nor could did he have the words to truly describe them. But he was filled with admiration for the dancers. "You are beautiful and so is your dance. But is this the end of the moon's path? I have come so far."

The closest of the dancers giggled, its light bouncing with the sound. "Oh no, Walker. You have not yet reached the end of the path. Why would you care though? Come dance with us and forget all else."

Oliver watched some of the dancers, swirling through the air. While he had first thought that they were pure white, he now noticed that each dancer was a bright pastel. Oliver was fascinated by their movements. "How could I become like you? You are light itself."

"If you wish to join our dance, you will become like us. There is nothing to it, you must accept the light into your heart."

The beauty of the light and the dance tempted Oliver even more than the previous encounters had. "Do you know how far I have yet to go? What happens at the end?"

"How should we know? We have chosen this." The dancer paused in front of Oliver. "We know not where the path ends, come dance with us."

Oliver shifted his weight from left foot to the right foot and back. "Could I really become one of you?"

"You can but you must choose now. The great dance moves on."

Oliver closed his eyes as he thought. The great dance was a thing of beauty. He'd never been a dancer but if magic could make him a being of light, then magic could make him a dancer. But if he chose this, he'd never know what the end would be.

"Fare thee well, Walker." Oliver's eyes flew open at the faint sound of the dancer's voice. It was already too late; the lights had receded back into the sky. He sighed, if only he had more time.

Time had never been a friend to Oliver. He was always late to work. He struggled to finish assignments on time.

"I wish I'd chosen you. I can't imagine that anything would be better and I'm not sure I can cope much longer." Then he shrugged, he would find out. He couldn't stay here so it was time to move on.

Ahead, the silvery path looked different though Oliver wasn't quite sure what the difference was.

As he grew closer, he knew what the difference was. He could feel the heat and hear the crackling noises that meant fire. Great silver flames rose from the path, he could feel the heat from some distance away.

"Going back means that I die. Going sideways means that I die. But going forward into that? I think that will kill me too."

It seemed strange to Oliver that he'd begun the night with the intention of dying and now his desire was to live. It seemed unlikely that he was in a dream; he could smell the breath of the hellhound, he both saw and heard the lightning. If it were a dream, it was the most elaborate dream that he had ever had.

Oliver took a deep breath to prepare himself for the fire. He immediately began coughing, the hot air from the flames torturing his lungs. Three steps ... two steps ... one step.

His swimming trunks caught fire the moment he stepped on the flaming part of the path. The next step and his skin was flickering with the flames. Another step and every nerve in his body felt as though they too were engulfed by fire.

To either side was water, cool wonderful water. Oliver's body needed to be in water as it had never needed it before.

It took strength of will that Oliver didn't know he possessed to stay on the path. He screamed, surprised that his body was still capable of the action. Each step brought more agony, more pain than he'd ever imagined. He couldn't understand why he wasn't a pile of ash, a mere cinder on the silvery path.

Faster than the fire had begun, it ended. Oliver took a step and the flames vanished as if they had never been. He almost fell to his knees in relief, the pain that threatened to consume him was gone. He glanced down at himself and found that not a trace of fire was left. His clothes and hands were not even singed from the flames which was both a surprise and a relief.

He looked toward the silvery path, only to discover that he had almost reached the end. The path was cut, clearly and distinctly. Beyond was the pitch black of utter night. Oliver could see no sky, no stars, no water. From his current position, it was as though the universe itself stopped.

Still, he continued forward since he didn't have any other way to progress. With each step, the blackness of the end grew closer.

Then he reached the place where the silver path stopped and the blackness began. Oliver took a deep breath before moving forward again, only to realise that he hadn't been breathing regularly for some time. He wondered if his heart still beat. Did it matter in the end? He thought he lived, perhaps that was all that was important.

Oliver took the last stride forward and what had been pitch black a moment ago came to life in a rainbow of colours. "Welcome." "Greetings and be welcome." "Welcome home." A swirl of voices surrounded Oliver. He blinked to discover that he was surrounded by the most beautiful people he had ever seen; not a flaw, not a blemish to be seen.

He took a step backward, away from the gorgeous people that he saw. "I don't belong here. I am not worthy of being in your company."

"You have earned your place here. Welcome home." A beautiful woman hugged Oliver then kissed him full on the mouth. A second woman followed the first and Oliver stood speechless. Then a man did the same, which startled Oliver. When he looked around, there were many perfect people all waiting to greet him. He had never felt such an outpouring of affection.

"What happens now?"

"Whatever you like," replied the man who had just kissed Oliver.

He stepped aside and a woman took his place. "We play, we dance, we sing. You have long since left your body behind. No need to worry about mortal concerns."

"How will I remember all your names?"

"We are the children of the moon and you are one of us. We have no need for names, you'll see."

The spirit that had once been Oliver nodded once. The last of his concerns vanished as he became one of the children.

The Middle Fate
By Tamantha Elliot

Meow.

Meow.

"Shoo."

Meow.

"Piss off."

The cat looked up with narrowed eyes.

Meow.

"You're standing in the middle of the road. Go left. Go right. Literally go anywhere else."

Meow.

"Fucking hell."

I nudged the cat with my toe. That earned me a hiss but the little black fluffy mass wasn't moving. I crouched down, bringing myself eye to eye.

"You're a little shit."

The cat sniffed my nose.

Meow.

With a stretch, it padded its way off the road.

"What the fuck?" I yelled after it. The cat didn't care. It just kept trotting along, straight into the pale arms of Attie.

"Nice try," she said, scratching the cat under the chin. It purred. Rude. Attie walked across the road, placing the cat back in the middle, directly in front of me again. Attie checked her watch and with a tap on my shoulder dragged me back across the road.

Meow.

The car sped down the road, the pair inside arguing, the music blaring.

Meow.

I didn't bother getting up. Lying on my back, looking up at the stars.

Meow.

Brakes squealed, the car swerved. BANG. Lights flicked on in a nearby house. The cat sniffed my nose again.

Meow.

"Are you proud of yourself?"

Meow.

"I'm just doing my job," Attie said.

"I was talking to the cat," I said, reaching up to give the creature a scratch behind its ears. The sound of slamming doors and rushing neighbours sent it running.

"That cat was doing its job, too," Attie said. "In fact the only one not doing their job here is you."

"I got bored," I said, sitting up, watching the carnage. I could hear the sound of distant sirens.

"Go home Sis, this isn't your jurisdiction," Attie said, walking onto the road, eyes ahead on the fast deteriorating threads hanging from the car, unnoticed by the gathering mass. Her gold scissors glittered in the car's headlights. I dusted myself off and removed the leaves from my hair. I turned my back on Attie, and started down the road, ducking and weaving between the golden strings of every new spectator, leaving the car and the pole it was wrapped around behind, the people accumulating in their pyjamas and the approaching emergency vehicles. I passed a young girl clutching a black cat. I paid no attention to them.

"Watch yourself, Miss Lachesis," the child said. "It's not your job to save them. We don't take too kindly to those who deviate." I looked back over my shoulder, eyes locking with hers. A parent called her back inside frantically. She tore her gaze away, running back inside. Only the cat kept its attention on me. Not that that's anything new really. Cats are interesting creatures, did you kno-

"Miss Lachesis," the woman who had yet to bother to introduce herself was tapping her nails against her desk. From the moment I sat across from her and the man - the man who presented himself just threateningly enough to enforce the seriousness of the situation, but not quite threateningly enough to constitute a defensive reaction - both all nicely pressed and suited up, she'd made her dislike towards me evident. I couldn't tell if this was a predisposition brought in from outside the courtroom, or if it had something to do with the fact that I sat down, looked her in the eye and smirked. Maybe both. "Is there relevance to this little…" she waved at the ghostly vision of myself, frozen in time, staring at a cat, "…story of yours?"

"Well it does lose some of its artistic meaning when you cut me off mid-narration ma'am."

"Miss Lachesis, please answer the question," the judge said, holding a hand up to the woman. She was wearing one hell of a foul glare.

"It must have some relevance. One of you possessed a perfectly fine child and turned it creepy." I waved towards the ghostly child projected in the centre of the court, mid run towards the house. "Look at her. She was terrifying enough before that. Both myself and that poor cat have been permanently scarred by that experience. Do you know how much it costs to put a cat through therapy?"

"Miss Lachesis, I don't think you quite grasp the seriousness of this situation," the judge said. He hadn't bothered to introduce himself either. Rude!

"With all due respect sir, I am taking this incredibly seriously. I find it disgusting that child possession is not illegal."

"Miss Lachesis, you have just indicated to the court that you did in fact receive warnings from the council."

"That's another thing," I said, leaning back in my chair, the wheels creaking slightly as I rolled at a snail's pace away. "That is the most bullshit excuse for a warning I have ever received in my life. You should really do something about your legal team. Oh wait. That's you guys. Makes sense. I'm actually surprised you sent professionals to arrest me. I was expecting an army of little fucking creepy possessed children." I leant forward, dragging my chair and I back to prime real estate in front of my desk. The wheels and their creaky-ness sent an ear-assaulting screech through the courtroom.

"Miss Lachesis," the man leant forward in his podium. "We all have better things to do, if you would please proceed with your account."

I waved my hand and the misty street blew from our view. The child and the cat wafted away one after the other. I tapped a few times on my desk. "You might have better things to do, but I most certainly don't."

Harvey Brooks was a fairly uninteresting man by most descriptions. He lived alone. Well not entirely alone, he had a dog. But a dog isn't a person. A dog generally doesn't talk back to you, they are terrible cooks, and you can't exactly teach them to play darts.

While a dog is of course a very suitable companion, human interaction is often required and unfortunately, it was something that Harvey got very little of. Unsurprisingly, most people found him dull. It only took one or two conversations to unravel the root of all Harvey's problems. In fact, Harvey was to remain uninteresting until the very day that his car would hit a truck at alarming speed, removing his head from his body – after that Harvey would become a very interesting person. A very dead, decapitated person, yes, but very interesting.

Harvey, of course, didn't know that his head was to be separated from his body. No, in his mind his head was going to stay very firmly attached. He was going to meet a nice girl – one his parents liked, and more importantly, one who liked his parents. They were going to have a charming life with exactly two kids and many dogs. Everything would be wonderful. The only time imaginary Harvey was going to be lying dead in a coffin would be after a very extended life. A hundred years of life preferably.

"Is this going somewhere Miss Lachesis?" The judge looked at me through the misty form of Harvey's aged weeping imaginary children.

"Sir, I am merely setting the scene," I said, leaning against the misty coffin holding dear dead imaginary Harvey

"Miss Lachesis, this is a trial not a play."

"With all due respect sir," I said ducking between the frozen figures of Harvey's fake family, looking over his podium on my tippy toes. "You asked me to tell my version of events, you did not specify through which means I was to perform that task."

"Most people would take to the stand and state their testimony," the woman muttered.

"Yes, but if you are going to be forced to rest your asses in uncomfortable chairs for hours on end listening to me speak, I might as well make it entertaining. I am even providing visuals. I am giving you all a show that you will never forget."

"Or, Miss Lachesis, you could make it quick."

"Sorry, am I mistaken. I believe you were present when they read the rather long list of crimes of which I have been accused. This trial won't be quick and as I am under oath, I must say that I intend to draw this out to excruciating lengths, because, well, I like the attention." I pushed myself away from their fancy little podium and winked at my sisters. Attie sat impatiently, her resting bitch face even more scowly than usual. Clo rolled her eyes, shaking her head in a way that only the oldest could pull off.

"Do you have siblings, sir?" I asked, twirling back to face him. He looked over at the woman with a confused air. "It's a simple enough question." I didn't even let him answer, "Because let me tell you something about being the other one. Your parents have a child. The first child. Their first child. And she's perfect their pride and joy." The stationary forms of Harvey and his family blew away, leaving the image of the happy little family. "Watch as they read a deeper meaning into everything she does - every blink, every laugh. One day she'll grow up to be important, a 'creator of life' or some bullshit like that. Then they have another one. Another perfect little girl, and of course the attention deviates from the oldest to the new child slightly as child number one has already had her first words, taken her first steps. Dear child number two is a blank slate ready for learning and, well, if they did so well with the first then, surely, they can keep going. So, cue child number three. And Gods is she pure perfection, the apple of everybody's eye. It's almost as if the universe spins its course around her." I growled, the image of the family spun dramatically, centring on little baby number three. "Child number one is a little jealous, now old enough to comprehend the emotion but she's also adapted what she'll go on to call 'good leadership qualities' which is code for being a bossy little cow." I spat the words over my shoulder. "Child number three doesn't care because she's the new perfect little bubble in everyone's world. So, what happens to child number two? She becomes the other one. Nothing too special. Just there. She'll get a job that no one cares about, all her achievements ignored. Like, come on, you all heard that one of us fucked up. When I walked in I saw it on all your faces: *who the fuck is she?* You know Clotho, you know Atropos. You know who they are, you know what they do. The beginning, the end. Then there's me. Child number two. No one has a clue who I am. I'm just a poor undermined young woman desperate for attention."

A chair scraped across the floor at an alarming speed behind me. It hit the floor, wood against wood echoing through the court.

"Are you honestly trying to blame us for your behaviour?" Attie yelled. I didn't bother looking at her – I knew exactly what she would be doing. Her posture. Her expression.

"I wasn't blaming but, hey, if you want to confess – would that stand up in court?" I asked the judge. He ignored me.

"Miss Atropos, sit back down," he boomed. I smirked. His angry gaze turned to me. "Miss Lachesis, it would do you good to not antagonise the people in this courtroom."

"I mean, I guess I can try. No promises of course. It is a family matter after all." I sat down on my desk, "Obviously, though, I'd find it awfully difficult to antagonise anyone while telling you all about dear Harvey Brooks"

"Fine, Miss Lachesis," the woman said. "You may proceed."

"Are you sure?" I said, clapping my hands together, leaning closer – centimetres from slipping off my desk. "Not going to cut off my narration again?" The judge gave me a warning look. I stole one more glance at my sisters. Clo was pulling the exact same face. A beautiful symmetry of pissed-offedness. My eyes slid off their faces onto the floor, the single gold thread looping and zigzagging down the aisle. I clicked my tongue against the roof of my mouth, spinning my attention back to the front of the court. I leapt off my desk, swinging off one of those stupid pillars on my way back to my stage. I pushed myself forth into the misty formation of Harvey Brooks' house, the construct building its way around me.

Little boring Harvey Brooks upstairs asleep in his bed. Little boring Harvey Brooks' dog – Spot – I fucking kid you not – asleep in his bed. All was still. God, this is starting to sound like a Christmas story. 'Not a creature was stirring, not even a mouse.' Which of course is bullshit because there were plenty, and are always plenty, of insects and other creepy crawlies moving around in every house. Right, my testimony. I had no reason to be in the uninspired house of Harvey Brooks, but I was. Kinda. I was at the front door. It was almost like a scene from a Rom-Com. I was the pretty young person standing in front of the door unsure whether or not to knock. Or in my case, unsure whether or not to break and enter. Only mildly different. I put my hand on the handle, tapping my finger on the cool metal. An owl hooted. I leapt back from the door. Probably a signifier that I knew that I really shouldn't have been doing what I was about to do.

The well-suited woman straightened her posture, opening her mouth. I knew that the whole not interrupting my narration thing wouldn't last long. "That's only an admission of guilt towards the breaking and entering. Not the whole other thing." I waved my hands in a sarcastic show of jazz hands. "I will admit that I shouldn't have broken into Harvey Brooks' home. However, we can all agree that it is a morally grey area when you are a being of somewhat omnipotent nature. Locked doors are like the 'do not tumble dry' equivalent. We are 'all seeing' and all that shit. All I did was enter a private residence outside the parameters of my job – I didn't even break. All I did was enter." The woman glared at me.

Anyway.

I straightened my clothing. Checking around for any children who may have seen my embarrassment. My eyes fell on the dickhead sitting on the roof. Staring at me.

"Really?" I hissed up at the owl. It tilted its head. "Was that really necessary?" It just hooted at me. I felt my eyes rolling before I even registered that it was happening. With a determined glare directly towards the bird I placed my hand on the door handle and turned. There was no resistance. I slipped into Harvey Brooks' house unseen by all but one asshole of an owl living on his roof. Of all the houses in the world to break into I had managed to choose the most boring one possible. Like he could have at least had a cool state-of-the-art gaming system, or coffee machine, or super fancy toaster. Anything. But no, his house was minimalistic. Who the fuck has shelves with nothing on them. The whole purpose of a shelf is that it holds things. How can you not have one decorative anything? Not a single porcelain pig or tiny ship or urn holding the ashes of some random family member. On top of that the colour scheme resembled that of a hospital. Like come on. Who wants to wake up every morning and go through as extensive mental journey of their last 24 hours trying to work out how they were hospitalised only to remember 'oh that's right. I live in a stupidly coloured house with shelves that DO NOT HOLD THINGS!'

There was a cough from the podium. Almost as if they'd given up on actually interrupting me with words now. They'd moved onto sounds of disappointment. I flicked my eyes up from the interior of Harvey's home, meeting the pure detest seeping from the gaze of the judge, paired with the growing hatred building up from his well-dressed neighbouring lawyer.

"I'm sorry sir, I am just very passionate about shelves," I said running my hand across the nearest bare one.

"We can see that Miss Lachesis," the judge said. The stenographer was hitting the keys on his little archaic typewriter with such a fury that I could only assume that he was putting my rant into capital letters. "But we are not asking you about the interior decorating, or lack thereof, of Mr Brooks."

I let out a loud sigh. "Fine. No more talk of shelves," I said, holding my hands up. "But I'll have you know that Harvey's ridiculously decorated house is one of the most interesting parts of him."

The scene inside Harvey's house sped up. As if on fast forward it flew through boring room after boring room, with me keeping my gaze on the judge as if we were in some sort of staring contest in which only one competitor was aware that they were competing. The wispy blue versions of Harvey's walls ceased their movement.

Much exploring led me to the conclusion that someone had recently robbed Harvey and he had yet to notice it, or he was in fact the single least interesting person to walk this planet. I found myself standing at his back door, staring out into his backyard. Little Spot wrapped up, snug in his bed next to the little doggy door. I kicked it with my foot. The door, not the dog. I am not a monster. It flapped back and forth. Spot stirred ever so slightly. Worst guard dog ever. I reassessed the back yard, surprised to find that Harvey Brooks actually had grass — like real grass, not astro-turf or aesthetically appealing pebbles. What am I saying? People with aesthetically appealing pebbles put things on their shelves. And sprouting from that grass was an actual, legit tree. I quietly slid open the glass door, once again finding no resistance. As I walked across the patio Spot finally decided to do his guard dog duty. Bark, bark, barking at the open door. I waved off the racket. I ran my hands across the lowest branch of the tree. It was a little more than a stick. Freshly planted. You could barely call it a tree, but at least it was something remotely ornamental. A light flicked on upstairs. Spot was still barking at the doorway. Harvey Brooks clomped down the stairs, muttering under his breath. Rubbing his eyes as he walked, he stopped dead. Looking at the open doorway, then down at his dog, then at the doorway again. As Harvey Brooks shut and locked his back door, grabbed a pestle and his phone, I snuck into his pantry. As Harvey Brooks called the police, I rummaged through his spice cabinet. As Spot growled at the pantry door, Harvey Brooks paused, pestle in hand swinging the pantry door open. I came face to face with Harvey Brooks for the first time. Harvey Brooks came face to face with an empty space. While Harvey Brooks rattled off his address to the operator I snuck back out the back door, leaving Spot barking at nothing once more. As Harvey Brooks looked at the door he was sure he'd closed, I began pouring copious amounts of salt onto the root system of his new cedar tree.

"So, Miss Lachesis," the woman said, walking through the image of the backyard, "you are telling the court that you broke into Mr Brooks' house and salted his tree?"

"Was that supposed to sound oddly sexual Ms. Wonttellmehername?" I said, making sure to circle away from her, "Because I can assure you that unlike some other beings that have entered these courts I do not spend my time screwing mortals. Besides, last time I checked tree murder wasn't illegal unless a) the tree had previously been a person, or b) the tree possessed some semblance of sentience. Both of which do not apply to the cedar in question."

"Is everything a joke to you Miss Lachesis?" She crossed her arms and leant against my desk.

"That's a good question," I said, "perhaps we should explore it further. Add it to the list of charges, Judge. Frivolous will slot in nicely between narcissistic and self-absorbed in the grand list of things people have called me in an attempt to offend me." I patted her on the shoulder, "but of course, we should really finish up my testimony for my first charge. I can't believe you would hold up justice like this, Ms. Wonttellmehername."

"It's Eunomia. Ms. Eunomia"

"Wonderful. As I am under oath I will politely inform you that I do not intend to remember that." I smiled at her, pushing her off my stage in the nicest way possible.

The police showed up. Boring. The police took Harvey's statement. Boring. The police found no signs of forced entry. Booooring. The police found nothing missing, partly because they didn't think to check Harvey Brook's salt supply and partly because Harvey had literally nothing interesting to steal. The police left Harvey Brooks' house. Spot stared at me through the door, not daring to venture into the backyard. Harvey Brooks slept shittily with a pestle resting on his bedside table. I sat next to the dying cedar tree, working from someone else's home. Ruler in hand, cross-legged in the grass, measuring. Golden thread, upon golden thread. Measuring. Measuring. Measuring. Do you know how boring constant measuring is? Like, I can't even begin to explain how boring a legit eternity of just measuring shit is. Measuring! I'm not even good at maths.

Then, Harvey Brooks didn't care that I'd killed his cedar. He just stood there unimpressed in his mediocre suit and travel coffee cup. His moderately priced, over polished shoes stood on top of my strings. That man tracked mud across perfectly straight and cut pure gold threads that I had been measuring for hours and I still continued my endeavour. That is the heroism that I cannot believe I am here being persecuted for today. He didn't stare at the tree in horror. He didn't lock himself inside. He looked at the dead tree. Then he looked at his watch. He muttered something about sorting it out when he got home and scurried off to work. He was certainly the sort of man who would scurry. I decided to move my measuring into Harvey's kitchen, where hopefully no one would stand on my hard work. Spot started howling as I entered the house. I growled at him.

"He's not even here," I said, stepping over the little furry thing. "'If you are going to be an ominous harbinger, at least do your job when he's home." I placed the salt back

into the pantry and started work on making myself a coffee. "Not that he'd actually think anything of it. Who acts so nonchalantly about a dead cedar in their backyard?" I searched through the fridge for anything but skim. No luck. "Like that's slightly foreboding right? A perfectly healthy tree suddenly dead." Spot growled at me, "I know it was me," I said, looking out at the dead tree. I started opening drawers. In addition to poor colour choices, and a crime against interior decorators as a whole, Harvey had absolutely no flow to his kitchen. There was no logical placement to anything. Like nothing at all. The kettle was boiling. Screaming at me. But I was opening cupboards and drawers here, there and everywhere in search of a mug. Guess what everyone? Harvey Brooks has no fucking mugs. Like in his entire house. I have since had a lot of time to check and there is literally not a single mug in that house. The man uses travel mugs and glasses. Who does that? Also, if you were wondering, Spot was still making a racket through all this. Although I do have to agree with his wailings. This lack of mug situation was a travesty. I had to put my coffee in a milk glass. Do you know how stupid that looks? It's just not practical. There is no handle! Glaring at my stupid excuse for a coffee mug I leant against the counter. I looked down at Spot, who would not shut-up. Like Ohmygod. "I need to up my game," I muttered, taking a sip.

I slammed the glass onto the bench. It wasn't supposed to be a slam. More of an annoyed placement. Letting the ether know that I was pissed. The glass cracked. With an angry growl, in a very cat-like movement, I swatted the glass off the bench. Coffee and glass sprinkled the floor. Spot whimpered. With my head in my hands I just stared at the glass. Watching the shitty coffee sink into the grooves of the tiles, a light brown sea with boats of sparkling glass, I glanced up at the clock, a smirk creeping across my face. Packing up my threads, I folded them away neatly under their respective names, replacing them with rows upon rows of Harvey Brooks' glasses.

Harvey Brooks trudged into his house muttering under his breath. He kicked his shoes off at the door and threw his briefcase at the foot of the stairs. I stood in the kitchen, leaning against a bench covered in glasses. Spot watched me from the other side of his doggy door. His little doggy eyes narrowed. I stuck out my tongue. I listened for Harvey's approaching footsteps. With a quick stretch, I held out my arm and swung. As Harvey turned the corner his cups flew off the bench. Smashing against the floor. A floor of broken glass and foreboding imagery. And what did Harvey Brooks' do? Yeah, he stopped dead in his tracks, but that was nothing new. A look of fear crossed his face, which of course has me thinking – good, he's finally got it – but no the fucker ran upstairs. Locked himself in his room and called the police…again.

"Blah blah, there's someone in my house." "Blah, blah, they're taunting me." I began slowly banging my head against the closest wall. "Blah, blah, I can hear someone

downstairs" I took a deep breath, pulling open a drawer with brute force. I began flinging plates at the wall.

The judge held up his hand, "Pardon?" I was frozen mid-throw, a plate in the middle of exploding a couple of metres from my form.

"I started throwing his plates at a wall, sir,' I said. His face dropped. "Oh, come on. What is with you people?" I slumped into my chair, the force propelling it across my stage. My deadpan expression watched the judge as I rolled on by. "Oh Lachesis, don't break and enter. Oh Lachesis, don't kill people's gardens. Don't break people's dinner sets, Lachesis. What's wrong with you Lachesis?"

"We've been asking that for years," Attie muttered from behind me. The judge glared at her. "She's a psycho" Attie cried. Clo shushed her. "Look I don't know why we have to sit through all this, look at her. She's clearly unstable." She leapt from her chair, throwing her arm in my direction. "She's turned the courtroom into a theatre. She's spinning around in her chair right now."

Yeah, I was. Head back in boredem, spinning circles next to the exploding plate. I stopped, a few momentary swings passed as I stared my sister down. "She's a psycho, says the chick who literally kills people for a living." I made a cutting motion in the air next to me and she glared one hell of a glare. I rose from the chair, kicking it towards the wall. I straightened my skirt and jacket and crossed my hands in front of me. "May I proceed?" I addressed the judge, purposefully placing my body in the way of Attie. Clo was trying in vain to calm her down, pulling her by the arm. Attie's fuming eyes caught something on the floor. In her brief pause Clo was able to pull her down. I followed her eyes, the rot crawling across the floor, I quickly snapped away.

"I do have one question that you have yet to address," the lawyer lady, what was her name, Enema? Eunomia? Whatever.

"Question time is at the end of the presentation."

The police rocked up again. Searched the house head to toe. All while I made sarcastic comments from atop the dining room table. Spot watching me like a hawk. A very dog-like hawk. I watched Harvey Brooks. The boring man who couldn't get a hint. For gods' sake. How many omens do you need to throw at a man before he gets the whole, 'you're gonna to die thing?' It would probably be better just to let his head get severed. The police, of course, came up with nothing. The only oddity present in the kitchen of

Harvey Brooks was now cold coffee trying to make a run for the door, but even that was a dead end. Their reach doesn't exactly extend to higher entities such as ourselves. And as Harvey Brooks sat on the couch, cradling a pillow and jumping at every slight sound, I knew that desperate times called for desperate measures. I walked right out the front door, making sure to close it on my way out this time. When I returned with my buckets of blood he was in a fit of nightmare-filled sleep with Spot standing guard on the other side of his bed. Picking the perfect wall, I began to make my mural. I pride myself on my calligraphy, you know. Everyone tells me I have wonderful handwriting. The alarm clock threatened to wake him up before I was done. It sat there, it's glowing green numbers illuminating the room. A silent, 'I'll do it, I'll wake him up. He'll catch you'. Alarms clocks are dicks and I was having none of that early riser bullshit. If that man was late to work, so be it. I threw it out the window, much to Spot's distaste.

I got no reaction from the court, almost as if they'd given up on my antics. Boring. With a roll of my eyes I continued.

Harvey Brooks awoke with a scream. Which I guess is the normal reaction to opening your eyes to find blood dripping from your wall. And I suppose that, no matter how nicely presented, the words 'YOU ARE GOING TO DIE' probably make that whole situation worse. But he wouldn't listen any other way.

He sprung from the bed, I sighed striding over to the door. I put all my weight against it. Spot growled at me.

"How do you not get it Harvey?" I said, as he frantically started trying to pull the door open. "The barking dog, the hooting owls, the tree, the kitchen wares!" The door budged a little, I barged into it. The sound of my body hitting the wooden door caused him to jump back, stumbling away from me. I had literally lost all fucks to give at this point. As Harvey Brooks toppled away from his door, I let down every barrier I had ever put up. I let them all down in front of boring, near decapitated Harvey Brooks "Today you are going to die! You are going to drive that shitty little car of yours into a truck. The top of your car is going to end up on the other side of the fucking road with your head still in it! Is that what you want Harvey! Who will look after Spot if you have no head Harvey?" I grabbed the collar of his pyjama shirt, "I measured your thread. I know when it ends. I tied it to you, and now I am watching it disappear while you blatantly ignore every single fucking sign I leave you. Do you know how long it takes me to measure those threads Harvey? Do you how long I have been sitting in an office, measuring threads for every single fucking person, on this stupid fucking planet Harvey? Do you know how long? An eternity Harvey, a Gods-damned fucking eternity and you ignored me like everyone else!" I growled. All the colour drained from his face.

"Who-who are you?" he stammered, I rolled my eyes and pushed him against the wall.

"Of course you don't know who I am. No one knows who I am. I am the person trying to stop you from fucking dying, but no…" I threw my hands up in the air, "…you just don't get it! How can you be that stupid?" Spot started growling- like usual, late to the fucking party. "And you just shut up. He didn't listen to you either." I glanced down at Harvey's thread, the gold fast receding, the dull boring brown underneath getting closer and closer. I groaned, pacing across the room. The boring dead man looked up at me in fear. Finally fear. I punched the door. My hand flew right through. But the sound that accompanied it didn't sound right. Too loud. Too metallic. Too much tire screeching. Too much like a car colliding with a truck, the roof of the car ending up on the other side of the road with the poor driver's head sitting inside. Screaming. There was a lot of screaming. I glanced down at the thread. The thread with a sliver of stationary gold. I flung open the door and ran through the house, skidding out the front door and down the street. Confronted immediately by the gore, the blood, the accident. And I laughed. In the middle of the road. Harvey Brooks ran out after me, stopping dead behind me. Almost exactly like the collection of neighbours, onlookers to the tragedy, looking shocked and tearful. Almost.

His eyes weren't on the accident that was supposed to kill him, but on me. Laughing in front of the devastation. The only person in the crowd to see me. The only one who noticed Attie march up to me. Scissors in hand. The only person to hear her scream, "What the fuck did you do?" as she punched me square in the jaw. And the only person to notice the two headless bodies in the car and know for a fact that it should have only been one.

The courtroom was silent. I took a bow. There was no applause. Just shocked silence. I spun around, basking in my silent glory.

"You are aware, Miss Lachesis, that you just confessed to all the charges against you?" the lawyer said, Her voice was clouded in confusion. Her eyes darted toward the judge who just sat there in stunned silence.

"I certainly did, Miss Eunomia." I sat back down on my table. "I am guilty as fuck," I said. "I'm guilty! I prevented the death of Harvey Brooks! I killed two innocent people before their prime, and I proved that our stupid Fates systems has faults. I won!" I screamed into the courtroom, my voice bouncing off the acoustics. Clo had her hand to her mouth in shock. Attie's attention fixed on the floor, her posture frozen. And I just sat in the middle, in all my smugness.

"Why?" Eunomia said. She didn't present the question in the tone of a lawyer, but in a voice doused in pleading.

"I measure the threads of every life. I know when every single person, God and all of the bastard demi-Gods on this mess of a planet dies, but you can't even remember my name. No one knows who the hell I am. I know when you are all going to die. I measured out your entire lives, but you would go through every year I measured not giving a fuck about me. The first face you ever see is Clothos' and her spinning. The last face you will ever see is Atropos' and her stupid scissors. But what about me! Just chilling in the background, invisible" I slipped off the desk and approached the podium, "But now, I'm unforgettable. There won't be a day in your boring little lives that you won't remember me. I will be fucking infamous. Everyone will be talking about me. I'm going to be trending!" Attie stood up behind me. Clo tried to stop her as she walked towards me, every step a struggle, her hands shaking. "No more fucking measuring. No more living in my sisters' shadows. No more being undermined, and underrated. No more of a system which gave me a job that no one wanted, a reminder that I am the member of this society that no one wants. Now I will go down in history.

"As the villain. A monster," Eunomia cried.

"But at least people will talk about me. They'll know my name." I held my arms out. In the corner of my eye I watched the receding gold, the thread behind it crumbling to dust. The age catching up. I cocked my head at the judge, sending him a wink. I saw the glint of my sister's golden scissors. I didn't close my eyes. I stared him down. With a smirk and that look in my eyes, waiting for my world to end with a single snip. I would be the face that would haunt him for the rest of his life. I measured a thread for every single God, demi-God and person to every walk this planet. I remember attaching my own, I remember looking at my life and hating it before it had even properly begun. But this, this is an ending for the ages. This is the death I worked for, this is the death I deserve. And what a way to go.

Finally, I am fucking unforgettable.

Downfall
By Marc Murkin

Lemistan whiled the afternoon away blowing smoke into the sky, waiting for heaven to fall. Scant hours after sunset, a new light appeared amidst the stars burning like the midday sun. It was like nothing he'd ever seen before. No celestial body such as this had graced the sky within his lifetime. No, this was finally it. The answer. So the prophetess's augury was true.

In a voice gravelly from pipe smoke, Lemistan recited the verse.

"During the seventh stewardship of Annwyn, the sons of green lion, descendants from the Shepherd that lit the path for men, will war with one another. We look on as moon cub slays its elder brother, soaring to higher glory. The sacred land settles the blood, ash and shadow, and peace will reign for the first time since the arrival.

"Words derived from the prophecy of Krisanthalus, the last Alvar of Annwyn," the old man whispered.

Lemistan did not avert his gaze from the omen in the sky. All eyes in the kingdom of Eyrkandia looked up with him and watched with fear. When his neighbours and the nearby guards let out shouts of awe and worry at the bloody sign, Lemistan didn't stir. There would be plenty of time for this old magister, who had waited years for this moment.

"The time is right," stated General Gorman Task. "Never before would I support the words of a pompous witch, much less the rambling of Lemistan and his dark brotherhood. But, my honour will wane before I admit that I was wrong."

Murmurs bubbled around the long table covered in maps and

miniature icons. Lords from all over Eyrkandia gathered around the table in Motleng Hall. Nobles from wealthy and backwater fiefs agreed amongst themselves. All but one man, who stood by the window, looking out at the red blaze of prophecy that pierced the sky.

Gorman walked to the man and placed a hand on his shoulder.

"Duke Antony, we cannot ignore this. This is a clear sign by the gods themselves. We must take this opportunity."

"Ser Gorman is right, Your Grace," said Lord Vahn. A foreigner, Vahn was also the youngest man in the room. But as Duke Antony's highest benefactor he was the most powerful in the room, second only to the Duke. Vahn looked up from his study of the maps on the table, his hands pressed out onto the provinces of Wylderdale in the south and Thar River to the west. "This is a good omen, and the sky is a window for all to see. We need not spread any dissent, the auguries of the prophetess are well known. No doubt your brother has seen the sign. He may already be taking action."

Antony remained unmoved, his eyes fixed. "No," he whispered.

"Pardon, my liege?" Said Vahn. All the nobles waited in silence.

Antony turned from the window, his voice raised. "No. My brother wouldn't know what to make of this. Inaction is his curse. Ever does he languish within his own mind, wracked with indecision. No, he will do nothing. Only what we want him to do."

"And what better time to act then now," said Vahn smiling. The gathered nobles agreed, thumping the pommels of their belt knives against the table. "The king sits on his throne, too afraid to act. We will take Darnon while he does nothing, straight out from under him!"

Cheers erupted around the table. Fists and knife pommels thumped the smoothed surface so hard the miniatures vibrated away from their placements. Everyone cheered except Antony and Gorman.

"Hear me!" Shouted Gorman, "hear me lords. Enough! The Duke thanks you all for your loyalty. But we cannot risk open war with Darnon."

"Ser Gorman is right," agreed Antony. Approaching the table, the Duke studied the kingdoms capital on the central map. "Motleng will always be my home, but no. Darnon is, and will remain the seat of power in Eyrkandia."

"Then we must draw him out," said Gorman.

"Yes," sighed Antony.

"Jon has not emerged beyond the gates of Darnon for months," said

Vahn. "He refuses to even acknowledge emissaries from my country. Father puts up with it, though it shames us all."

Antony whispered, but his voice carried across the silent room. "It will take something dramatic for him to emerge from hiding. Something unspeakable. Gods forgive me."

Antony watched the grim faces as each man took a moment to face a struggle within themselves. In the end, everyone lifted their gaze back to their King. One by one, they nodded.

"May the gods forgive us for what we must do."

Jon punched open the double doors of his throne room before the guards could react to open them for him. "Unbelievable," he shouted, storming from the hall. "When did this happen, Rone?"

Rone stumbled to keep up with His Majesty's long striding steps, attempting to lace up his shirt front as he went. "News came in the early hours. There's been smoke on the horizon since the evening."

"And you thought it best not to tell me? Could nobody have told me?"

"Forgive me, Highness. I've sent word ahead to the garrison; the mustering has already begun beyond the walls."

Jon stopped and looked at Pious Rone, his faithful servant. "You thought best to pre-empt me? You think I would not react to this travesty? In my own kingdom."

Rone bowed his head and remained silent.

Jon spat at the fine tapestry of the Arrival before hurrying on. Ahead the guards had ample warning to open the doors having heard of the King long before they saw him. Jon emerged from the great palace of Darnon, squinting against the morning light. High above the city, he swept his gaze across the many quarters of his city far below. He loved Darnon but he was also very angry with her. Jon scorned his city, and turned away. Leaning out over the wall, he watched the smoke plumes that stained the edge of the southern horizon.

"Brynlast burns, Rone. It burns! Why didn't you tell me? Why didn't you wake me? I've sat lethargic, still clutching to winters edge. I slept while homes burned, people fell to iron and flame. Meanwhile I sit idle, shitting down from my lofty perch on the mountainside."

"Forgive me, Highness."

Rone knelt before his king for far too long. Jon rolled his eyes, and with each breath he exorcised the rage that bellowed within him. With a groan, Jon pressed his hand atop the shoulder of his most loyal servant. "Get up Rone. Damn it all. Damn the Arrival and this entire world and all who dwell within it! You did well to alert the garrison and muster our allies. I just hope they get here in time."

Releasing a frustrated sigh towards the heavens, Jon Derayus, King of Eyrkandia, finally noticed the fiery wound in the sky. It gazed upon him like an angry eye, exultant in its impending victory. The words of the prophetess are true then. The gods of fate and fools punched him hard in the stomach and kneed him between the eyes. "Son of a bitch!" Jon greeted the morning.

"Lemistan, you're finally here."

Duke Antony stood in the middle of a thick copse of trees, cold and confused. The gloom dulled the shine of his plate mail underneath a heavy winter cloak. Mist rose with each breath, winter's chill had not relinquished its grasp on the realm yet.

"Yes, Your Grace, I'm here."

"And not a moment too soon. I need you by my side." Antony paced as though he marched down a line of soldiers, but it was one wizened old man. "The others don't believe it, but I fear my brother will be decisive, and sooner than expected. His anger will not fade, not after what we did at Brynlast."

"That may be true," whispered Lemistan, "I'm afraid I will not be taking part."

Antony moved forward and lowered his voice, lest his bodyguards overhear. "What did you say? Is this why we meet under a canopy of shadow? You mean to flee the field of battle when I need you. What did I do to earn such betrayal?"

"It is nothing of the sort, Your Grace, you must believe that."

"Then what's the reason?"

"The part I've played - the part played by my order, is to remain a secret. The guild remains your most steadfast supporter. But as before, our support is to remain a shadow under the mountain that will be your rule."

"I don't understand," said Antony, "I gave your master my word, that I'd openly support the craft of your guild. To sway the minds of the people. I do not break promises, nor do I intend to forget my friends once I am king."

Lemistan bowed low. "We wholly trust that you will keep your promise.

But in the shadows we must remain, for now. I hope despite this, your promise of support will remain, when you grant us the title to Broad Hill."

Antony waved his hand, "Yes yes, you'll have your land to rebuild your order. You have my word. But I'd be remiss not to ask that you provide aid to me in the coming battle, even from the shadows?"

Lemistan crossed his arms. "It's a great risk, Your Grace. The words sung from the prophetess take shape in the present. And the omen is clearly in your favour, as bold as the sun rises. Far be it from me to steal victory from you when you're destined to take it yourself. But, I will share with you something that may save lives."

Lemistan whispered his secret to the prince. Once done, the old magister took Antony's hand within his own. "Godspeed, King Antony."

"Godspeed Lemistan. Come see me in Darnon when this is all over. You've done so much to get me as far as I have, I regret my harsh words." Antony spun on his heel and left the copse without looking back, as prepared as he was ever going to be.

"Godspeed indeed," murmured Lemistan. Even in the gloom, high above, he could make out the red blaze from between the leaves.

Jon had to admit that Rone had proven his worth, despite the constant battering to his patience. News of Brynlast burning spread faster than Rone's horseback messengers. Once Jon's warhorse Dextres was ready and cantering out the gates of Darnon, the king's closest allies had begun forming warbands in the open fields. Despite the good progress, Jon hadn't stop cursing the entire time trip down the mountain.

"My own brother, the rose knight. The Blazing Lion of the Morning seeks to take my place at the throne. Let him come for it I say, it's cold and uncomfortable. They call me a tyrant, my heart breaks. I may die before his followers reach me. Traitorous little bastard."

"It will not stand," shouted Lord Manderly, riding at his side, his cheeks puffed and red. He reminded Jon of a potato stuffed into a metal cup. "Wylderdale stands with you! For you, we'll cut the traitorous little milksop down, I swear it."

"You'll swear nothing of the sort," replied Jon, reining Dextres as he spoke. His voice loud and commanding in the way that men close shut their mouths and listened. "Hear me, gathered lords. My brother, the betrayer, is to be spared, if at all possible. He remains my brother, and the lord of Motleng. I know many of you disapprove, but rest assured, justice will come for Brynlast. For the burned homes and the people slain. We march not for vengeance, but justice."

Jon urged Dextres onward before Lord Manderly could even sputter another bootlicking response. The ground shook as the gathered warbands followed their king on foot and on horseback.

"Rone, send word to the rearguard and all who've yet to reach muster that we march with all haste south to Brynlast. If they're late they can guard the gates for all I care."

"At once," Rone nodded and parted from Jon's side. No sooner had he left, Jon found a new companion in his place, astride an able brown courser.

"Calen, my friend," said Jon curtly.

"Jon," replied Calen with a fine salute from horseback. He was rarely one to care for titles. "I've been waiting on the mustering field for weeks for you to come out and play. Where is Garian?"

"Garian is safe, at the border with his uncle James."

Calen made a face. "The border, safe? Jon, we're not at peace."

"He's safer there with family. Safer than he would be here. I'd not risk my own son in a battle that intends to end my line."

"Sounds like you're starting to believe." Calen looked up at the sky, at the red comet. Jon forced himself not to look with him.

"I didn't stay that. But yes. See how you get when a death sentence looms over your head for half of your kingship."

"As if you'd let me be king."

"No. You'd probably manage it better and be smug about it."

Silence spread between the two. The type only made comfortable from years of friendship. Growing up playing sword in the gardens, to lords of the realm, nothing changed.

"I'm surprised at what you said back there," said Calen. "I didn't expect you'd leave Antony alive."

"Oh he will die, Calen. By my hands alone. I've been king long enough to know it's a fool's game. Antony gets the high chair, while his allies get rich and fat off treats dropped from the table. Gorman Task and his other allies feed him shit and nonsense, now tell me who actually rules? He thinks I will do nothing, and for that they will pay."

Antony rubbed his eyes, too long had he spent looking over a map of the area. The Duke's closest advisor crowded the tent.

"Rangers report that Jon has emptied Darnon," said Vahn, "preparations are underway."

"Thank you Vahn," replied Antony. "No doubt Pious Rone gave him the much needed nudge out the door."

"He's a devout man, it's true," agreed Vahn, "but Jon is not. I don't understand why Rone devotes himself to such a man, and Jon puts up with it."

Antony pinched the bridge of his nose. Everything was starting to move. "Jon believes in nothing and everything. That's exactly why Rone is there."

"I'll never understand your brutal Eyrkandian ways. Barbarians all, present company excepted. I have news on our other endeavour."

Antony looked hard at the map, not at Vahn. "What news then?"

"Crown prince Garian is with the Glenhalls on the western border. He's vulnerable. I have men poised to cross and take him. The red sign in the sky was their signal. He'll be alive, as you wished, though I don't understand why."

"Garian's only crime is to be my brother's son. He's a good lad. He'll agree to renounce his right by inheritance, and I'll let him live out his days somewhere warm."

"Or he will die," growled Gorman from the darkness.

Antony looked long at his general. He'd almost forgotten he was in the room, sitting in the shadows. "He will renounce."

Gorman lit a pipe, and shrugged.

Antony pointed to the map, a hand south of the tipped marker of Brynlast, with Wylderdale beyond. "We'll cross the bridge at Merrins Crossing and secure it with our main force. Then a contingent of our best men will cross at the hidden ford in Havens Wood."

"I had no idea about this ford, Your Grace," said Gorman, smoothing out his moustache. "And I thought I knew these lands better than anyone. I doubt the usurper does either. It's a brilliant stratagem that will cut off any escape when things turn sour for them."

"Yes, well done, Your Grace," said Vahn. "I never knew you to be quite the pathfinder."

Antony held back a grimace. Shame filled his stomach. He wished Lemistan would've been here to share his own ideas.

"How many are gone?"

Jon tried to be motionless while his squire Tobias and Rone helped him into his armour.

"At least a third of the men." Calen's face burned and his blonde hair was wet against his face. His gauntleted hand gripping the hilt of his sheathed blade. He was in full harness for much of the day, reviewing the forces. "Freden is gone, as is Lanning and his warband. I've not heard from Tonnig either. It appears that some of the more scattered levies from the backwaters preyed on the timing and fled too. I've not had time to get a full account."

"To the hells with them," growled Jon. "If I see Ser Freden standing with my brother, I'll cut him down myself. He hopes that is his fate."

"Jon, in all honesty the sooner this ends, the better. The men are talking."

Jon turned, making life difficult for Rone and Tobias as they worked the buckles on his greaves. "The men are talking? Lords above, what could they be talking about? Could it be they're talking about the blazing comet in the sky? Or maybe the words of the prophetess and her wretched guild of wizards, who claw at the words of a long dead Alvar. Or, could they be talking about the fact that based on her prophecy, they're fighting on the losing side?"

Calen shrugged.

"Damn it Calen, I know. It occurred to me that it was foolish not to call James from the border."

"The Marquess is serving his duty," reminded Calen, "protecting the border, and your son."

"He would've wanted to be here. You know, he doesn't believe a word of this prophecy.

Calen for you to come at my call, you don't believe?"

Calen rested his hands on Jon's shoulders, it was the closest thing to a hug that their armour would allow. "I'll follow you to the end. Nor does it seem wise not to risk the heir to the throne, prophecy or no."

Jon sighed as the familiar weight of his armour finally settled over him. "I would've liked to see him one last time."

"Jon."

"I know. But how can I stand tall with that blazing thing in the sky, reminding me that I'm going to die. Let's get this over with before we're the last two standing in the rearguard."

"The last three," cheered Rone as he finished armouring his lord.

Jon scowled as he watched Rone strap a rapier to his belt.

Antony sat solemn by his campfire. Hundreds of fires dotted the field all around him. For the first time in many years, Antony was unsure of himself. Lemistan leaving unsettled him, despite the information gained to turn the coming battle.

"What troubles you Your Grace?" Said Vahn.

"I've doubts," Antony said finally. "Brynlast hangs heavy on my heart. What divine right do I have after committing such atrocities?"

"Brynlast was full of dogs, loyal only to your brother. The people love you, Your Grace. Once this is over, you will make reparations and all will be well. My country will help you, once the Marquess is gone from my border."

"I fear the queen and her family may not leave Darnon in peace."

"Then we will evict them. After we're finished here."

Antony looked long into the fire, searching for answers. "I've incited civil war, against my own people. Will I not be seen as a warlord?"

"The people love you, you know this. You'll see once this is over, and we march onto Darnon victorious. This was the time to act. The signs were, I should say are, quite clear." They both looked up into the blazing inferno that remained in the night sky.

"Your Grace!" Shouted a scout stationed at the fringes. Approaching the fire, he stopped to catch his breath. "Your Grace, your brother has forced a march with only a fraction of his army. He's already passed by Brynlast."

"Damn him," said Antony, rising up from his seat. "He's moving faster than expected. Are we ready?"

"We're not at full strength either," frowned Vahn. Antony believed it was the first time he saw creases mar the prince's face. "In a few hours Jon will take control of the bridge. Even now it will take time to move all the fighting men across, let alone secure it."

"Then the hidden ford remains our only advantage. We will cut off any chance of escape before the rest of his army arrives."

"It's a good plan, King Antony," Vahn bowed low, "if Jon keeps up his march, many will not arrive in time for the battle. It seems that your brother rides hard towards death."

"Or he's sparing many lives," sighed Antony. "Alright Jon, let's get this over with."

Jon rubbed his face. He mentally prepared himself before lowering the faceplate of his helmet. He needed time before his vision would dim into a narrow slit. It felt like his scowl never left his face since the comet's arrival.

"Jon," shouted Calen, riding up the line.

Jon looked at him and said nothing, his face haggard and drawn.

"Ranger reports have come back with sightings of the Wolf of Thar. He sides with the enemy."

"Shit! That bastard!" Jon continued to curse and sputter and spit until his throat grew hoarse. "Well I can expect the whole bloody east of the realm following his heels then. Where is he?"

"Uncertain, he has two standards raised. One at the vanguard, the other to the rear of Antony's forces."

"That's not like him. Everything about this feels wrong. Go to the flanks and put a fire up their arses. If the Wolf is out there somewhere, that's where he'll strike."

"I'll stand with you!" said Calen.

"You'll go to the eastern flank. Keep my men's courage alive. Find my son, should the worst happen."

Calen saluted and rode off to the east, down the line of knights on horseback, raising cheers as he passed.

"How is one supposed to ride to his own death?" muttered Jon. The doomed king watched as the sun rose, competing for glory against the red death. "It shouldn't have to end this way."

Jon remembered that he was not alone in a field. Surrounded by men and women who pledged their allegiance, their very lives, to him. Jon looked over each of their faces. Many expressions were grim or conflicted, as they fought within themselves. Jon wished it was the gut-wrenching fear that overtook everybody on the eve of battle. But he knew it was over the idiocy of standing on this field next to a man condemned by the gods to die. Their loyalty would forever mark them as traitors, if they survived the day. He watched, expecting for them to scatter to the four winds, but they didn't.

"Ser Tomas," Jon called finally. "Sound the advance."

Ser Tomas Edgar blew long on the horn of Gamling, and its clear resounding note echoed across the fields.

"Eyrkandian sons and daughters," shouted Jon. "I thank you for your sacrifice. Long have I ruled. Long too have I endured death above my head, poised for this very moment. I choose to face it. If it must be so, then I choose death!"

Screams mingled with wave after wave of arrows whistling in the morning air. The sounds were soon lost under the thunder of hundreds of mounted knights at charge. At his side Ser Tomas again blew his horn, before letting it drop to his side, taking up his spear.

"Martelle, my love. Forgive me for not having the courage to say goodbye." With raised sword Jon lowered his faceplate, pressed his knees into the flanks of Dextres. He rode to his doom. Cursing the gods, Jon galloped alongside his allies as they braced for collision. To his right, Ser Dartus crunched into an opposing horseman. The impact sent both horse and rider down in what sounded to Jon like a quick death. Jon moved to avenge Dartus with a swing of his sword, his steel cutting his opponents nose through to his brain. The act of vengeance slowed Jon, and his allies surged forward all around him. Ser Tomas hew a path for his warband to follow, taking up the cheer. Death. Death.

Jon was going to die, but he would bury himself under the corpses of his enemies first. He spurred his horse into danger. His bloodied sword sang through the second and third line of enemies, leaving screams in his wake. Jon rode upon a pocket of unsuspecting archers not prepared to face him and mighty Dextres. The King's sword rose and fell, and all he could see was red. Red of blood, of the comet, bleeding out of bluest sky overhead. In a moment of reprieve, Jon spied the red plated armour that could only belong to his brother, the rose knight.

How fitting, he thought. If he is to die, let him die by his hand, the bloody chosen one. Jon charged towards his brother, screaming like a demon, cutting down anyone who stood in his way. The King's spirits lifted at the sound of men screaming 'Derayus', either side could be cheering. For him or his brother. For his life, or death. He brushed the thought away, and drank in the feeling, more out of defiance than anything else.

Jon struggled with his sword, his arm turning to lead. He rested his arm in front of him while his horse took him the rest of the way.

"Brother!" Challenged Jon, his sword raised again over his head. "Face me! Let this end."

The red knight looked up towards Jon, but only for a moment. Jon desired to see the fear in his brothers eyes, but his face was covered. He was cutting men down around him with deadly precision, but he was surrounded.

"Yield! Jon shouted, but his voice failed him as he gulped for air. Nor could he call a halt to the soldiers in frenzy, who surrounded Antony and dragged him from his horse. Jon could do nothing but despair as several blades pierced his baby brother's armour,

Jon finally screamed when he caught his breath. He tore at his faceplate, desperately tugging at his crowned helmet.

"Make way for the king," someone shouted as Jon approached. He fell more than dismounted as he rushed to his brother's side, who lay helpless in the blood-drenched mud.

"Move," he grunted, pushing aside a man in bloodied brigandine. Jon's own soldiers surrounded him. Many had lost their horses, but they were gaining ground against the enemy.

Red of blood covered over Antony's armour and sleeves. It was more likely his armour was the only thing keeping his insides from spilling out. Hands slippery with blood, Jon made short work of the buckle on Antony's helmet. His hands shook as he lifted the faceplate.

"Fuck! Antony, where are you? Face me! Finish this!"

Antony fidgeted in his borrowed armour. He felt vulnerable without the red plate that made him the rose knight. "At least I have you," Antony whispered to his trusted warhorse, scratching at his ear.

The woods were thick on both sides of the ford into Bardon Wood. The warband found it was difficult for more than three horseman to stand together, let alone in any kind of formation.

"Any wonder this ford is so well hidden," said the Wolf, a massive man wreathed in black armour, and guardian of the east. He sat comfortable atop a monstrous horse two hands higher than Antony's own. "We'd best have everyone cross now."

Everyone perked up at the sounds of steel and death echoing from the west.

"We're late!" whispered Antony, looking over at the Wolf. "Time we move before Lord Highcourt is wiped out. We'll round on them in full force."

"Alarm!" Someone shouted.

"What do you see?"

Nobody replied except for shouts of anger and pain as a swarm of men on foot rushed from the woods."

"They'll give us away. Charge them down," shouted the Wolf. He howled his anger with every swing of his axe, giving credence to his namesake. But Antony hesitated as he watched a knight to his right fall from his horse with a spear in his heart. The men that spilled out of the woods across the ford were little more than town levies. Dressed in mismatched pieces of iron and boiled leather, they wielded farm tools and axes. On foot they outmaneuvered the cavalry force, which lacked the room to be effective.

"We've got to get out of the woods. Go!" The howl of the Wolf thundered amidst the trees, and all who heard it took pause. They abandoned the crossing.

Antony held tightly as his horse carried him closer to the battle. He pushed on to help with the retreat. Ser Freden's horse collapsed, full of arrows, the knight trapped underneath. He was overrun before Antony could command his horse about.

More levies appeared on the southern side of the river. Arrows flew by Antony as he rode on calling to his men. A line of spearmen blocked the way, waiting to pierce the horses out from under them.

"Derayus!" Howled Wolf. Many took up the cry, but it was far fewer than what they started with. Antony hesitated. His horse took a few wild steps, uncertain. Antony could see the comet in the sky, the omen that set everything into play. The comet was beginning to fade, passing from the heavens. The gods cast dark clouds, and their opponents closed in around them.

Surrounded, his opponents pulled Antony from his horse, but the levies lost grip as he fell. Before being trampled Antony rolled aside. His warhorse bucked and kicked, cracking the spine of one of his attackers. Antony rolled up, drawing his sword and faced two men. Their axes would be put to better use chopping kindling, he thought with confidence. His armour held, but the pain in his shoulder told a different story when one got a lucky strike in.

The levies he faced seemed unskilled in combat, especially against a swordsman. Noble sword duels meant nothing in the chaos of a real melee, and despite Antony's fear, his training took hold. Every breath, every swing meant life or death. The levies should've had the advantage of numbers, but they were not trained to fight together. Antony sidestepped left, his sword going right. The levies got into each other's way. Antony responded and brought one low with a single swing, his blade tore into patched brigandine. The Duke pulled his sword from the man and reversed the swing back into the first man. The levy threw punch at Antony, screaming hysterically. The blow was absorbed by Antony's armour, but the man's pitiful wailing jarred Antony and his response. He back-pedaled until he had room to thrust and stabbed the levy in the stomach, changing the screams into gurgles. Antony won, but his sword was stuck in the man's gut as he fell.

"For the King! Derayus!" howled Wolf. Fewer men cheered, instead concentrating on their own battles. The Wolf was trying to rally the men, but Antony wore borrowed equipment. Nobody would recognize him but for the signet ring. That was a detail nobody hat time to observe with bloody weapons and guts flying around.

"For the King!-" Wolf's cries cut short as an arrow shaft thumped into his chest. He already bore several arrows in his armour, but this one made him stagger. Antony caught glimpse of the bowman, already with another arrow nocked and ready. He loosed, and the breath from Wolf's lungs failed him, and the towering giant fell heavily from his horse. The cheers ended as the lord from the east fell like an ancient pine struck by lightning.

Without sword or shield, Antony drew a knife from his belt and moved towards the bowman. The bowman met his gaze evenly, drawing another arrow. The ground was unsteady, but Antony tried to change his direction to keep the bowman's aim unsteady. The bowman released. Antony flinched and swung his knife in front of him but the arrow flew wide. Antony was too close now, and the bowman threw down his bow and drew an axe. The man looked strong for a simple levy, but he was no different to the men he'd already bested.

As the forces on both sides began to thin, duels between exhausted men began. They met with a clash of metal, crashing again and again until someone died. Antony's opponent had patience, holding his guard well and striking with caution. Antony lacked the reach with his belt knife, and the bowman's axe looked very sharp.

"Derayus!" Shouted the bowman, "For the king, for Eyrkandia!"

Antony retreated from relentless attacks. He barely deflecting the axe away with parries of his knife. The flurry of swings caught Antony off guard and for one moment he began to despair. This bowman was a fellow countryman. A simple man, answering the call of his king. Did he deserve as much?

The bowman began to tire, so Antony pressed the attack and closed in.

He could not defend against the different angles and received many cuts to his arms and legs. Antony lunged forward. The bowman stepped back, but it wasn't enough. Antony sunk his knife into the man's side. The bowman flinched and groaned, but he didn't fall.

"Eyrkandia!" screamed the bowman. He swung his axe down, cutting into Antony's arm at the elbow. Antony cried out without sound as fire lanced up his arm. He tried to pick up his blade, but his fingers did not respond. They remained with the knife imbedded in the bowman's side. Antony watched in horror at the bleeding remains of his harm. Staggering back, the Duke of Motleng wanting only to fall. His chest exploded with pain. He watched as blood leaked from the seams of his armour where the bowman's axe cut through his cuirass. As he fell the bowman collapsed on top of him. Prince and countryman, both dying, comforting each over in their final moments.

"For the king," the bowman rasped at the king's brother, never knowing who he was.

Before Antony's vision faded into nothingness, he saw the red blaze of prophecy reflect in the bowman's eyes.

Jon could barely contain himself. "I'm alive!"

The king stood in a field surrounded with dead men robbed of their lives. Jon watched the still eyes of Ser Gorman Task who masqueraded as Antony. A traitor, and his brothers closest friend and advisor. Jon had no idea where his brother could be. Did he flee, or could he still be here, somewhere? High above him, the red comet that only a few days before cut the sky like a wound, had now faded into morning.

Extinction
By Joelle Cronin

D plus 102

The blood-stained sand gave way to the murky blackness of the incoming tide. Emerson struggled forward through the water, suppressing her panic as the sand dropped off beneath her feet. An unidentifiable object floated close to her face as she swam, its rancid odour forcing her to gag. She pursed her lips, terrified of what or whom she might ingest. The boat she strove for bobbed in the distance as the wind grew. Emerson's leaden legs struggled to respond; her strokes were becoming sluggish. Although her body was struggling, her mind was racing.

She let out a tiny choked scream as her foot hit something slimy and rigid below the water. It broke her concentration and she failed to brace herself against the rolling waves. The black water crashed over her and she spluttered as she vanished underwater for a few terrifying seconds.

Emerson wouldn't let herself be beaten by the water or the overwhelming doubt in her mind. She swept her fringe from her eyes and continued. The water she'd ingested was nauseating and she paused twice to vomit. Her eyes burned and she strained to keep them open. As the boat - her tiny beacon of hope - loomed closer, her strokes became instinctively stronger. Her excitement was short lived. Emerson came to a sudden stop in the water and glanced around, her heart pounding in fear. She heard the unmistakable sound of something in the water approaching her from behind. Whatever it was, it was strong and powerful and flew through the sea effortlessly. She held her breath but exhaled as she realised the figure was a man. He didn't pause or acknowledge Emerson as he passed and he was soon at the boat, grasping at the waiting hands that welcomed him. His head was covered in platinum blonde hair, streaked with black regrowth. Once aboard, he disappeared, ushered below deck by the waiting soldiers.

Emerson hadn't expected him to help her. She certainly wouldn't have helped him, had their roles been reversed. The end of the world had made everyone selfish, and justifiably so. Those kind-hearted men and women who had dared to pause to help had perished within the first few weeks. Emerson only had herself to worry about now, and she was content with that.

She reached the edge of the boat and gazed up at her rescuer, an African man, his skin as dark as the night sky. He leant forward, extending a hand towards her. She kicked and propelled herself out of the water, her arm outstretched in desperation. He caught her forearm and with one smooth motion he pulled her upwards and out of the filthy sea. A second set of hands appeared, snaking around her waist, pulling her into the safety of the boat. The African let her go and immediately resumed his position, his keen brown eyes scanning the water for more survivors. The owner of the second set of hands held her, keeping her from collapsing onto the deck. Her legs, wrecked from the brutality of the swim, shook underneath her. The second rescuer towered over Emerson, his kind face covered with an untamed, grey-flecked beard. The wooden floor was wet under Emerson's bare feet and she curled her toes in disgust as she realised it was covered in a fine layer of slime and mould. She took a moment to regain her breath and glanced around the deck. There were people scattered around the edges of the boat, scouting for swimmers.

The boat had been poorly maintained, it appeared shabby at best, but Emerson couldn't care less. It floated and that was all that mattered. Small groups of people huddled on the filthy deck, their faces pale with despair. Soldiers, armed with automatic weapons, paced the deck in silence. The pungent smell of mildew wafted over Emerson as she surveyed her new surroundings. The serenity was the most stirring observation she made. Her life hadn't known such calmness since long before the Prion had been discovered. Emerson herself had never heard of such a thing until it began to dominate every news cycle. The Prion was found hiding within the brains of almost every living mammal on the planet. Almost every brain; Emerson hoped she was the exception. The collapse of the human race at the hands of a tiny, misfolded protein began insidiously. The first to die were the unborn; a subtle omen unheeded until it was too late.

Her wet clothes clung to her malnourished body and she shivered as a strong gust of wind swept over her. She took a few moments to brush a stray strand of seaweed from her shoulder and pushed her roughly chopped hair off the back of her neck. Her hair had never been this short, but long hair had become unmanageable and she'd been forced to take to it with a pair of blunt scissors.

Emerson was escorted below deck by an armed soldier to where an older woman, dressed in a bright pink and yellow dress, began to fuss over her. She checked Emerson's vital signs, studied her eyes with what appeared to be a small magnifying device, and took a blood sample. Emerson let her work in silence, aware of the rifle aimed at her back.

"Pass," the grey-haired physician said eventually, dismissing the solider with her announcement.

The soldier left immediately and Emerson was ushered on to another small table manned by a young worker with enormous arms and shoulders. It was obvious he had been some kind of body-builder in his previous life. Emerson had seen and met plenty of them at the gym she used to attend. He took Emerson's details, filling in a form as she answered his questions. Then he plucked out a permanent marker and wrote a four-digit number on the back of a dog-tag and handed it to her. She glanced at it: 6625.

"This is your identification number. This verifies you have been tentatively cleared of infection via a visual examination. You will now be taken to a quarantine holding zone until the results of your blood test return. Should they be negative, you will be allowed to integrate into the Pearlwood Safe Zone. Keep this identification tag on your person at all times and produce it immediately when requested. You may now move along to the bathrooms." His speech was perfectly rehearsed, as though he'd said it exactly 6624 times before.

Emerson nodded and immediately donned the tag, tucking it under her damp shirt. The East Coast Quarantine Zone was rumoured to be located aboard the Horizon, a luxury cruise ship commandeered by the military and anchored off-shore in a classified location.

In the cramped bathroom, Emerson freshened up before returning to the deck to take in the last few minutes of sunlight. A soldier handed her a threadbare blanket and she gave him a grateful smile. The boat had begun moving during her time below deck. Anyone still in the water or on the shore would be left behind.

Emerson took a seat next to a young family who were sitting in silence by the anchor. They glanced at her but didn't speak. No one spoke to each other much anymore. Emerson wrapped the blanket around her shoulders and stared wistfully out to sea, drinking in the rays of the setting sun as the boat began its journey to the Quarantine Zone.

D minus 290

Emerson's eyes glazed over as her aching feet tread wearily on the cushioned leather belt of the treadmill. The machine was moving at an unimpressive rate, a clear reflection of Emerson's lack of enthusiasm about the mundane activity. She glanced up from the illuminated monitor to stare instead at the blank television screen mounted on the wall in front of her. In the polished surface, she could see vague reflections of the people moving around behind her. She scowled as she recognised one of the svelte figures lingering by the front counter. She grasped the handles of the machine to steady herself and twisted around to glare.

Maddison Amery was one of the most awful people Emerson had ever met. She always prided herself on being beautiful and fit, and found pleasure in degrading anyone else who didn't meet her own personal standard of beauty. They had attended high school together several years prior but Emerson doubted that Maddison remembered who she was. Maddison was five months pregnant to an older, influential lawyer and her attitude towards other human beings had worsened since she'd been inundated with pregnancy hormones. Emerson hadn't seen her around in weeks and had hoped the woman had moved on to the newer, exclusive fitness centre which was unashamedly poaching clients from every other gym in town.

Emerson and Maddison had never exchanged a word within the confines of the gym. Emerson was quite certain that Maddison didn't even know she existed. Her mere presence was toxic enough to make Emerson uncomfortable and dredge up unwelcome memories from her high school days.

Emerson slowed the machine to a crawl and clumsily hopped off. She staggered as her legs struggled to adapt to the stationary nature of the tiles beneath them. She beelined for her locker, throwing her sweaty towel over her shoulder and grabbing her belongings. Maddison moved out from behind the counter where she had been gossiping and made her way towards the change rooms.

Emerson turned to leave but moved only one step before her mouth dropped open in surprise. Maddison was as slender as a twig. Her baby bump, which was disproportionally large a few weeks previous, was gone completely.

Emerson immediately felt guilty, as though her own negative thoughts about the woman had led to her misfortune. She knew the baby was dead. Babies born that young didn't survive. She walked towards the exit, pausing to fill her bottle from the icy cold tap by the door. As she waited for the bottle to fill she couldn't help but overhear an employee speaking to another client.

"It's so sad!" the employee gushed, clutching her hand to her chest empathetically. "Imagine having to give birth to a dead baby. It's devastating!"

Emerson blanched at the appalling comment.

The client smacked her hand on the counter. "You know, she is the fifth woman I've heard of in the last few weeks that's had this happen to them. All of them have either miscarried or had a stillborn. Something strange is happening. Perhaps there's heavy metal in the water again and it's hurting the babies?" They nodded at each other before the client spoke again. "Thomas and I were thinking of trying for a baby ourselves," she said, her face unenthused by the concept. "Though, I'm not sure it's a good idea at the moment to be honest. I'd rather go on a holiday. I was considering checking out that new luxury cruise ship. The one that travels the world. The Horizon, I believe it's called?"

Emerson finished filling her bottle and passed the women on her way to the exit.

"I'm so jealous," the employee gushed. "I've always wanted to go on a cruise but I just can't afford it. It doesn't help that the kids are begging me to take them to see that African Mummy exhibit at the museum this weekend. It's $15 for entry, per person!"

Emerson left, sliding her sunglasses down over her eyes as she stepped into the glaring sunlight.

D minus 182

BIRTH RATE PLUMMETS, DOCTORS BAFFLED

Emerson's eyes gazed over the bold headline that populated the entire front page of the crumpled newspaper. The older man sitting opposite her ruffled the paper as he read, his gnarled hands wrapped around the edges.

Emerson glanced out the window over his shoulder, taking in her current location. The bus was close to the city now, a few short minutes from Emerson's destination. The bus was in poor shape, its suspension in dear need of correction. Emerson could feel every bump and shudder deep in her bones as they travelled. She sighed and wondered what type of car she could buy if she only ate canned soup from the dollar store for the next six months. She'd have to splurge on fruit and vegetables at least once a month to avoid scurvy and malnutrition, but she could budget for that.

The bus hit a large pothole and Emerson flew several inches out of her seat. Her arm whipped out and she instinctively grabbed the closest thing to steady herself. Unfortunately, the closest thing was an overweight man with an outrageous handlebar moustache who was crammed into the seat next to her. Emerson apologised profusely, plucking her earphones from her ears as she did.

"Don't worry about it, love," he said, his plump fingers gripping a tablet. Emerson could see he was reading the online version of the daily newspaper, the same paper the man opposite them was reading. Emerson couldn't help but read a few words on the screen as she settled back into her seat. The screen showed a news article about the momentous discovery of an ancient mummified body. It had been found inside a meticulously sealed tomb in Africa almost 12 months previously. Emerson wasn't particularly interested in the topic. She found the talk of dead bodies and human remains disrespectful, and couldn't comprehend the interest in such a morbid topic. The editor of the local newspaper was obsessed with the discovery and had campaigned successfully to have the remains displayed in the local museum as a part of the international publicity tour. There was not a country in the world that wouldn't see the remains visit them at some point over the next few years.

The rest of the bus ride passed without incident and Emerson was soon walking into her workplace, an upmarket boutique clothing store. It was located in a prime position along the main street of the mall. Her presence was immediately welcomed by her frantic co-worker, Clarice, who was manning the sales counter.

"Oh, thank goodness!" Clarice announced, disappearing towards the back of the store, leaving Emerson with the customers. Emerson plastered a smile on her face, dropped her handbag to the floor behind the counter and accepted a dress from the first woman in line.

Emerson dealt with the queue of customers before hunting for her co-worker who had retreated to the storeroom.

"Where is Chelsea?" she asked. Chelsea was the store's manager. She was also eight months pregnant and due to go on maternity leave in only a few weeks.

"No clue. She didn't turn up this morning. I tried calling her and left three messages but haven't heard back yet. Luckily, I've got keys to the safe or else I'd have been screwed. I've been here by myself since 9am." Clarice was stuffing a sandwich into her mouth as she talked.

"Did the baby come early?"

Clarice held up her phone and shook her head. "Nope, nothing on Facebook. Besides, she would've sent a message letting us know. This is so unlike her." A moment later, Clarice's phone began to vibrate and she exclaimed as she saw the ID on the screen. "Oh, it's the store's owner. I called her too when I couldn't get onto Chelsea. I've only met her once or twice since I started here. This will be interesting. I don't want Chelsea to get fired."

Emerson left the room as Clarice began her disgruntled tirade at their employer, an aging woman named Jenna who floated in and out of the store whenever she felt like it. Emerson set about cleaning up after the morning rush and worked diligently until Clarice stormed out.

"Okay, I don't know that woman very well but that was the weirdest conversation I've ever had." Clarice raised an eyebrow, disdainful. "First of all, she sounded like she was drunk – slurring her words like a sailor – and secondly, she had no idea who I was or who Chelsea was."

Emerson's interest was piqued by Clarice's comment. "Yeah, she's been very distracted lately. She's been doing odd things and has been forgetful. She forgot to pay me last week and when I worked with her yesterday she kept giving out the wrong change to customers. Not just once either. People were complaining all day."

"Can you get dementia at 60?" Clarice asked. "Because that is the only logical explanation right now. Yeah, it's either dementia or the Curse of the Mummy!" she exclaimed and dissolved into hysterical laughter at her preposterous thought.

"Don't laugh, girl." Emerson and Clarice spun to face the store's lone customer, an immaculately dressed woman in a vintage style dress. Her face was covered with a light touch of makeup; bright red lipstick emphasising her thin lips. Her face was lined from age and her voice was soft and raspy. "Terrible things happen when the living disturb the dead."

Her piercing green eyes fixed on Emerson, who had been stunned into silence by the woman. Clarice wasn't laughing anymore. Her face was pale, her mouth down-turned in distress.

The woman turned and left. Emerson unclenched her fists, her heart pounding.

D minus 50

Emerson forced a smile as she handed the customer the handles of the paper shopping bag containing their multiple extravagant and unnecessary purchases. Rich people were insufferable sometimes.

"Thank you, dear," said the young woman, clearly affluent going by her impeccable clothing and nails. She was likely the same age as Emerson, so Emerson doubted the money she was spending was her own. The rich woman called out to her friend who was browsing the row of crystal Christmas ornaments. "Come on, Jillian, I've got to make it to the drug store before they close!"

The pair left and Emerson pursed her lips at the mess they'd left behind for her to clean. The rich woman's friend, Jillian, had tried on and discarded over twenty dresses in the 45 minutes she'd graced the store, but had left with only a pair of cheap earrings from the sale rack.

"Speaking of drug store, have you gone to get yours yet?" Chelsea, the store manager, asked as she stooped to grab a pair of discarded heels.

Emerson shook her head. Between work and study, she'd barely had time to sleep. She'd picked up an additional 20 hours of work a week after the store's owner had been taken sick for the past few months. They were advertising for another sales assistant but were yet to receive any applications.

"Go now," Chelsea urged and subconsciously rubbed where her own baby bump had been a few months earlier.

Emerson recognised the sorrow in Chelsea's voice and actions, and nodded dutifully. "Okay, I'll duck down to Meadows now while it's quiet here."

The pharmacy was busy and Emerson picked through the crowd. The store was full of panicked people buying toilet paper and bottled water. She joined a short queue near the consultation rooms and was given a questionnaire attached to a clipboard. She answered the questions thoroughly and was soon ushered into a tiny room where a female pharmacist was sitting in front of a computer. Emerson handed over the clipboard and the pharmacist scanned her answers. She confirmed Emerson's name and date of birth whilst attaching a blood pressure cuff to her arm.

They sat in silence while the machine whirred away. The result must have been adequate because the pharmacist nodded approvingly as she entered the data.

Emerson left the consultation room ten minutes later clutching a large paper bag filled with a six-month supply of the oral contraceptive pill and ten doses of the emergency "morning after" pill. Her head was full of counselling and advice about preventing pregnancy at all costs.

Pregnancy had been officially banned two weeks previously and the Government was now funding free birth control for every female of child-bearing age. There had been an astronomical surge in non-viable pregnancies over the past six months. 95% of pregnancies were ending in a spontaneous abortion and the 5% that made it to delivery had a mean survival rate of 17 days.

The pandemic was global; every country across the world was reporting similar trends. There had also been a correlating rise in unexplained deaths and undiagnosed debilitating illnesses. The illnesses were characterised by rapidly deteriorating cognitive function. Despite the overwhelming supply of funds being channelled into research, scientists and doctors were yet to find a plausible explanation. The implementation of a management plan was only just beginning.

Emerson took her first pill as she walked back to the boutique.

D minus 7

Emerson perched herself on a stool behind the sales counter. The store was empty and had been every day for the past week. She had straightened every rack of clothing and steam-ironed everything she could get her hands on. She was now waiting for the end of her shift. She wondered why she had even bothered to turn up at all. The entire mall was deserted. Something highly contagious had confined most people to their beds. The symptoms were unlike those present in previous pandemics. No one was sure how the pathogen was spreading. In fact, no one was sure what the pathogen was.

Most of the symptoms were confined to the central nervous system. It began with forgetfulness, confusion, dizziness, before progressing to hallucinations, changes in motor function, and an inability to form words or sentences. All cases ended in death.

Emerson's attention was diverted to the radio playing softly beside her. The music had been interrupted by a news bulletin ordering a mandatory curfew. Everyone was to go home and remain there until further notice. Emerson packed up the store, blowing out the candles on her way out the door. She headed home, dodging an intoxicated homeless woman who stumbled towards her, gurgling and crying.

D Day

Emerson set her head down to rest on her knees. She was curled into a small ball and hiding in the corner behind her bedroom door. She remained deathly quiet, her ears listening to the horrific noises coming from the corridor beyond the door. The radio emitted only static now but Emerson dared not move to switch it off. She glanced at her phone but it had become nothing more than a brick. Both internet and cellular reception had been lost the previous day. The last news bulletin she'd heard before the signal had disappeared was that a scientist in South America had finally uncovered the pathogen; a Prion. Rumours of its origin were already rife but Emerson couldn't help but remember the words an impeccably dressed woman with thin lips uttered to her six months ago.

The streets outside were filled with bodies, many of which were still moving despite having been shredded by bullets fired by a desperate and scrambling military a few hours previous.

Emerson couldn't be quite sure what was happening around her but she was overwhelmingly confident about one solitary fact: the world, after struggling to hold on for over twelve months, had finally begun to die.

The Black Bell
By Stephen Ryan

The heavy rain falling washing the cobble stone street clean. Breakwater with care rides his horse through the quite streets of the night. The oil lamps light along the streets gives faint shadows. Warm and dry under his long oil skin cloak covers the back of his horse and his wide brim hat keeps the rain of his face. A few people walking along the streets all with their heads down trying to stay dry under their cloaks. Reaches a fork in the road and stops his horse. The right fork will take him to the Kings castle. The King and his summons. Breakwater felt his stomach churning it was only faint, but deep down something was wrong. The raven on his left shoulder seem to pick up Breakwater feeling. Its seems the King has to wait. Turns his horse down the left fork, the roads lead down the steep hill. The sharp sound of the horse hoofs on the wet cobble stone echoed off the buildings. In the distance to the left in the oldest part of the city the silhouette of an ancient tall tower still stands. A bell tower with a large black bell sits in silence. Not far down the road movement catches his eye. As he approaches he finds a family of two sheltering under a small shop awning. The father stands in front of his family, the two kids behind their mother. Breakwater could see by the look of their clothes that this family wasn't street urchins. "By your leave sir we have no nothing." The feeling in Breakwater gut told him this was the place he needed to be. "I can see that. Now tell how this came to be."

"I paid me rent to the collector, got me ticket and I thought all's well. Come sun down the owner came by saying we'd not paid. I's shows me ticket he calls fraud and his thugs throw us out."

"Who is this land lord?"

"His name be Stone sir; he is rotten to the core. he has no heart and feels nothing for anyone. I have no means to fight in court, the law only believes the one with gold." Breakwater reaches under his cloak and takes out a small pouch of coins. "Here, this should be enough to get you to the King palace. Go to the back gate and hand this medallion to the guard. One of Kings men will talk with you. Tell them what has happen. I recommend you do, not lie but you will be safe." He looks down at the pouch of coins and feels the weight in his hands. "If they ask who you be?" Breakwater gives a cheeky smile. "Somebody you don't need to know. Now where does this Stone live?"

"You'd be seeing his work from here sir, he lives in that big building on top of Millers hill." As Breakwater turn his head to see where he was pointing the Black Bell rang fills the night silence. For a moment, the streets stopped. Breakwater turns his horse around. "Get your family to Kings Palace."

Henry Stone sat working in his office "That Bell again. Why is it every time that thing rings it makes me jump?" The Butler places the port tray down onto the small table. "You would think the priests would ring that thing at more reasonable hours. "Sir. that is the Black Bell. the priests won't even go anywhere near that tower." He pours a glass of port and places the glass to the side of his master. "Well, why can't somebody go into the tower and stop that bloody from ringing."

"They would sir but the tower has no doors and any attempt to scale the walls has always ended in death."

"That thing has been sitting in silence for centuries and it's only now the last two score years the always seem to ring." The Butler refills the port glass. "Excuse me sir do you know the true story behind the Black Bell?" Stone places his quill down. "Please fill me in."

"This story in short goes like this. A white wizard came across an injured child. He tried to save his life, but the locals would not believe him, and accused him of murder. Anyway, before they were about to execute him his final words were. To prove my innocence a bell tower on this spot will rise. When one person comes in to right a wrong the bell will ring once. The second bell will only be for the guilty and the third bell will toll upon sentence or before death." Stone picks up his quill. "I would believe that but magic died out years ago." "That may be true sir, but every time that bell has rung there has always been someone found guilty. It's considered a bad omen" Stone glance at his butler, and sighs. "Well lock up and that will be all for the night."

"Very good sir." Leaving the office, the butler walks down the stairs and checks the main doors. He looks through the glass panes of the doors, the rain still coming down. At the end of the court yard outside of the gates. He saw the dark shape of a man mounted on the back of a horse a raven flew down and landed on the horseman shoulder. He smiles to himself watches man rides away.

Next morning the sun breaks through the clouds. drying the wet streets. Stones office. Buzz with activity. With clerks carrying files and filling in ledgers. One the Clarkes looks up curiosity, watching a rider trotting into the court yard. With an agile move slides of his mount in front of the hitching post. Without pause he advance to the front door. The raven takes off as he alight from his horse and lands on windows ledge. "Oi aren't you going to tie up your nag?" Breakwater said. "No." Enters the main foyer, He saw a small line of people in front of the main clerk. See's the stairs, Breakwater ignores the line and starts ascending. The clerk looks up to see strange man ascending the stairs. "Sir, sir you can't go up there without an appointment." Breakwater ignores him. At the top of the staircase he finds a large heavy door inscribe with the name 'Stone' in gold.

Without knocking he opens the door. Finds a stout man with a florid complexation sitting behind the large wooden desk. It was at the moment Stone heard the second bell. He flinched. Breakwater closed the door behind him, slides the bolt in place. He then took the closest chair and wedge it under the door handle. He turns and stares at Stone. "You heard it, didn't you?" Breakwater intone. Sweat started to appear on Stone face as the larger man approach him. "I-I don't know what you're talking about. Stone places his hands on the desk. "I'm a busy man if you have not made an appointment I will ask you to leave." Breakwater hears heavy footsteps running up the stairs. They tried the door handle it would not open. They yelled through the door asking Mr Stone are you okay. Breakwater yells back. "Not for very much longer." Then they started to ram the door. "You know when he gets through you're a dead man." Breakwater shrugs the threat off. "Good. Until that happens we have some matters to clear up." Stone huff, "We have no matters to talk even beyond you leaving." A large thump hits the door. Breakwater leans over the desk and stares Stone in the face. "This is your one and only chance to repent before the Kings auditors and men arrive."

"You think I'm scared of auditors, they always check my books and have never found a coin out of place." Breakwater raise an eyebrow see's the sweat on Stone face. "If you have nothing to fear why are you sweating?" The door pounds again. Breakwater stands back up and looks around the office. "My teachers always taught me, the guilty always keeps incriminating evidence close by." The loud thump hits the door. "Do you know who are dealing with?" Breakwater continue to smile. "The question you should ask yourself, Stone, is who are you dealing with." Another crash hits the door. Breakwater looks out of the window. Over the courtyard to see a black carriage followed by the Kings men on horseback. By this time the door hinges start to give. "Your time is running out, Stone. are you going to give up the ledgers the auditors don't see?" In one quick movement, he kicks the chair, and draws the dagger from his belt. Unbolting the door when thug fell into the room, Meeting breakwater dagger. Breakwater drives the dagger under his rib cage killing him. Letting the thug fall to floor Breakwater eyed the Chief Clarke mouth open in shock. "Go Away." The clarke bolted. Cleans his blade with a cloth the auditor with the kings' men appear at the door.

"So Breakwater I suppose you will be claiming self-defence for this one?"

"Well, Glen I did try to keep him outside but he was incessant on breaking that door down to come in and kill me."

"At this stage I'm not seeing any evidence, and you know how the King value his time." Breakwater turns to Stone. "last chance to come clean. Keep in mind I recognise the craftsman work of your desk and I will find the hidden panel with the ledger." Takes Stone by the ear and leans in close. "If I do find this ledger Stone, there is a horse outside not tied up. It can out run any of the Kings horses." Breakwater pushes Stone aside crumbles to floor. He sits behind the desk and swipes everything off and lets it spill onto Stone. Covered in paper and dripping ink. Slides out a panel Breakwater holds up the ledger. "I told you I find it." Stone slaps the wall a passage appears he rolls out of the room before anyone can react. the Kings men rushed to the panel. "Let him go he won't make pass the main gate."

Breakwater walks over to the window and watches as Stone, with a lot of effort climbs onto the horse and takes off. As the horse nears the gate. Breakwater lets out a sharp whistle. The horse stops dead. Stone flew through the air before he hits the gate he hears the third bell toll and his eyes widen in horror. As he impales himself on the spikes on top of the gate. Breakwater and Glen who were watching this unfold made painful faces. "Told you he wouldn't get pass the main gates."

"Well that may be fine but I wanted him alive so we can question him on where he has been hiding the money."

Raven flew through the window and landed on Breakwaters shoulder. Breakwater points at the secrete passage. With one solid kick smashes the panel reveals a room with more ledgers and bags of money. "looks like enough money there to fund a small army." Breakwater gives Glen a pat on the shoulder. "Well now that is all over with I best be on my way." As Breakwater was about to leave the room the Kings men stood in his way. "Oh by the way Breakwater they weren't here for Stone, they here to make sure you get to see the King. you know how he hates his summons ignored."

"Honestly Glen I was on my way." Glen smiled

"You better hope the King swallows that one."

Dark Miracle
By Terry Mullins

The Montrose Event was perhaps the most singular happening in human history. A massive solar flare had erupted from the sun, and screamed on a path to envelop the earth. Despite many over the years cautioning about of this type of flare, the powers that be blissfully continued to run things the way they always have. Their responses ranged from, "let's do a study on this" to 'the likelihood of this happening is remote', even the inane "God wouldn't let something like that happen."

Some refused to believe the flare was coming, thinking it was a way to get them to drop their guard. Some thought it was true, but saw opportunity. So, powers of the readied their militaries.

But strike it did. It lasted a few hours, inflicting tremendous damage. Satellites were knocked offline, sometimes permanently, sometimes not. On earth, those who were still flying soon were not, some landing, all coming down to earth. Radar installations, communication nets and any power plants still operating crashed, with catastrophic effect. Auroras were seen to the equator.

And then it was gone. Power and communications were restored. Then it was discovered that the solar storm had left a legacy, a change that was poised to set the world on its collective ears.

The Montrose Event started the age of Super Powers. Men and women were gifted with abilities out of myth and fiction. It was called a miracle. But as time would tell, the flare was an omen of darker times, and those powers were a dark miracle, for the people that gained these abilities were not saints, but ordinary. Now they were more.

It was a lovely summer day, with a cool breeze blowing, unusual for this time of year. A storm brewed in the distance, but it was not yet threatening. Melissa, Andrea, and Karl were playing. They were not supposed to, as their parents wanted them inside. But the afternoon was clear, the air was fresh and school had been shut for the day. Something called the 'great flare' was going to happen, something that meant little to the eleven-year old children. 'After all, not much will happen. Scientists always get it wrong. Dad said so' Melissa had said, parroting her father's words, that she had heard earlier that day.

But at last, the daylight fading and the storm nearer, they headed home. As they were walking, Andrea's mother met them. 'Andrea, where have you been? I was worried.'

'Sorry Mum. I forgot.' Andrea apologized. Her mother's face was drawn and worried. Andrea thought, why is she worried. The flare thingy isn't dangerous. Dad said so. Her father, the local member of parliament, was a distant man, who didn't show much affection to his only child. Andrea hadn't been told directly about the flare, she had overheard him talking on TV.

Her mother smiled, and shook her head. 'Never mind, you're here now.' She turned to Melissa and Karl. 'You two off to your…'

A sudden flash of light took their attention. In the twilight, a great rippling light crossed the sky, an advancing field of fire, all green's, blue's and purple's dominating. It was silent, and was made even more visible by every artificial light near them going out. The storm rumbled, the clouds lit a strange pink colour, lightning flashing, accenting the strange hues of the heavens. Then, in the distance, a large explosion ripped through a power transformer, high on a power pole, shedding sparks as powerlines fell. Andrea's mother whipped around, saying 'Kid's, down!' But the children were already falling, overwhelmed by a, noise. A passer-by yelled 'my god, look at it. The sky is on fire.'

Later, Andrea said she heard a sound, like a bell echoing in her head. Melissa said she heard a crack of lightning and Karl heard a shout of joy. The last thing Andrea saw for some time was the panicked face of her mother, kneeling beside her, her mouth saying something. Her name she realised.

Ten years later, and a lifetime away, Andrea opened her eyes, as a voice said, 'somethings happening Doctor.' The head up display of her helmet relayed a multitude of information, everything from ambient temperature to news camera footage in the area. It was quiet, high on the Alchemist Inc building, the roof festooned with solar panels and satellite dishes. Ten stories high, it towered over this part of town. Below the distant riot seemed surreal, flames and people and police moving in a strange dance. It was a clear night, with a full moon and blazing stars. High up on the tower, there was only the merest trace of the smoke and heat from below.

Standing there, three figures observed the scene, through a holo projector, displayed in front of them. 'Looks pretty bad,' commented a tall, well-muscled man. 'Covenant believers and a full police response, by the looks.' He was dressed in a dark blue outfit, with lightning bolts running down his sleeves and legs, his head covered by a hood and goggles. A respirator hung loose. Turning to the others he said 'Bad time on the streets. The Patrol will be out, monitoring the situation. Do you think she'll make it?'

'Maybe, maybe not Surge old boy. That's up to blind chance' the second man said. He was dressed in what looked like a business suit, but one that had been recoloured in many different hues, a modern day motely. His face was covered by a white porcelain mask, which sported a merry smile, but his eyes seemed empty. He gave a chuckle 'If anyone can beat the odds, it's Tricky.' He started to whistle, off tune.

Surge gave him a sour look. 'You have a strange way of being helpful, Prank.' Prank chuckled again.

'Have faith. She will be here' came the synthetic, nearly insectoid sounding voice of Andrea. Covered in white armour, with red high-lights, she was fully sealed, protected by synthetic muscles and dense armour plating, and a high end human machine interface. Turning, she faced the two of them, her helmet seeming inhuman in the dim light, her eyes glowing a dim green. 'The distraction of the riot, and the site's low security, increase the odds of success. And Tricky is reliable, and very fast. In fact.' She turned to the street, her eyes glowing green as she watched, her sensory input processing new information. 'There', she pointed.

All three focused on the street. Moving down it a pair of high speed figures burst into view. Lavender St was a long, straight and clear road, walled by offices, shops, and parks. The group focused, and they saw a young woman, dressed in yellow and orange, being chased by a fast-moving slab of muscle, all in black, twin machetes in his hands, a pistol at his side. Above them, moving dangerously fast in the built-up area, was a spider themed aircraft. Cutter and Arachnia, heroes of the patrol. Chasing Tricky.

Andrea leapt of the side of the roof, letting gravity's acceleration take hold, her onboard computer tracking her fall, as she switched into tactical mode. 'Surge, blind Arachnia's craft, Prank, get to the street.' She calmly said over their comm links as she fell. And so, Andrea, the so called super villain known as Doctor Artifice, entered the fray.

It was always strange to Andrea when she entered a gestalt with her battle computer. Her senses expanded, with facts and figures running in front of her eyes, and she didn't so much read as absorb the data. Time seemed to slow, seconds dragged by. Trying to explain it to others was difficult, and all she could say was that it was like a series of images.

Descent commencing. A burst of energy spat out from Surge and Prank,followed down the building with a loud 'Yahoo!'.

Antigrav belt activating, jetpack ignited. Artifice's fall became controlled as her flight systems took hold. Arachnia's vessel staggered as Surge's EMP blast hits it, glowing streams of energy crisscrossing the hull. Around the area, lights fail, and come back on and for an instant her display flickered. She filed a note about it. Her shielding needed some work. Prank, seemingly danced down the side of the building, slowing his fall, catching a window here, a ledge there.

Weapons suite online, targeting. Tricky, moving at nearly two hundred kilometres an hour, stepped onto the bonnet of a car and leapt, spinning as she flew, hurling flashbang grenades behind her. Cutter, sprinted past those before they could detonate, duplicating her manoeuvre with a shout. The car they both used as a launch pad staggered under the double impact, its car alarm filling the night with sound. Blurring with speed, Cutter closed on Tricky, moving to both cut her path off and cut her body.

Targeting systems locked. Smiling with anticipation, his blades started to swing. Tricky tried to dodge, with little hope of avoiding the attack.

Lasers firing, Mini missiles away. Both shoulder lasers slammed into Cutter's arms, throwing off his aim and causing him to stumble. He slammed into Tricky, entangling the two of them. The pair of them hit the road and start a shattering roll, splitting the pair apart. Six of the mini missiles slam into Arachnia's craft just as she started to fire her auto cannons, their shells pock marking concrete and shattering windows as the vehicle spun under the missiles impact. The spider craft sharply turned and fled down a side street, trailing smoke and flares, seeking to avoid contact as the surviving mini missiles pursued.

Both tumbling speedsters continued their bruising roll. Prank landed on the ground with an elegant tumble. As part of the same action he hurled a small sphere at the tumbling pair. Striking the ground near them, it exploded with a loud pop, and covered them with a restraining goo, slowing their slide. Surge himself jumped to the street, landing as if ten stories was nothing as he converts his kinetic energy into a flash of light and a loud thunderclap.

Doctor Artifice, placed her battle computer on standby, and moved over to Tricky, cutting her jets to land. Both the speedsters had ended up against the wall of a building. 'Surge, Prank watch Cutter.' Quickly, she pulled out a spray dispenser and used it, causing the goo on Tricky to dissolve. Pulling her away from the still entangled and struggling Cutter, Tricky gave a gasp of pain.

Looking up and seeing the white and red helmet of Andrea, she smiled. 'Hey. Sorry, but I ran into company.'

Artifice nodded, 'So it seems'. Cutter struggled and began swearing at the group, the bindings holding him, and the world in general. Artifice sighed. 'Prank, if you would.' The entangled hero went silent as a large calibre pistol appeared in Prank's hand, the barrel of which was pushed into his throat.

'Cutter, if you don't shut up, I will take immense pleasure in shooting you.' He stated in his carefree way. But the eyes behind his googles were cold, as was the tone of his voice. Cutter shut up. Another goo grenade was used pinning him completely to the ground. Prank got up as the rest started to move away and waved at the entangled hero. 'Ta tah,' he sang as he hurried after the others. Cutter started swearing again, though much more quietly.

'Surge, take Tricky. We need to withdraw for now.' Artifice had completed her scan of Tricky. 'Two cracked ribs, a lot of bruising. A day or so of healing for her.' Already, she was scanning the area, tracking Arachnia's vessel as it wheeled around the streets, tracking the signals being transmitted. 'Arachnia is calling for assistance. We will have the Patrol here in minutes. Prank, stay and observe. We'll take the others to safety.'

Prank flipped a salute to her mockingly and said 'Okay dokay. I can do that little thing. Meet you all later.' He moved to the side and faded into shadow.

Surge picked up Tricky, cradling her as Artifice grabbed him, ignited her rocket pack, and started flying. 'Oh Tricky, did you get the package?'

'Oh yes. I got it.'

Her face hidden by her armour, Andrea smiled. 'Good.'

Prank slipped back to the safe house the group was currently using, moving from shadow to shadow. The Patrol, accompanied by special service police, cleared the scene of their little battle, freeing Cutter and taking evidence. When they finished, so he left. Obviously, there would be no immediate pursuit.

He paused in a shadow for a moment, to reflect on things. It had been a wild few years. The world was going to hell in a hand basket, and all was dark and gloomy, with no light but the one of an oncoming semi. He shook his head. This wasn't like him. Or more correctly wasn't like him now. As a child, he was introspective, quiet. Then came the flare. A voice of sheer joy is what he heard at the time, and a new self just appeared. The Prank. He took off his mask, with some effort and looked at it. His other self. With the mask off he could just think. With it on he preferred to act. Strange, he didn't use to have to have the mask on to bring out the Prank. He just did it. Now it was harder. He shook his head.

Stupid, he thought, *best get going.* Putting the mask back on, he looked around. The night vision in the googles allowed him to see the darkling world as if in near daylight. No one was following. He waited a few minutes, and backed track himself a bit. Something? A flicker of movement scratched his vision. Hmm.

Prank faded into the deep shadows of the building near him and shifted. Shifting was something he didn't like doing much. True, it was a way to disappear and reappear, teleporting if you liked the term. But it was cold when he did it, and strange voices seemed to speak to him, just out of earshot. Old Doc Artifice had measured the time it took for the shift, and said it was close to instant. But it always seemed longer. It was tempting to linger a bit to make sense of it. But Prank felt if he did, he might never re-emerge.

Still, it was handy. He emerged inside another shadow, overlooking the alley. He glimpsed something. Ah! A drone. Annoying things, and no way for him to know who was controlling it. It could be a news service, a fan group, a spy agency or even the government. Best not to take chances. The drone lifted and quietly moved to his last known location. Prank smiled, and shifted again to a different shadow. Only the voices remained.

Minutes later he arrived at the safe house, pushing the doorbell. A small camera examined him and the door opened. He waved at the camera and entered. A few seconds later he was descending in a high-speed elevator to their real base. If someone was still tracking him, they would have fun searching an empty house. An excellent prank.

Melissa, known in costume as Tricky, tried to relax on the bed as the autodoc examined her. She flinched as the robot gently touched her ribs. 'Hmm, yes. Field diagnosis matches. Two cracked ribs, bruising across much of your body. Some grazing. Hmm.' Melissa had often wondered why Andrea had designed the autodocs so that they chatted and commented as they worked. Maybe it was to make them less imposing. Five-foot-tall cylinders, surmounted by cameras and with multiple retracting arms, each with different tools and grippers, they were somewhat daunting. The voice was supposed to humanized them, she supposed. It didn't work. The auto doctor finished its examination, giving her a strip of tablets. 'With your accelerated metabolism, recovery should be completed inside twenty-four hours. If you feel discomfort, take two painkillers. If symptoms persist, see me tomorrow. You can go.'

'Thanks, Doc.' She said. Ozzie, changed out of his Surge costume and lying on the nearby lounge, smirked as she got up. As far as he was concerned, thanking a machine was foolish. But Tricky felt it was appropriate. He went back to watching the news, while Andrea was examined the file Melissa had recovered. Or stolen, depending on the point of view.

'You are welcome child' said the autodoc, and it handed her a lollypop from its lollipop dispenser. Melissa got to her feet, pulling on her shirt and accepting the lollipop, and walked over to Andrea, ignoring the now laughing Ozzie.

'So, what do we have' she asked the busy woman.

'Several points of interest.'

'Such as? My lord, pulling information out of you is like drawing water from a stone.' Melissa sniped.

Andrea turned her head towards Melissa, opening her helmet. She smiled. In a normal, non-synthesised voice she said 'You raided a university archive. As far as I can see, we have two hundred and four thousand, six hundred and twelve files, on topics ranging from anthropology to zoology. Even I am going to need a little time to go through it. But yes, I have identified some files that will be important in both our near and far future.' She touched her on the face. 'Are you OK?'

'Good as new by tomorrow. But you already knew that.'

'Physically yes, but that is not what I am talking about. Cutter got closer than I liked. What happened? The Patrol should have been nowhere near you. This information was not that secure.'

Melissa shrugged, immediately regretting the move as pain jabbed in her side. 'I don't know. It was quiet, only a couple of guards around, a few researchers still working. No one near me.' As she spoke, Andrea brought up the schematics of the building Melissa had entered. 'The codes you gave worked, and it took about five minutes to complete the download. But when I exited the building Cane Toad and Cutter jumped me. Nearly got me too, but I flash-banged Cane Toad and ran. Arachnia joined in and I bolted towards you.'

'Hmm.' Andrea fully removed her helmet, and ran her fingers through her hair. 'Why just those three? The Patrol SOP would have called for a full team to engage a known felon, which is five to six members, not three. And they would have had special service police support' It seemed strange to hear her normal, synthesised voice.

Melissa winced. The Patrol was the national "Hero" group, the super-powered arm of the state. Most of them were ok, but some were, well, dicks. 'No, no SSP, and just the three of them. Do you think this wasn't sanctioned?'

'Perhaps. Get something to eat and drink. I shouldn't be long.' Andrea refocused on the screen, pulling in and analysing information.

As Andrea worked, she ruminated about the past. Part of her gift, her talent, her power if you liked, was a memory that never forgot. But sometimes she could put a memory to one side. Archive it, as she once joked. Ever since the flare. She could also multitask like very few others. So, as she worked, she remembered.

It had been six months after the flare, with large parts of the world going up in flames, both figuratively and literally. Andrea hadn't been to school for a long time, and hadn't seen her friends for longer. There was no point. She now knew and understood everything a student should know at high school graduation and beyond. It was all so easy, now. But her parents were troubled. Her father wanted to keep her "gifts" a secret, and mother wanted care for her. Andrea was sad about what she had done to her parents. She heard the arguments.

Before the flare, Andrea and her parents went along to church every Sunday. Afterwards they went together only a few more times. Her parents had not quite understood what had happened to her, and she had been learning at an accelerated rate for weeks. Then when they were sitting in the church she asked, fairly distinctly 'There is no objective proof for a deity like this. Why are we coming here? It's boring.'

Her father stared at her, stunned, his face growing red. Her mother stammered a moment and said, 'Andrea, be quiet!' Andrea didn't know what was wrong. She had always been told to tell the truth. Her father said nothing, but at the end of the mass had calmed him down.

He said to Andrea's mother, 'take her to the car. I'll be along.' Then he turned to talk to other parishioners. Her mother was quiet as she took her to the car.

'Mum, what's wrong?'

'Dear one, you cannot say things like that in church. You just can't. Your father is very angry at you.'

'But...'

'There are no buts, young woman! Sit quietly!'

Andrea obeyed. Her father came back to the car and asked, 'who told you such false trash, Andrea? To say that in church. Lord save me, where did you learn that, that falsehood?' He finished nearly yelling at her.

Andrea was stunned, but she realised to reply would result in more yelling. Her mother said to her father, 'dear, let us talk about this at home.'

She was banished to her room, and banned from television and the internet. So, she sat and thought. She heard her parents arguing in their room. Lying down on her bed, she listened.

From that day, she was forbidden to access the internet as 'it has given you false ideas that will be purged', but within a day, she had, with the use of an electronics kit for kids, an old keyboard, and her television set, circumvented that. She didn't want to lie to her parents, but she needed to know. But all she found were more questions.

Then school started up again. Due to the troubles, schools had been shut down, but as a "return to normality' the local church school, Saint Mary, was opening. When she arrived, Melissa was not there, and no one would tell her where she was, just that "she was sick, you should pray for her." Karl's family had moved away, she knew that. So, she was friendless. And the lessons were, boring. She already understood the whys, wherefores, and answers.

Within two weeks, Andrea had learned three things. One that Melissa and Karl were gone forever, that school had nothing to teach her, and she was super powered. She had repaired a computer in class, got every answer correct and built a robot. She demonstrated she could bypass computer censor blocks and showed that she was quicker and fitter than even many of the boys. Other students avoided her, and the teachers were nervous. After that her parents took her out of school. Everything came to a head that Sunday night. Her father rarely talked to her, but the reports from the school about her meant he had to. Both him and her mother sat at the table, facing her.

'Andrea, we have been talking to the school. And they have said you are different.'

'Yes father' she said. This was going to be unpleasant.

Her father was uncharacteristically uncertain, so mother spoke up. 'We are going to have you assessed, my dear. It's the law. So, you will be going to a special hospital for a few days. We will need to pack a few things.' Andrea had heard about being assessed. It had a bad reputation.

And that was that. She never directly spoke to her father again, only saw him on television or at a distance. The next day they left and entered a small hospital on the outskirts of Sydney. A doctor, and a lawyer spoke to her and her mother after three days of testing, after which her mother signed some papers. The lawyer, a tall, thin man with a sour face said, 'she can be on her way today. It's best to do this quickly. We have a car to take both of you to the train station.' Her mother nodded. The saddest day of Andrea's life.

Andrea blinked, and bought her main attention to the here and now. Melissa was shaking her arm. The sad memory faded. Part of her gift. She never forgot. 'Andrea, do you want some food?'

'Oh. Yes please' she said absently. Andrea restarted working on the computer, and Melissa went into the kitchen to cook.

'Ozzie, you want something?' she asked as she did.

'Nah, I'm good,' he replied. He relaxed on the couch, changing channels with a blink of the eyes. He looked back at the others quickly with fondness. Good friends, even Karl. He considered himself lucky to have them. In the world of today, you needed to have friends you can trust.

After the flare, Ozzie had become a controller of electricity, and other electromagnetic forces. It became his play thing. His mother and father had taken him onto shows on television to demonstrate what he could do. Electric Oz they called him. Made a lot of money doing it. Later he said, 'Lord we were stupid. All it did was to make me a target.'

While he was showboating, the world was imploding. North Korea, then China, and all the places in the world where grudges were deeply held. Some places just ceased to be nations. Then came the Harris Act.

The Harris Act was the Australian Government's response to the super human crisis. Under it, all superhuman individuals would be incarcerated, until they were considered safe to return to society. Powered children became wards of the state, those older were just imprisoned. It wasn't called that, but it was. He was rounded up quickly, his mother and father forced to give him up. They, and others like them, screamed bloody murder, calling it legalised abduction, and gathered support for a legal challenge. It might have worked.

Then came the attack on Brisbane by the Desolation, a group of supers bent on destruction. All legal avenues at that point evaporated. Well, that was the past, and he was no longer in the government's care, though they really wanted him back. They had proven that on many occasions.

But, because of it they all met. Doctor Artifice, Tricky and Prank, though when he met them they were Andrea, Melissa, and Karl. In the institute.   A chime sounded, alerting them. Someone was coming down the lift. Karl got up and moved to the security panel, and checked the monitor. Karl. Good.

A few seconds later, the door opened and he emerged. 'Hey.'

'Hey back. Anything interesting happen?'

'Not a lot. Cane Toad and Arachnia freed Cutter, and left. A drone tagged me on the way back, but I lost it. Might not be a bad idea to scan the neighbourhood, though.' Karl took off his mask, and looked up. Seeing Melissa cooking, the smells of bacon, eggs, beans and onion drifting through the 'Hey, Mel, can I have some?'

'Yea, oh endless stomach,' she replied fondly. 'I'm making extra.'

Karl undid his utility belt, dropping it on the table, and placed his pistol beside it, and went to help tricky. Karl moved back to the couch. Soon Melissa and Karl joined him with plates of bacon, eggs, onions and baked beans. And toast. 'An early breakfast' Karl commented. Melissa had placed a plate beside Andrea without a word. Without breaking her gaze, Andrea began eating, typing or using the mouse with the other hand.

Ozzie watched her for a moment as Melissa joined them. 'That is eerie.'

Karl clipped him on the shoulder, as Melissa glared at him. 'You do know she can hear you.'

He grinned. 'Didn't say it was a bad thing.' Then discovering his appetite, he tucked in.

They settled to eat, without much conversation, watching the television. Behind them Andrea scanned, typed and analysed. Of course, she heard the conversation of her friends, and while working she began working out comments she could make later, while at the same time she processed the information before her, and charted their strategic path forward.

Then…What was that. She refocused, her eyes narrowing. A name. Doctor Armstrong Jones. A name she remembered well. Nine years ago. She remembered it with pinpoint accuracy.

Andrea was dressed in a blue dress, a backpack on her back and a suitcase beside her. Her mother was with her as they waited in the train station with a few other children and parents. Outside was noise, the sound of protestors. There was fear in the air, Andrea could taste it.

It had been a week, before the assessment. Her parents just seemed to stop loving her. Her father wouldn't even talk to her unless to give orders, and her mother wouldn't look at her. She was tested, and obviously found wanting. She took it unemotionally, but something finally broke inside her. She could now discuss quantum physics at a doctorate level, could understand and argue both philosophy or literature. It meant nothing to those who were supposed to love her. In her room on that last night she cried quietly.

Now she was at the train station. There were policemen wearing armour, and carrying rifles. Andrea wasn't certain if they were to protect her, or guard her. Outside protesters screamed for "the devil children, the freaks" to be gotten rid of. People she had never met hated her. 'Why do they hate me mother?' she asked. Her mother, somewhat flustered replied.

'They are afraid. People like you are dangerous. It best that you go to where it will be safer.' She suddenly realized what she said and corrected herself, 'I mean where you'll be safer. Of course. Please be quiet, dear. Ask your father when he comes.' And that was Andrea's last conversation with her mother. Her father never showed.

The children's names were called out, and when hers came up her mother said, 'Go on. Your father and I will visit you.' They never did. Later Andrea worked out why. He father was part of the 'lock them up' political movement, and she was a liability to him. Sending her to confinement showed his willingness to sacrifice for his ideals. Her views were not considered.

The train trip was quiet, with some children crying, others sitting in a stunned silence. The guards patrolled the passageways. She never really spoke to anyone for the entire trip. The trip took three days, or there about. The train stopped, and exchanged guards, and took on more children. The terrain outside grew dryer and turned into desert. Finally, they arrived. They exited the train onto a concrete platform. There was a bus nearby, a bus that was unusual, for the windows were covered in bars. And all the armed guards were still present. A rollcall began. A somewhat overweight man with a greying hair and a large moustache stepped forward.

'Children. My name is Doctor Jones, Doctor Armstrong Jones. I know this has been very scary for you, but you have nothing to fear here. But you all have abilities that set you apart from most people. You are here for both you and us to learn about your abilities, to determine that you are safe, and send you home. Now everyone please get on the bus, and we will take you to your new home.

You have nothing to fear here. The first lie.

Her reverie took her less than a second. She smiled. It was not a kind smile, but was one that promised that someone soon was going to be unhappy.

'Attend, everyone!' she ordered. The others, had finished their food and were quietly talking and watching TV.

'What's up' Karl asked.

'I have found someone, someone we all know. Someone who owes us dearly.' She put her helmet on, and assumed her other identity, Doctor Artifice. With the helmets neurological links, she converted the files she had located to a circling holographic image centred on the table. The room grew quiet as they absorbed the information.

Ozzie spoke first. 'Doctor Armstrong Jones, you miserable, child abusing bastard! He's alive? You know where he is?'

Artifice's synthesized answer was short. 'Yes, and yes.'

Melissa, her eyes grown huge, said 'Where, where is he?'

'He is living in a tenured position at the Alexander Harris Memorial institute. His name has been changed, but it is him. These three files are video images of him visiting an astronomical symposium. On the Montrose Event. He is now called Doctor Arnold Carter.' She started to play one of the recordings, muted. After about twenty seconds, she froze the image. Then she isolated a shot of the audience, zooming into a pair of men, then onto one of them. The hologram split, placing an older image up. 'I have a ninety-eight percent correlation. It is him. Now the question is, what do we do?'

There was silence for a moment, as the four considered the issue. Melissa said. 'He is a monster who made monsters out of children. He has no right to live free under the sun.'

The others paused in a little shock. Melissa was perhaps the most nonviolent of the group, quite often being a peace maker within the team, and in their dealings with others. For her to suggest what she seemed to be suggesting was a shock. Prank found his voice first. 'Assuming a nineteen twenties gangster voice, he said 'so yer want him ta be pushing up the daisy's, sweetheart?' His mask assumed a stern look.

Melissa, caught out by her own comment, looked flustered. 'I…don't know. But he must pay. Perhaps if we publicly reveal him to the authorities, he could be sent to prison.'

Andrea shook her head. 'I don't think that will work, Melissa. Look at the person beside him.' She removed the old image of the doctor from the screen, expanded the image somewhat, and focused on the man beside him, who was sitting talking to the doctor. The hologram split into three side by side images. The first was the original shot, the second reveal a man in his twenties, tall and well-muscled, with black, shoulder length hair. The third show a man in a black and blue uniform, with the crest of an exploding star on his chest.

Surge swore, and Prank's fists clenched. Melissa sighed. 'Nova. It's definitely him?'

'Yes', Andrea said. 'Nova, or as we remember, Brenden Georges. Another fine product of Doctor Jones's experiments. And head of the Patrol'.

All of them remembered the detention centre, the tests, and trials, but Andrea remembered it all as if it happened yesterday. The facility seemed at first to be much like a school at first, albeit with armed guards. The children were divided up into classes and were assigned teachers. But they couldn't leave, and there was an area they were forbidden to go. The special section. But every now and then students would be taken there to work on "expanded classes." They never came back, except for two students. The first was Brenden. He was a couple of years older than Andrea when she and Ozzie met him, a stern and strict child. And he was a dick, in both their opinions. The second student was her.

Andrea's abilities drew her to the close attention of Doctor Jones, and after a month he had her assigned to him for closer analysis. This turned out to her being used as a living computer, and she attended the good doctor as he worked. She asked him once why she was spared the lessons the others had. He looked at her and started asking her a series of questions, ranging from current quantum theory, to biology, to deep philosophy. Then he asked her, 'If you know, and by that, I mean understand, the answers to the questions just given, what could school lessons give you?' She had no reply.

So, she was now an appendage of him. Strangely, so was Brenden. He was a quiet boy, but very focused on the rules, as he saw them. The primary rule was, it seemed, that Doctor Jones made the rules. And Brenden's gifts were extraordinary. Great strength, strong resistant to damage, and the ability to fly made him a perfect example of a tank type power, or more specifically a flying tank.

Time passed, months flowed on into years. Andrea read and learned vast amounts at this time, as the Doctor believed she would be of the greatest use to him as his personal information and analysis source. She also learned several other things. That Brenden had no problem being a dick, and that the doctor used her friendship with Ozzie as a lever to control her, (He had at first tried to use her parents in this role, but soon found out that she didn't care much about consequences to them). Then he discovered Karl and Melissa's importance to Andrea.

The special section was carrying out scientific investigation that crossed the border of legality and morality, in the search for understanding of, and application of super powers. And both Karl and Melissa were in the middle of it.

She found out one day, as she was working in the workshop. Both

Doctor Jones and Brenden walked in. 'Andrea, a moment of your time.'

Andrea froze a second. This would be unpleasant. She was only supposed to work here under supervision. *Brenden again*, she thought. Assuming a blank face, she said 'Yes, Doctor?'

'What are you working on?'

Her mind thought quickly, finding a story that was nearly true. 'An idea I had, doctor. It is an attempt to make a small drone, a walking type that can scale walls, windows.'

'Ah. Why?'

'I thought it could be useful. In cleaning, remote repair, that sort of thing.'

'Ah. May I see it.' Andrea passed him the tiny robot. It was a big as a bottlecap, with multiple legs, a marvel of micro engineering. 'It seems somewhat flimsy. Brenden, test its resistant to damage.' He passed it to Brenden. He held it between his thumb and index finger, looked at it for a second, then crushed it. No emotion crossed Andrea's face. 'Ah,' the doctor continued, 'not that useful.' He sat down across from her, as Brenden stood behind him. 'We should, I think talk about your violations of the rules, Andrea. You have been given much here, and yet I sense defiance in you.' He stared at her for a moment, Andrea staring back. 'Ah. Come my dear, I have something to show you.' He stood up, gesturing to Andrea to do the same. She stood and they all left the room.

They moved through the white corridors of the special section, occasionally meeting other researchers, who greeted Doctor Jones with good mornings and smiles, with the Doctor responding with their names and a friendly nod. It suddenly occurred to Andrea that behind the friendly exterior, the façade of amiability, they were all scared of this man. After a time, they entered an observation room. The room had several screens on the walls, and tables filled with computers. Two lab assistants were working in the room, and on their entrance, both stood respectfully.

'Ah. Gentlemen, I need this room for a short while. Please set your devices to automatic recording and take a break. I'll let you know when to come back.'

Both said, 'Of course, Doctor Jones,' and after a short amount of typing on their computers, left the room.

After they left, the Doctor sat at one of the terminals. 'Now, Andrea, the special section is purposed with investigating the powers and abilities of people like you. This is only one such facility, of course. There are others. But this is the only one investigating the young in this matter. This section contains those who have been determined as too dangerous to be released, or who have abilities we may need. Let me show you a few of these subjects.' He deactivated the screens, except for two. On them she saw both Melissa and Karl. Karl was huddled in a ball, in the middle of an extremely bright room, and Melissa was running on a treadmill, sensors attached to her body. She looked tired, and Andrea realized that she was close to collapse. 'Subjects 124 and 214. The girl has what the simple call "super speed", and the boy, Ah. He is interesting. He can transpose himself from shadow to shadow.'

He looked at Andrea. Her blank face had been replaced by a pale, clenched one. 'Ah. You know subject 124 or 214? Or both?'

'You know that I do, Doctor.' Tears ran from her eyes, but she, with an effort, resumed her blank face. 'What you are doing here is illegal, Doctor. Even under the Harris Act. Would you like me to site the relevant laws and regulations?'

He smiled, a friendly smile and chuckled a bit. 'No thank you. Pfft, laws are transitory things, changed at whim by people who are ignorant. I serve the needs of science, and my goal is the betterment of mankind. I am not bound by such trivialities.'

'You are an evil man.' She realized that was a mistake as Brenden's hand closed on her shoulder and squeezed. There was an audible crack, and a massive jolt of pain, and she screamed, collapsing to her knees.

'Ah.' The Doctor knelt, and quickly examined her. 'Ah, a broken collar bone. Brenden, that was an overreaction.'

'Sorry Doctor.'

'Ah. Well, these things happen.' He stood. 'I guess we can let this one go, but please be careful in future,' he said, patting Brenden on the shoulder. He looks at the weeping girl. 'Ah. Andrea. I am in a decision point at this moment as to the future experiments to be carried out on Subject 124 and 214. Maybe more invasive procedures? Also, I have decided to bring a new subject into the special unit. Subject 301. You know him as Ozzie Phelps. I wonder what we will learn.' He smiled again. 'Let me put it bluntly to you, my dear. Your behaviour will influence my decisions here.' He looked at Brenden. 'Take her to the infirmary. A broken collar bone is nothing to sneeze at.'

At that moment, Andrea came to a decision. Despite the pain, her emotional state, she thought clearly behind it. She had to escape. And take her friends with her.

Memory, Andrea thought, back in the present. *Sometimes I think it's a curse.* The escape was easy, though dangerous. What Doctor Jones hadn't known was that the tiny robot destroyed by Brenden was not the only one. By the time he discovered her efforts, she had already built twelve of them, and a small device, an ear bud, to communicate with them. And they built more of themselves to her instruction. Also, she lied about what they could do. She called them assemblers. Nano technology that wasn't Nano. They could eventually make whatever she wanted. Six months after her collar bone being broken, they all escaped, with most of the "students." The good Doctor was missing presumed dead, in the burning wreak of the special unit. Four years they had been in that place, they entered as children. When they left, they weren't.

She looked at the others, and they all looked at her. 'He owes us. We need to find him, and make sure he isn't hurting anyone else, see he faces justice. We are called villains, but that is only because the villains are in charge. Go sleep. Tomorrow we prepare. Tomorrow night we act.

The next night, all of them were in an empty building close to the institute. After the troubles, many businesses had closed, leaving many deserted structures. All of them were in their combat costumes, and were checking their equipment. Artifice turned to her companions, her helmet sealed. 'According to my sensor drones, he seems to be alone in his house, watching TV I think. Security seems light.'

'Sounds like an easy attack. He is unsuspecting, and we can be in and out in minutes' Surge said, as he checked the magazine on his pistol.

Artifice stayed silent. Melissa sensed she was uneasy about something. 'What's wrong, Doctor? Everything seems to be going to plan.'

Prank answered instead of Artifice. 'It's too easy. He should have much more security.' His mask imaged concern.

Surge stopped his weapon check. 'You think it's a trap.' He had learned over the years that if Prank thought something was off, things were definitely off. 'Maybe we should back off.'

'What? But we are so close.' Tricky sounded like she had been just informed her puppy had died. She turned to Artifice. 'Do you think that?'

For a long moment, Artifice said nothing. Then, 'I am extending the sensor drones search pattern. This will take a few minutes. I am also going to risk sending one into the house to do a direct visual inspection of Doctor Jones.

Outside, Doctor Artifice's drones scattered. These drones were small, less than five centimetres across, and disc shaped, upgraded versions of her originals. They were silent and as invisible as she could make them. They moved out on their expanded search areas.

One however slipped into the house, under the front door. Quietly it moved into the lounge room, where according to the heat scan of the house, Doctor Jones was. Artifice focused her vision, through the drone, onto the static figure. The Doctor seemed to be sleeping, wearing a nightgown and slippers, with a folded-up newspaper on his lap. The drone at this range could sense his heart pumping, and could the sound of breathing. Artifice gathered the information. It seemed alright, but Prank was right. She went back over the gathered sensor information. Then it clicked.

'It's too regular.'

The others stared at her. 'What...' Surge started.

'His heart beat, his breathing, it's too regular, too artificial. It isn't him. It isn't even human.'

'Shit' Surge muttered. 'Then it is a trap. We should leave, now.'

'No. The trap is wider than you think. My drones are picking up a significant force of police gathering around us. I have located Arachnia's spider ship, camouflaged in a court yard, two blocks away. Prank, go onto the roof, see if you can see anything.'

'On it.' Prank's mask showed a grim determination on it as he stepped into a shadow and vanished.

'Tricky, check the building, see if we have been infiltrated. Surge wait with me.' Tricky gave a loose salute and shot away.

Surge, his face hidden behind his hood and googles still manage to show concern. 'Are we in trouble?'

'Yes. On my command, I want you to generate the biggest pulse you can. Push your limits, Surge.'

Prank reappeared. 'There's no one on the roof, at the moment, but I can see some aircraft orbiting us a few kilometres away. Helicopters I think.' Even he was starting to show tension.

Tricky returned. 'There's no one else here.'

Behind the opaque face plate of her helmet, Artifice smiled. 'I don't think they know we are here. Or at least not here precisely. Prepare to move.'

'As soon as we move, they'll be over us like a rash.' Prank cautioned.

'I know. But if Doctor Jones is behind this, he will want to gloat. He wants to beat us, show he is our superior. Maybe even get us back under his thumb. Our response is obvious.'

'Is it?' Melissa sounded confused. Pranks mask showed a puzzled look.

'Oh yes. I'm going to trigger his trap.'

Minutes later the front door of the target house exploded, and the white and red armoured form of Doctor Artifice entered. In seconds, she had entered the lounge room, and a bolt of energy slammed into the head of the sleeping figure. For an instant, nothing happened. Then metal sheets slammed down, cutting off all egress from the building. A hologram formed in front of her.

'Ah. Doctor Artifice I assume. Or perhaps we can be less formal. What do you say, Andrea?'

Artifice cocked her head. 'Well if you want me to, Armstrong.'

The image of Doctor Jones winced. 'I think you should keep calling me doctor. Unlike you, I have earned my title.'

'No, I think I'll keep calling you Armstrong. Armstrong the child abuser. It has a nice ring to it.'

'You seek to provoke me. You will not succeed. Ah. Two points; you are trapped, and there are enough explosives in this house to kill you. I advise you to remove your armour, disarm your weapons and cease all communications. I had hope to collect all your little band, as it is likely they are nearby. So, finding them should not be too hard a task. And if they get away, they'll be little threat without you leading them.'

'Oh, Armstrong.' Artifice's sing song synthetic voice was mocking. 'You have made the same errors you did years ago.'

'What is that?'

'You underestimate me, and you are arrogant. And you are still an evil, evil man. We will find you Armstrong. And there will be a reckoning of your crimes. All of them.'

For the first time she could remember, the doctor looked angry. 'I see no further point to this conversation. Nova, take her!'

One of the metal screens dropped and Nova, smashing through the window so revealed, pounced on Artifice. Or would have, if he hadn't passed straight through her. Surprised, he slammed into the opposing wall, punching through it into another room.

Her flickering image looked at the shocked face of Doctor Jones. 'What's the matter, Armstrong. You look like you have seen a ghost. Two can play at deception.' Then the image vanished.

Fifty metres above the house, Artifice activated a link with her neuro net, triggering the radio detonators on the explosives in the house, whose frequency she had determined before her hologram had entered.

The explosion was truly epic, with the shock wave buffeting her, shredding her cloaking field. Below her she could see Nova blasted out of the fireball that was once a house, trailing flame. With an angry scream he shot upward, seeking to attack. The collected police forces started to react to her defiant presence. She smiled. If this worked she and her friends would be legendary.

'Surge, now!'

Hidden on the roof of the building they had prepared in, Surge was seated in a lotus position, focusing himself for his greatest ever pulse. Beside him, Tricky had her medical kit at the ready, and Prank was ready to support him. When the signal came through, he focused on a patch of sky, a thousand metres up. And pushed. As the energy came out of him he screamed. A flash occurred, and it expanded in vast hemisphere. The approaching helicopters quite literally fell out of the sky, and even Arachnia's flyer staggered as it was rising, crashing into a building. Radios sizzled and died, radars burned out, cars lost power. The perimeter of the effect continued to expand, spreading the damage as lights failed. The effect was felt for tens of kilometres, and it still expanded. Above them an aurora appeared, in greens and purples and blues. Surge collapsed, staggered and gasping, into Prank's waiting arms. Tricky quickly took his pulse, and found it, weak and thready. But strengthening.

Artifice's armour systems flickered for a moment. She had studied Surge's pulse ability for years, and had shielded her systems as best she could against it, but even that was overcome by this pulse. For an instant. She noticed the aurora blazing above both herself and Nova. *An omen*, she thought. *Yes.*

Suddenly she changed her plans as information flowed into her mind. At this point she had originally intended to evade, and she still could. But she wasn't now. The Aurora above her, so like the one that caused the dark miracle that cursed this world, was her sign, her omen. A stand was needed. Nova was going to fall. She was going to win this.

'Too long, Brenden. For too long no one has opposed you. It is just you and me, now, you useless dick! Come on, show me what you've got!' Nova screamed and charged into her with a crash of power, causing them to whirl around in the sky. Below the police and few civilians in the area stared in wonder at this clash of supers, heedless of the danger.

As Nova shot up towards her, Artifice was already dodging, her battle computers predicting and projecting tactics. Ducking under his haymaker, she slammed two punches into his rib cage, and broke away. Her fists could dent plate steel, and shatter rock, but the effect on Nova was simply to wind him. They spun around the sky, exchanging blows, but most of Nova's missed Artifice, while hers didn't. As the exchange of attacks continued, Artifice noticed this.

It confirmed in her mind was that Nova was a bad fighter. The reason was simple. Nova was lazy. True, he could throw a tank, and rockets would bounce of him. He was exceedingly fast, and could outfly a jet, but it was obvious he hardly ever trained. What was the point, as in his mind no one was his equal. But Artifice had trained for the last six years, and had fought many times. Some battles she won, others lost, but she learned in the way only a mind like her could. At this point she was possibly one of the best hand to hand fighters in the world, backed up by cybernetic muscles and a predictive battle computer. Nova, to his shock, suddenly found he was on the defensive for the first time in his experience, his attacks dodged or blocked, and he was taking hits that were beginning to hurt. 'Can anyone support me?' he called on his comm. link. There was no reply. He didn't understand his radio had been fried by the pulse, that his teammates were trying to escape their crashed aircraft, and the police below were significantly demoralized by the events unfolding. He was alone.

Nova launched a vicious kick into her midriff, which she rolled with, taking his leg in her hands. Warning signals flashed in her vision as she rode the kick going into a spin, then slammed him into the ground, the people below diving for cover, as debris scattered.

Nova recovered, standing quickly, launching himself into the air at Artifice. She reacted, falling back, and flushed her missile racks at him. A cluster of explosions crashed over Nova, jarring him but he still climbed, seeking his tormentor. Artifice felt rather than heard her missile pods reloading, and realized she was going to take a hit. She accepted that, and strove to make a problem an advantage. With lightning speed. she slammed her arm into a block, striking between Nova's hand and elbow, reducing the attacks power, and deflecting the strike somewhat, but the impact spun her. Warning signals flared. She noted, absently, that the armour on her left shoulder was badly damaged. The pain was bad, but she accepted it as the price for her counter.

For Artifice's battle computer had recognized a weakness in his defence, and flipping behind him, she smashed the back of his neck with a double fisted blow, driving Nova head first into the rubble of the house below. The noise was incredible, dust and smoke rose from the crater where he hit. Her pods reloaded, she followed up with a full flight of missiles and both shoulder mounted lasers, the lurid red light brightening the scene with a hellish glow. Guided by her battle computer gesalted mind, she followed up, powering down feet first onto Nova's chest, cracking ribs.

Nova couldn't believe this. He was in more pain then he had ever experienced, he was dazed and confused and couldn't see properly. His lack of combat training showed. He found himself on his back, with Artifice straddling him, her knees pinning his arms. All he could do was try to breath.

Artifice's face plate opened and he saw the face of the girl he had victimised years before, her eyes hard and cold. 'Hello, Brenden. It's been a while' He couldn't believe it. He was beaten by her!

'Stupid bitch, couldn't face me in a fair fight' he snarled, trying to shake her off.

That got a laugh, as she easily countered him, slamming his head onto concrete, with an audible crack as the cement fractured. 'You're not trying to say if I was out of my armour it would a fair fight? That reminds me, I owe you something.' She struck with devastating force on the space between his neck and shoulder. There was a sickening crunch, and he screamed in pain. 'Payback. Remind your master, slave, we are coming for him.'

With that she shot up, the rockets on her pack blazing as she sought both altitude and speed. He lost her in the rippling aurora as he lay there, in too much pain to move.

The dust of the battle had cleared, and the lights were restored. The Patrol gathered around their fallen leader, stunned at what had occurred. The Special Service Police kept their distance, but Nova was certain he saw condemnation in their eyes. The paramedic working on him finished the support dressing on his shoulder and offered something for the pain. He didn't reply, and one of his team mates thanked her. She shrugged, packed up her kit and left.

The team gathered their defeated leader and flew him back to their base, an ex-military facility on a small island in Sydney harbour. The specialized medical group there set his broken collar bone, concluding that he also had several cracked ribs. Still he said nothing.

Finally, they left him to rest. Quiet at last. After about five minutes someone entered his room. Doctor Jones. Nova said hollowly, 'I failed, Doctor. She beat me, I could hardly touch her. How? It was Andrea, from the Institute. She's just a weakling, a know it all geek.'

Doctor Jones, sighed, sitting beside his bed. 'Ah. My boy, you lost a battle, but not the war.' He sat back and sighed again. 'Yes, our little trap failed its objectives, but we have learned much. They have revealed a lot of their capabilities, and our next plan will be better for it.' He patted Brendon gently on his good arm. 'Focus on healing. Ah. We do have other priorities, so we leave the pursuit of these criminals to others for a time.'

Brendan shifted. 'She said they were coming for you. She means to kill you, I think.'

'Ah. She and her allies are coming for me. Good. Let them come. I...we will be ready for them. Together we will give them the feeling of utter defeat.'

In the half light, Brenden saw the light glint of the Doctor's glasses, his eyes like pools of darkness. He shivered.

'Count on it, my boy.'

Arrival of the Ravens
By Michael Huddlestone

Kameko knew what was coming. It had been foretold by the tea leaves days earlier. By noon the birds had begun to arrive. The flock had spread their numbers across the village, each house had at least a trio of the black winged creatures perched on the roof. The villages had taken little notice of them, but Kameko saw the truth. It was their frayed feathers that betrayed their true purpose. Their arrival was the final omen of the inevitable.

The villagers did not listen to her when she tried to warn them. To them, she was just the village's crazy old lady. They would smile and nod to her while casting their judgment and looking down on her. One of the field men had even thrown her to the ground demanding she ceased her raving as she was scaring the children. The children should be afraid, they all should. Kameko had tried but the weight of their children's deaths, all their deaths, would rest on squarely on the souls of their parents. Her hands were clean.

Kameo packed what little she had into the cane basket at the rear of her bicycle. He felt the raven's black soulless eyes watching her as she began to make her way out of the village and into the forest. Venturing deeper into the woods, the ground became softer, the bicycle became harder to push. Mud pulled at the tires as though it was in league with ravens. Kameko had no choice but to keep pushing, she would need the bike once she left the cover of the trees. The road was long and windy to the nearest temple, too far to walk before nightfall. Kameo dared not travel at night. Other evil entities roamed the gloom of the night, looking for the lonely travellers.

No forest animals stirred, any animals that remained were well hidden as if they knew what was coming. The forest was silent. The only sounds were the fall of her footsteps in the soft squelching mud and the racing beat of her heart pounding in her ears.

Something stirred in the woods. Kameko stopped. She recognised the sound; the Ravens were coming. She ran, leaving the bike in the mud, leaving all she owned in the world behind her. Was she too late? Darkness began to spread through the forest. Tengu was coming.

The darkness took chase, shadows swept to the left and right, racing to block her departure from the forest. Outside of the woods, she would be safe, for the moment at least. She had to make it out of the forest.

Not too much further, Kameko thought to herself between her quickening breaths. The shadows that flowed beside her began to break off into fragments. They grew as they moved came closer to her, taking on human form. These were souls now a part of Tengu's Legion, turned evil by his touch. He grew in power from every soul of the living he took.

"They cannot hurt you." It was the voice of her long dead mother, "just keep running." Her voice always guided her, as had done during her life.

As Kameko glanced back, a woman now ran beside her. She was young, beautiful, full of colour and life. Her light blue satin dress glittered with gold flecks in the occasional beam of sunlight that broke through the canopy. Kameko knew her from the village though her name escaped her. The woman smiled. Kameko's pace slowed.

"Run Kameko!" her mother's voice screamed at her. Heeding her mother's warning, Kameko turned her gaze back to her destination; the view of the open fields could be seen in the distance as the forest began to thin out. Despite her age, Kameko still had some pace from her youth, she was a woman who always kept active. She began to put some distance between her and the young woman.

"No!" Kameko heaved out between breaths. The woman's eyes rolled back in her head reveal only the whites of her eyes. Black colour spread like ink from the bottom of her dress turning the blue of the fabric into frayed black cloth. The gold flecks now burnt scorched marks into the fabric. Her smile widened unnaturally, tearing at the corners of her mouth. Inside the gaping darkness of her mouth serpent-like fangs descended from her once white teeth, now stained in a dark crimson colour.

"Alone, away from the source, they cannot harm you." Her mother spoke again seconds before the woman lunged towards her. Kameko's body wanted to avoid the attack but her mind held her strong, forward to the clearing. The demonic soul passed through her as she ran, chills swept up her spine, then the woman was gone.

Larger beams of sunlight broke through the canopy as she fast-approached the clearing. Glancing behind she saw the wave of shadows behind her was gaining fast. Her aged legs ached with pain, but they did not falter. The black mass behind her bubbled as it passed along the ground. Faces called out for her, and arms reached out begging for her to join them. Closer and closer the sunlight came. More fragmented souls detached themselves from their master, each screaming at her as they tried to make her stumble.

In the sunlight ahead, a silhouette of a man appeared. His features, while not quite clear to her, held gave her a familiar sense safety.

"Run Kameko. Run!" He called out to her. She knew it was her brother, Shoichi. As if that was enough to make her go on, her weary legs found a new strength and her pace quickened. His features became visible. He was smiling, waving her towards him. Her heart ached. Only mere metres now stood between her and her brother who stood on the edge of the border of the forest. Before her mind could keep up, her body slowed. Her legs giving way brought the old fortune teller to her knees. Pain surged through her body, her old bones broken by the fall. She looked up, just an arm's length from her brother. She reached out to him, as she stared up at the man, he smiled. Her hand fell to the ground as she finally remembered. Shoichi had died five years earlier. One word escaped her lips as she exhaled.

"Tengu."

"I've been looking for you, Kameko." The man's deep voice boomed through the woods, shaking every tree to its core. A violent wave of darkness swept over Kameko as the sea of shadows engulfed her. She screamed as they tore at her with claws, teeth, fangs, consuming her into their dark solitude of slavery. Kameko joined the ghastly faces of the dead villagers who had been consumed earlier. None escaped. The forest became silent once more. A single figure stood looking over the clearing setting his sights on the spires of smoke rising from the next village. The lone call of a raven broke the silence, as though speaking to him. The man turned and smiled.

"Soon."

An Act of Grace
By William Elliot

H ow is she?'

'Settled now, she's still confused, but much more coherent than she was.'

'Thank God for that. Do you think it's genuine, or is she playing us? You know what her kind is like?'

'I'd say genuine. She's clearly suffered some form of trauma, and she *was* weak with exposure. It would have taken days to walk here. It's not surprising she can't tell reality from fantasy, though. The poor thing has lived out there all her life.'

'All good and well, but we need to keep a lid on this. The last thing we need is the press stirring up the populace with superstitious rubbish. You need to take her back, as soon as possible.'

'Me? Surely your people would be better able to do that.'

'Hmph. Not this time, outside of my jurisdiction. They put the whole area under the jurisdiction of the presidential guard decades ago so we didn't have to deal with the nut cases. If any of my people get involved I have to go through official channels and that will take time, not to mention give the whole thing too much attention. Better if a 'caring' citizen merely drops her back.'

'What about this talk of omens then? Do you need to speak with her before she leaves?'

Grace pressed the pillow to her ears, tears streaming down her cheeks. They were going to take her back. She didn't want to go back, she'd only just got here two days ago. The mere thought of it made her stomach clench with fear.

A cat meowed and the window blew open, frame smashing hard against the wall of the little room, jolting Grace from the bed. It must be midnight. This was the third night in a row it had happened, the previous two spot on midnight. Instinct replaced fear as she leapt up to fasten it, the chill night air blasting her diminutive frame. It was only early fall, yet freezing outside. Not that she really cared. Her sense of feeling had gone along with her appetite.

Sighing in resignation, Grace flopped back on the bed, making no attempt to cover her ears. She was way too anxious to sleep now, and besides, they might say something about the omens. Dr Grahame was talking to someone in her sitting room, just down the hall. She had a modest cottage on the north side of the little town that straddled the major route from the western borderlands to the Citadel in the east. The monastery where Grace lived was a full day's journey up into the mountains to the North. Up there the rooms were tiny, barren and cold. By contrast the cottage felt opulent and snug.

The man's voice was deep and resonant, but unfamiliar. He'd not visited Dr Grahame since Grace had arrived. 'No need. Superstitious nonsense, that's all. Early fall has been bitterly cold before, and it wasn't the bloody legions. And red skies are hardly a mystical event. They're just a bunch of crackpots that would like nothing better than to be the centre of attention, not even a recognised religious order. I don't know why the authorities don't just shut them down.'

Dr Grahame's voice was brusque and clipped, as it always seemed to be in company. While taller than Grace, most people were, she was petite all the same. Tonight, she would be dressed in the drab attire preferred by middle age spinsters, affecting a stern demeanour for her visitor.

She also had little time for what she called silly superstitions, confirmed by her next words. 'I agree, but superstition runs deep here, no doubt from too much exposure to that… hmm sect'. The problem was, those silly superstitions were Grace's reality. She quite liked Dr Grahame — she was nowhere near as stern as the Sisters, and had been nice to her — but she was wrong. She had to be.

Grace peered toward the ceiling as she considered. Not everyone thought as Dr Grahame did. Some of the older people had already fled to the Citadel, and more were thinking about it. Whether from 'superstitious' beliefs or more 'real' fears for safety, there at least seemed to be agreement that is was the shooting star that had caused it. Nearly a month gone now, the fiery messenger had crashed to earth beyond the northern mountains, hitting with such force the very earth shook. Then, five days past, the sky had turned bright red for a full day. The newspaper – Grace had never read one until two days ago – had been filled with stories all week, with all sorts of explanations about the cause. They were all wrong, though. Grace new the truth. The legions were coming and death would reap the lost souls.

The man grunted in response, 'All the more reason to get her back there where she can't do any damage.'

Grace lay in stunned silence, the picturesque little room at complete odds with the heavy dread in her heart. The veil had not been breached since the time of the Great Fall almost five hundred years past, when humankind in their arrogance had sought to usurp God. Soulless reivers swept across the world, raping and butchering as they went. Each horde commanded by a necromancer and supported by wraiths, capturing the souls of the slaughtered before they could cross over to the afterlife.

She shivered in fear, hugging her knees as tears rolled down her cheeks, window rattling in the cold wind. She had never seen the legions of course. None living had. She had been schooled in them, though, and seen the murals in the Great Hall. She knew what became of those lost to the legions.

Grace's pale skin all but glowed in the failing light and the cold wind teased her short, black hair as she popped her head out the window. They had been travelling all day and the mighty gates of the monastery were finally rearing large before them. There had been a savage head-wind until noon when the barren plains finally gave way to rugged mountains, slowing progress and making conversation impossible. It had made for a dull trip until they reached the relative sanctuary of the mountains, providing respite from the wind.

That had been fine by Grace. Still a little numb with shock, the rocking of the little carriage as it navigated its way along the pothole strewn road towards the monastery allowed her mind to drift. She had never been in a carriage before. The seats were more comfortable than a wagon, but it still bounced around with every hole and bump. It was warmer than a wagon though, particularly on the windy, barren plains.

Shoulders sagged in resignation, she would have been poor company for the first few hours anyway. She didn't want to be here, of course. The legions were coming, life as she knew it was about to end, and they were heading the wrong way. She had spent her entire 18 years in the monastery and now she was going to be forced to spend her few remaining days of freedom there before being raped to death by the reivers, and that was if she was lucky.

Once they had cleared the windy plains, though, Dr Grahame had teased her into conversation as they pottered along the poorly maintained road that traversed the mountain pass. It had started with her caste marks, the tiny marks tattooed on the inside of her forearms. Everyone had them of course, inked at birth to denote caste and expanded over the years as they gained mastery of their trade. It had been thus since shortly after the Great Fall, so all knew their place under God. For someone like Dr Grahame, they were a source of pride, elaborate and colourful. By contrast, Grace's markings were an announcement of her shame. She had no trade, no skills and no caste, at least no caste that mattered.

'I've never seen a caste mark like that before,' Dr Grahame had asked, her thin face showing genuine compassion. The question had stung all the same though, forcing Grace to look down at her arms in embarrassment as she swayed with the motion of the carriage. One tiny black line across the inside of each forearm near the wrist, these were her caste marks.

The smell of Dr Grahame's expensive perfume had wafted across the carriage, underscoring the gulf between them, sharpening her shame. Grace had looked up, eyes glistening as she held back tears, 'I don't know. I was abandoned at the monastery as an infant with no markings at all. After my fifth birthday, Sister Marcia tested me for a month and then meditated for a further month more before giving me these. She never explained which caste I was, but I can tell it must be the lowest of the low.'

Dr Grahame hadn't said anything, but Grace could tell what she was thinking, sitting there, straight backed in her expensive, lace trimmed travelling coat. Two things in caste marks denoted social standing, colour and complexity. Grace had neither. Even the untouchables had more intricate markings than she.

'How about a change of subject?' Dr Grahame's voice was soft with compassion and understanding. 'What can you tell me about the omens?'

Grace had relaxed a bit. This was at least something she knew about. Everyone at the monastery did. Dr Grahame seemed to know quite a bit about them too, even if she didn't believe them. Not many outside of the monastery did, apparently. Some of the older folks in the town close by perhaps, but almost no-one further afield, at least according to Dr Grahame. Grace couldn't believe it, couldn't believe that everything she had been taught wasn't true.

'They weren't lying to you, Grace. I'm sure the sisters believed everything they said. Indeed, many people would have taken those scriptures literally, even half a century ago. Not anymore, though. We're more enlightened now and understand that they are really just a metaphor, a primitive peoples way of explaining things they couldn't understand.' Grace knew what a metaphor was, and she didn't think the legions were a metaphor.

Now, as Grace popped her head back inside the carriage, Dr Grahame was asking her about her childhood. She shrugged, fidgeting with the braid on her dress as she looked down, 'There's not much to tell, really. I grew up at the monastery, working as a servant until I was old enough to be accepted as a novice.'

Grace grimaced at her own words, heart filling with such self-pity she didn't even notice the carriage had stopped. She'd been an ordinary servant and a complete failure as a novice. Eventually looking up, she noticed a barricade across the road with guards on each side.

'Good evening ladies.'

Grace started in shock, heart in her mouth, before immediately jumping from the carriage and falling to her knees in supplication. Dr Grahame remained sitting, but tipped her head slightly, quickly adopting her signature terse posture, 'Good evening to you too Captain.'

His voice was deep and soft, with an edge of sharp steel, belying the casual tone of his greeting. It belonged to a captain of the presidential guard, the legendary soldiers that protected his eminence. Grace desperately wanted to lift her head to see, but dared not. She was so far beneath his station she dared not even look upon his face. Only those of the elite castes were admitted to the presidential guard.

A large, calloused hand gently cupped her chin, lifting her head to look into brilliant, grey-blue eyes. Grace's heart skipped a beat and her face flushed, warmth flowing through her. Short brown hair framed a chiselled, tanned face with a closely cropped beard adorning a strong jaw. His deep voice melted her inside, vibrating her very soul, 'I expected you to be cold as ice, so lightly dressed. You're warm though, very warm.'

Grace felt her face flush again, but held his gaze, unabashedly. She couldn't drag her eyes away from those brilliant grey-blue orbs even if she wanted to. 'I don't feel the cold sir', she managed to mumble between shallow breaths.

The captain extended his other hand to help her stand, still cupping her chin. Fire raced through her, igniting feelings she had never felt before. Her legs felt weak, yet still she held his gaze. He smiled, accentuating his strong jaw and perfect teeth, 'Captain Samuel Marcus at you service miss. And what might your name be?'

Grace blushed again, mouth dry with nerves, head in danger of swooning. She swallowed and managed to respond, relishing the feel of his fingers under her jaw as she spoke, 'My name is Grace, Sir. I have no last name as I am an orphan from the monastery.'

He winked as he broke eye contact, turning towards Dr Grahame. Grace's heart fluttered. 'And what of madam?' he asked while extending his hand to help her alight from the carriage.

Dr Grahame tilted her head as she stepped down, 'My name is Isabelle Grahame, Captain, of Abbottown. An anthropologist by profession.'

The captain's eyebrow rose in response, 'Is your field of study anything to do with the Great Fall by chance?'

Dr Grahame snorted politely, her skirts swishing around her ankles as she moved, 'Of course Captain, it *is* the most studied period in history after all. My particular speciality is the culture and cause of the fall.'

Grace followed their conversation with interest as she stood close beside the captain, close enough to revel in his musky smell and the sound of leather armour creaking over well-toned muscle. It left her breathless and flushed, yet positively buoyant.

That's why Dr Grahame knew so much about omens but didn't believe in them, she was a scientist. Grace has heard about scientists. According to the sisters, it was scientists that had caused the Fall.

It hit her as she glanced at Captain Marcus again, eyes once again drawn by his handsome features. The name Marcus! Looking at the Captain in profile, Grace could see the resemblance. There was a Lieutenant Marcus in the northern militia that regularly visited the monastery. He looked much like the captain, only younger, barely older than Grace herself.

The connection dragged an elusive memory from Grace's subconscious.

'No!'

Grace recoiled more from the rebuke than the slap.

'He's gone, past the threshold. There's nothing we can do for him now.'

Grace nodded, tears in her eyes. She knew it was true. Lieutenant Marcus's soul had passed to the great beyond. Not even the most gifted of healers could save him now.

Sister Joan grabbed her shoulders, gripping hard with her calloused hands, 'Focus Grace, there is much to do. You must flee before it's too late. Now go, get to the town and warn them, the legions have come.'

Grace leapt to her feet. Shaking with fear and wiping the tears from her eyes, she raced toward the west door.

The memory faded and Grace looked up at the captain, tears running down her face as she sniffled and trembled with sorrow, voice barely more than a whisper, 'He… he's passed, your kin. His soul crossed to the great beyond.'

The Captain looked at her in surprise, clearly not expecting it, 'You were there.'

She nodded.

His eyes hardened, like glistening ice, 'Did you see him cross, actually see him cross.'

Grace shook her head, knowing what he asked. It was common to say the deceased had crossed to the great beyond, but only the sisters could actually see the soul leave the body. Grace had the talent apparently, even if she had completely failed in all of her studies. 'No, but Sister Joan did. I was there as she tried to save him, but it was too late. She only stopped because he had passed.'

The Captain let out a sigh of relief, the tension draining from his shoulders, 'Enough talk for now. The two of you will join me for dinner and stay here tonight. You won't be able to remain at the monastery beyond then, but it's far too late to return to Abbottown this evening. Grace desperately wanted to ask him what had happened, and why he had asked that question. Looking at his eyes though, she dare not. Dr Grahame looked on in shocked confusion, mouth slightly agape as the captained turned and offered his arm.

A chill ran down Grace's spine as she crossed the threshold of the Great Hall, images of blood soaked walls flashing through her memory, too quick to catch. It had been turned into both a temporary headquarters and camp site for the captain and his men. On one side of the room a large table was covered with maps. On the other, a similar table had been set up for dining. The food actually looked pretty good, but Grace's stomach cramped with nausea. She'd had no appetite for days.

Declining food, Grace took a seat on one of the elegant timber benches running the length of the wall. It ran the full circle of the room, broken only by the four entrances, one from each wing of the monastery. From above, the complex formed a cross with the Great Hall the jewel in the centre. This evening, though, even the magnificence of hall felt muted. The stained glass windows high in the soaring ceilings still shone with a kaleidoscope of colours in the failing light of dusk, flashing rainbows across the marble floors, but is wasn't the same. It felt wrong. Neither Dr Grahame nor the soldiers seemed to notice, though. The Captain had even taken off his armour and gun belt, although leaving the pistol beside him, close to hand. It was probably more habit than anything, but it was comforting all the same.

Grace hung on every word of their conversation over dinner, hoping to find out what had happened, where the sisters were. The captain wasn't sharing though, at least not yet. So far he had only engaged in small talk with Dr Grahame, although even some of that was interesting. Grace hadn't known the monastery had been built as a form of defence. She knew it sat astride a pass in the mountains, but hadn't known it controlled the only pass for hundreds of leagues in either direction. Apparently, anyone coming from the wastelands to the north would have to pass though the monastery.

'That's actually why it was built,' Dr Grahame sounded like a Sister in lecture mode, 'Just after the Fall. The logic was, if the legions returned, they would come from the northern wastelands again. It's a sort of castle. Of course, it would never stop actual legions of the damned, which is why the contemporary view is that the legions were merely foreign invaders. Not creatures from the beyond.'

Eventually, Dr Grahame broached the subject Grace had been too scared to raise. 'Did something happen at the monastery, Captain,' she asked, glancing over her glass of wine while trying to keep the anxiety out of her voice.

He looked at her with penetrating eyes, but didn't respond.

Dr Grahame motioned to Grace with her eyes before plunging on, 'Grace turned up at my house four days ago with her memory of the past week gone. The comment earlier was the first memory I've heard her utter. I was taking her back to the monastery to find out what happened.'

Grace nodded in confirmation from her pew on the bench, head down, wringing her hands in her lap, 'I'm sorry. I don't know why I can't remember.' Raising her head to look at the captain, throat thick with compassion, she added, 'Was he your brother, Lieutenant Marcus?'

The Captain nodded, his eyes were soft with grief, his voice tight with pain. 'He was. That's why I was headed to the monastery, we lost contact with his squad a week ago. I buried them yesterday.'

A guard squad was well armed and well trained. It would take more than mere bandits to dispatch an entire squad. Grace's stomach clenched tight as images flashed through her mind, 'Reivers!'

Dr Grahame supressed a slight chuckle, 'You must forgive Grace, Captain, she has taken the teachings of the sisters a little too literally.'

The Captain grimaced, his eyes tightening. He eased himself forward in his chair, 'Only, I'm afraid she might be right on this occasion. An entire battalion of them, complete with necromancer, as far as I can tell. The ugliest, scariest things I have ever seen, even dead.'

Dr Grahame looked at him mouth agape, her ferret like face flushing, 'You're not kidding, are you?' Grace's face had gone paler than normal, eyes wide as saucers, fear clutching her stomach tight, 'What about the sisters, did they get away?'

The Captain shook his head, sorrow carving lines in his perfect face, 'I'm afraid not. They all perished.'

Grace crossed herself in the way of the sisters, but held her tongue, chest tight, making it difficult to breathe. Memories teased the edges of consciousness, impossible to catch.

Dr Grahame, more clinical, raised an eyebrow, 'And where are these reivers now, Captain?'

Voice casual, the captain pinned Dr Grahame with ice hard eyes, 'Dead, all of them and I have no idea how. Not the militia though.'

Grace's gut clenched and she felt a cold fear run down her spine as memories bubbled to the surface. *Panting with effort, she raced past the prayer room. Running was something she could do, something she was good at. Not like healing. She sucked at healing, even though the sisters said otherwise.*

Dr Grahame's eyes lit up with interest, 'What did the corpses look like, and the ground around them?'

The captain frowned, surprised at the question, 'Like dried out husks, the life drained right out of them. The faces of the reivers looked peaceful, though. The necromancer – he pointed to the graphic renderings on the wall of the Great Hall – at least what I'm pretty sure was a necromancer, looked terrified. As for the ground around them, it looked fine.' He shrugged, 'Why?'

Grace gasped. Fear gripped her chest so tight she thought she would surely suffocate. Her head spun. The souls of reivers weren't their own. They were soulless creatures brought to life by a stolen soul held captive by the dark arts of the necromancers, deformed and tormented. Death brought release to the flesh, but not the soul. They went to the stealer of souls, leader of the legions, for all eternity. Every tainted soul left its mark, though, in life and death, ingrained into the flesh, poisoned and toxic. Tainting everything they touched, even the very ground on which they trod.

'Legend and superstition, Captain,' Dr Grahame replied in her knowing voice, 'the blood of the damned is supposed to taint the very ground. Clearly your reivers are somewhat more mortal than the legends suggest.'

The captain gave Dr Grahame a grim smile, 'Perhaps, Doctor, but they made quick work of a squad of trained soldiers and they are nothing like anything I have ever seen before.' A faint smile tugged at the corners of his mouth, 'Would you like to have a look for yourself? We have a few specimens on ice.'

Dr Grahame examined the reiver with fascination, her face lit with excitement. It made her look far younger and far less like a ferret than her usual dour demeanour, causing Grace to reassess her estimate of the doctor's age. They were in one of the monastery cool rooms, used to store food, the bodies of a reiver and a necromancer atop preparation benches. Grace blanched at the thought of food ever being stored here again, her stomach churning, almost causing her to flee. Instead, she forced herself to look at the horrid beast, breath shallow with fear.

The beasts were huge, each over two metres tall and thick with muscle, even drained of fluids as they were. Oversized human hands terminated in razor sharp claws and the unnaturally wide mouth sported huge incisors like a wild boar. The nose was also like that of a boar, a fleshy snout below beady black eyes.

Flying through the entrance to the Great Hall, she bounced off a hard, armoured body before crashing into the hard stone wall. A hideous goliath with dark, weathered skin and a bald scalp blocked her way. Turning toward her, it froze her with beady black, savage eyes. Bodies lay scattered across the blood slick floor.

'Oh my God, it's true,' Dr Grahame's voice was high and quick with excitement, 'They're not real. Well, they are real. Real flesh and blood, but they're not born. These creatures where made.'

'What?' Captain Marcus's eyes were wide with shock, mouth agape, voice loud against the stone walls, 'What do you mean, *made?*

The shock in the captain's voice completely evaded Dr Grahame, she was oblivious to everything around her. He was just about to repeat the question when a soldier approached and whispered in his ear. The captain's face drained of colour and his Adam's apple bobbed as he swallowed hard, 'Seal this place tight until I return. Nothing gets in or out.'

A trickle of icy dread settled in Grace's stomach. They were coming, she could feel it.

Grace's heart ached and tears ran down her cheeks. Dead, they were all dead. Looking up at the reiver with numb, frightened eyes, she barely registered the knife as it plunged deep into her stomach before twisting. For the first time she saw it, actually saw it, a soul preparing to cross the threshold into the afterlife. How ironic it was her own.

Left alone with just the doctor in the makeshift morgue, Grace couldn't handle it anymore. She had to get out. Breath shallow with fear, she made her way back to the Great Hall and the soldiers. The captain had departed, but left most of his men to secure the monastery. No matter how well trained they were though, a handful of men would be useless against what was coming.

Grace had sat in the corner worrying over Captain Marcus for three hours, anxiety gripping her chest like an iron band. He'd gone north with a few men to see what his scouts had found, and not yet returned. She didn't want to be alone with nothing but her imagination for company, but had little choice. She couldn't bear to look at the corpses and didn't want to get in the way of the soldiers as they prepared for a siege. Now prostrate on the cold marble floor, she tried to lose herself in prayer as her chest got tighter and the dread in the stomach heavier, along with a burning need she couldn't identify.

Eventually urgent voices penetrated her devotions.

'They're no more than 15 minutes behind us.'

'What about Seamus and Norbit?'

'Gone, sacrificed themselves to buy us time to escape.'

Grace glanced up in time to see two blood soaked bodies being carried into the room. Their moans marked then as still alive, but barely by the look of it. One was missing a leg below the knee, blood soaking the ineffectual bandages wrapping the stump. The other was whole, but crisscrossed with gouges deep enough to rip through armour and penetrate the soft flesh below. Even smeared with blood, Grace recognised Captain Marcus, fear for him strong in the back of her mind. Now though, it had been joined by a burning rage.

The beast turned, leaving her slumped against the wall, her life force ebbing with each pump of her dying heart. With every ounce of remaining strength, Grace lunged, grabbing its arm and lashed out with the only weapon she had. Its eyes grew large as it felt what was happening, but it was too late. Ignoring ever sacred tenant, Grace gritted her teeth and draw forth its life force, strengthening with every second. She didn't expect to save herself, lacking the skill even if it were possible. She didn't care though, as long as she killed the vile beast before her.

And in that moment between death and oblivion, the very instant her own soul crossed the threshold, she did what could not be done. She drew the beast's very soul from its body and into hers, just before her own soul snapped back across the threshold from the great beyond. Grace's pupil's dilated as her consciousness exploded, her whole being awash with ecstasy. She had never felt so alive, so complete. She looked down at the drained husk before her through cold, dark eyes and hungered for more.

The chaos before her drifted into the background as a cold clarity of purpose engulfed her, bringing with it a penetrating calm, infusing her entire being. She knew who she was, what she was, what she had to do. She gave into the burning need inside, a deep, burning hunger. She ached with it as she walked past the chaos around her, lightly touching both of the injured men as she passed. No more than a gentle brush of her fingers, too quick to notice as she casually strolled down the dark promenade to the northern gate. A solitary soldier manned the gate, his brow slick with sweat as he awaited the approaching legions. She could hear them now, whipped to frenzy by their necromancers.

She didn't say a word as he turned to bar her way, nerves taught in fear. She didn't have to. One look at her eyes was enough, two jet black portals to the abyss. He swallowed and stood aside as she pushed open the huge doors and slipped into the night, then locked them soundly behind her.

The sun shone bright against a deep red sky, already beginning to erase the bitter cold of the night before. Dr Grahame bent down to examine the wraith, weary from lack of sleep. Whether the blood curdling screams throughout the night or fear for Grace she couldn't say, but she had slept not a wink. The screams had stopped just before dawn, the ensuing silence even more chilling. They had to go out, though, had to look for Grace. She had to know for sure.

At two and half metres tall it was bigger and even more horrifying than the reiver corpses littering the ground around her, the necromancers too, for that matter. Even as a drained husk the creature sent a shiver down her spine.

'You were right, you know. They were grown, not born.'

Dr Grahame jumped in shock, heart beating hard and hands shaking.

'They were made in the years leading up to the Great Fall, precipitated it in fact. But you suspected that too, didn't you.'

Grace sat calmly on a large boulder, bodies strewn around her, her pale skin as smooth and perfect as the finest porcelain, accentuating her dark eyes. Even in the morning light her irises were so large and so dark as to make her eyes looked completely black. The light breeze teased her short black hair as she glanced around.

'No souls, though. The souls were stolen from people and imprisoned in the reivers by necromancers centuries ago.'

Dr Grahame stood frowning, still coming to grips with the concept. So many questions leapt to mind, but the one her lips uttered was, 'Souls. Do we really have souls?'

Grace shrugged, 'I can't really say, but there is a spark of consciousness within us, imparted in the womb I suspect, that is part of us, yet separate. Without it we lack something, something vital.'

'Where are they now, returned to the afterlife, or wherever souls linger after death?'

Grace's face sagged a little, her voice little more than a whisper, 'No. They were too twisted, too tainted to cross to the beyond. They had to be extinguished. In a way, though, they still live on in me.'

Dr Grahame blanched at the implication, mouth agape in shock, the wind whipping her brown curls across her face, 'You destroyed them, all of them. There must be thousands.'

Grace shrugged, 'Tens of thousands, actually. It had to be done, though.'

Dr Grahame's face drained of all colour and her hands started to shake. 'But how?' she asked, knowing the answer but not wanting to believe. All around her vibrant, living creatures had been drained of every scrap of vitality, every ounce of life.

It's all a matter of energy really,' Grace answered matter-of-factly, 'Draining them utterly of all life force was a convenient way to kill them, one of the few weapons at my disposal, but also provided the energy I needed to extinguish the damaged souls. I didn't need all of the energy, though.' She gave a ghost of a smile, 'On the plus side, I won't have to eat for the next few hundred years.'

Dr Grahame swallowed hard, not sure whether Grace was joking. As Grace turned to walk away, Dr Grahame noticed her forearms. Two bands of black ink extended from the underside of each wrist, circling her forearm in opposite directions twice each before meeting again at the tip of her elbows, stark against her pale white skin. The insides of her forearms were adorned with the most intricate markings she had ever seen. 'What do I tell Captain Marcus? He likes you, you know. He'll want to see you again. Not to mention he will probably want to thank you for healing him and saving all our lives.'

Grace turned briefly, a wicked smile lighting her face, black eye's shining, 'Tell the good captain I'm heading north to see what else the comet might have thawed out in the wasteland. If he comes looking for me for the right reasons, he'll be sure to find me.'

Dr Grahame watched her go, snippets of ancient scripture fitting together in her mind, *And death shall walk the earth reaping the lost souls, staining the sky red with the blood of the slaughtered.*

Red Sky
By Adam Stringini

The ocean bled crimson light into the night sky. It always did when a God surfaced from depths unseen to shed its nascent form. A small ramshackle vessel cut through the black water, its ancient and now little understood reactor humming. The vessel's three living occupants hurried about the rusting deck, illuminated by the red glow, readying themselves. Corroded containers of gathered alien tissue sloshed as the vessel moved. Their sharp stench cutting through the salty air. The ten dead piled aboard the vessel helped secure the containers, their tumorous bodies buffering the impacts each wave bought. The weary metal of the vessel groaned as it drew more from its aging reactor-heart, increasing its speed. On the roiling horizon floated the vessel's unexpected target, the shed body of an alien God, both food and fuel for the remnants of mankind.

"Blessed, blessed you are on your last night my sleeping friends!" Oma proclaimed to the piled bodies of the dead. His voice rising above thrum of the reactor-heart and the crash of the metal hull against the water. "The brilliance of the Gods fills the sky and their offering of flesh is too generous this night. Your journey to return to the Gods below will be swift and welcomed!". The remaining wisps of Oma's lank hair thrashed about as the vessel cut through the water. At the stern of the vessel, Akin scoffed as he readied a drag net line through battered pulleys. At the helm, Luk fixed Akin with a discouraging gaze. Akin's jaw clenched under the stern gaze and his line feeding became unnecessarily forceful.

"To pass into the realm of Gods on such a night!" Oma continued. "Truly they favour you!"

"All that yelling and he hasn't readied a single net." Akin said, his tone tense.

"You'd have more ready if you stopped complaining." Luk said as he adjusted the patchwork vessel's course while scratching a patchy, unkempt beard. Akin dropped his stare from the preaching Oma and busied himself with rigging another net. Akin's deft hands secured the lines and coiled the leads as salty spray wet his pale, pot-marked face. The night's chill stabbed at him but Akin smiled. Being so close to the vessel's thrumming reactor-heart bathed him in a piercing, but tingling warmth even if a phantom taste of metal filled his mouth.

"Fear not sleeping friends, I am here to ensure your final voyage is one of peace! Let the brilliance of the Gods below and the radiance of the sky above embrace you!" Oma said as he spread his bony arms wide and tilted his pointed face to the sky.

"Don't," Luk said raising a finger from the helm to Akin.

"If he talks about the Gods without lifting a finger to help one more time."

"You will do nothing Akin. The both of you have beliefs and the both of you have hands. I don't care what a person's beliefs are just as long as their hands are moving." Luk said.

"His hands are raised to the heavens, mine are on the ropes." Akin said. "Shouldn't you care about his beliefs?"

Luk's bald brow furrowed and his jaw tightened briefly. "His hands will be the last to touch the dead before they sink beneath the waves. His hands prepared the dead with knife and rocks to ensure a fast journey beneath the waves. Oma has used his hands Akin. Let the man be."

Akin bristled and looked to the horizon. Though he loathed admitting it, the sky's red glow was particularly beautiful. Ribbons of crimson light, seemingly solid, lazily drifted up from the black depths and scattered amongst the clouds. The red shadow of a God's brief time above the waves. Akin felt the tension in his chest release and his potted jaw slacken as the night sky rippled impossibly infinite shades of red. Luk caught Akin's relaxed look and spoke.

"Why let Oma anger you when his praise speaks of the same sky you see?"

"Because there are thirteen people on this ship and twelve are pulling their weight." Akin said still watching the stained sky. Luk raised his eyebrow.

"Ten people on this vessel will never gaze upon the sky again, or anything for that matter."

"Yet even the dead work to protect our haul of the Gods' flesh with their bodies Luk. Oma talks to clouds." Akin shifted his eyes from the red vista to the wisped haired, bony man at the bow of the ship. "Why bring him Luk? Why not Gult? He at least coils rope with one hand and helps the dead pass with the other."

Luk frowned again. "Akin, why do you have so much hate for the man? He performs a service for us just as you do."

"He speaks to clouds and the dead. You and I help fill the bellies of the people and fuel the reactor-hearts. Which sounds more like a service to you?" Akin said his tone hardening once again.

"The God's flesh we sift from the water is given from the same Gods Oma praises. It would be wrong of us not to give thanks Akin."

"Can we not give thanks while pulling the sift-nets? Or do you pull rope with your teeth Luk?"

Luk sighed and scratched at the scabrous skin of his scalp.

"You provide for the living Akin. Oma, the dead. He is the left hand to your right." He retorted.

"He thanks the Gods as if they throw their shed bodies onto the deck for us!" Akin said, his voice rising.

"They may as well. You look to the God's light for guidance to their Gods' flesh as do I. Red sky at morning, sifter take warning-" Luk began.

"-Red sky at night, sifter's delight. I know the saying." Akin said interrupting.

"Then you should know the foolishness of your hatred Akin."

Akin heavy signed and resumed his sky gazing. The vessel groaned again as Luk adjusted makeshift controls to maintain the flow of power from the reactor-heart.

The vessel soon neared the floating flesh of the Gods. The mucus-like mass stretched dozens of times the vessel's length. Its utterly alien scent overpowered even the brine of the sea and decay of the dead.

"Drop the net!" Luk said. Akin sprang to action with gritted teeth. Oma stood mouthing a prayer and touching the nearest dead as his hair danced in the wind.

The fine net dropped and swelled like a distended belly as it sifted the Gods' flesh the black water. Luk and Akin's arms burnt and their backs ached as they hauled the swollen net from the water and swung the bent crane arm onto the deck.

"A barrel Akin!" Luk said tying off the guide rope and readying the release line. Akin approached the remaining empty barrel at the stern of the ship, each chest height. He tilted the nearest and began to roll it back to Luk. Once secured in the deck's recess Luk drew the release line and the Gods' flesh spilled into the barrel. The Gods' flesh was coloured a pale bone and shot with shimmering grains of a silvery not-metal if seen in the light of day. It shone with a wet sheen, yet water beaded on its lumpy surface. Like the reactor-hearts it bathed those near it in a piercing warmth and caused the phantom metal taste. Under the light of the stained sky however, the Gods' flesh was a vibrant ruby whose metallic specks seemed magnified. Akin stared transfixed as the Gods' flesh poured, yet tumbled from the fine net. A smile split his pot-marked face as Luk caught his eye.

"It is so fresh it's warmth is almost hot!" Luk said. Akin nodded as he sealed the barrel to secure the precious Gods' flesh and rolled it with a grunt to the bow. Akin approached Oma and the two men stared at each other, their dislike palpable.

"The Gods honour us with a bountiful haul Akin. Have you taken time to thank them for their selfless act?" Oma said. Akin rolled the full barrel to an empty space pretending to ignore the priestly man's question. His calloused hands curled into fists before eventually replying.

"I'll thank them once I have sifted it all."

Oma sneered. "All they ask of us is their praise Akin. Praise is easier than hauling a net."

"You wouldn't know." Akin said storming to the stern.

"For someone who directly receives the gifts of the Gods, you do keep your praise quiet." Oma said in Akin's wake.

Luk's look of a reprimand made Akin shrink and abort his reply. Luk thrust the release line into Akin's hands and then clamped his vice-like hands onto Akin's shoulders.

"Enough Akin. We are out too far and too late at night to have you two at each other's throats now." Akin returned his stare as best he could, but faulted and turned away. Luk sighed and resumed Akin's role. The first net filled four barrels, the second and third net filled three and the fourth net two. Each time Luk approached Oma at the bow they shared a brief exchange. Oma spoke animatedly and Luk simply nodded in response. Akin ground his teeth as he watched.

As the hour grew late, the light faded in brilliance. The Gods were continued retreating deeper into the ocean than man ever could. The sky was a cinder of pale red and darkness threatened to swallow the vessel by the time Luk coaxed yet more power from the reactor-heart to light now sharp smelling deck in a cold white.

"That is the last one." Luk said standing to regard their haul. "We haven't filled our barrels like this for months!"

"Such a gift! Such generosity! Who are we to deserve it?" Oma said.

Luk and I do. Akin said to himself. Luk walked to the bow and clapped Oma on his pointy shoulder. "See our friends home to their rest Oma. It is almost dawn."

Akin saw Oma nod and return a clap to Luk's meaty shoulders. Luk returned to the helm and Akin resumed his spot nearby in the strange, skin piercing warmth of the reactor-heart.

"Akin?"

"Yes."

"Please allow the dead to pass without a word. They deserve as much." Luk said.

"Of course they do. I am not a fool Luk."

Oma began his service to the dead on bow as Akin and Luk watched on. They watched as Oma praised the Gods below and gently pushed the dead one by one through a hatch on the bow. As Oma spoke of the Gods' Sire arriving from the stars to birth their Gods in the ocean's depths, Luk broke the silence at the ship's stern.

"Akin do you know why I now choose Oma over Gult?"

"Why?"

"I have never heard a man tell the stories of our Gods like him before."

"You cannot be serious Luk."

Luk turned to look at Akin. His eyes were hard, yet kind. "I am."

"Gods below Luk! What difference does it make? The story doesn't change." Akin said loudly. Oma briefly glanced at the stern before continuing his praise for the Gods.

"Exactly my point Akin."

"What is your point?"

Luk signed and scratched his bald head. "Hearing the same story again and again is like sailing the shoreline over and over."

"I don't understand Luk."

"Akin, if you sail the same routes again and again eventually you don't think about the journey. You only become distracted with thoughts of the journey's end."

"I don't see the problem."

"What if, because you claim to know every rock in the shoreline, you stop minding your heading and run aground on new reef? You wouldn't make it the end you were so busy thinking of." Luk questioned.

"Luk, what has this got to do with Oma's story telling?"

"If you hear the same story again and again you will eventually stop listening. If you stop listening you will miss new wisdoms. If you miss new wisdoms, the Gods will find you unworthy and float you back the surface. We need people like Oma, Akin. We need people to tell tales in new passionate ways or we will lose the wisdoms still to be found." Luk said. He breathed deeply from the salty, sharp air as he watch Oma continue the rites of the dead.

Akin ground his teeth. His face's pot-marks grew taunt as he snarled. "The Sire came from the stars and crashed into the ocean, causing a wave greater than any before to wash away the unworthy. It laid its brood in the depths unseen by man and then shot back into the stars finally destroying the Once-World with a second wave greater even than the first so that the worthy could start again. The brood grow to become our Gods one by one and send their shed flesh to the surface to feed our bodies and fuel what is left of the Once-World. When our Gods grow to the size of the Sire, they shoot from the depths at dawn so that their waves wash away any who are still unworthy. They take with them the dead who we send to their depths inside their bulk to live amongst the stars. That is your story Luk. There is no more wisdoms to be found. If you eat and fuel the ships with the Gods' flesh, survive the waves as they leave for the stars and sink beneath the waves when you are dead, you are worthy. End of story."

Luk did not reply immediately. The boat was silent save for Oma's sermon at the bow.

"You are right Akin." Luk said. Akin blinked and turned back to Luk, smiling.

"You think I am right about the story's wisdom?"

"No, just right about the story. You have sailed the shoreline too well, you are blind to new reefs."

"You said you do not care what a man's beliefs are as long as his hands are moving Luk." Akin said.

"You are good sifter Akin. You'd be better if you listened to Oma. Leave it at that." Luk said. He stared at Akin with a soft expression, but hard eyes. Akin dropped his gaze to the deck.

Oma's sermon had stopped. Neither man at the bow had heard it end. Akin looked up from the deck and Luk's hard stare to see Oma's outreached arms. Each dripping from fingertip to elbow in Gods' flesh and an empty barrel on its side, contents drained through the hatch in the bow reserved to the dead to pass. Another barrel was opened, its contents threatening to spill. Akin's words caught in his throat causing him to splutter as his heart threatened to burst his chest. Luk simply stammered. Akin's and Luk's outbursts caused Oma to turn and regard the two. Oma smiled as he beheld the animal rage of Akin.

"What are you doing?!" Akin bellowed and lurched forward. Luk's strong arms arrested his charge.

"Oma what are do-" Luk said struggling to hold Akin. Oma's smile faltered slightly.

"He threw it away!" Akin roared.

"I gifted it back to the Gods to show we are not greedy and unworthy Akin! Luk! Control him!" Oma retorted.

"AKIN!" Luk bellowed. Akin stopped his struggle in shock. He had never heard Luk yell. Still with a large hand on Akin's chest, Luk regarded Oma.

"Oma, what have you done?"

Oma lowered his stained arms and straightened. "I have done my duty to the Gods as you have done yours Luk."

"How does that duty to involve throwing away the Gods' gift Oma?" Luk's voice was lowered.

Oma smiled. "You cannot see the reason Luk? Of you and Akin I did not think I would need to explain it to you."

Luk faltered for a brief moment. Akin saw his opening and took it, launching forward again. To his surprise, Akin found his balance off centre. He was swung into the side rail and grunted as the air was pushed from his lungs and fell to the deck. Spluttering, Akin looked up to see Luk's now fierce stare boring into him. "Do. Not. Move." Luk uncharacteristically threatened. Luk then turned to Oma and in the same tone stated "Explain yourself. Now."

"I will forgive the tone because I know your anger lies with Akin and not me Luk," Oma began.

"Do not speak for me Oma."

"Enough Luk. You sound like the barely rational Akin."

"Akin did not just throw away our hard-earned catch Oma." Luk said.

"Throw away?" Oma yelled. "Throw away?? Gods Below Luk! How could you see it that way?"

"How else is there to see it?"

"See it through the eyes of the worthy Luk! The Gods test us with this bounty. The months have been lean and now we are given such a generous offering? Why else other than to test who is greedy, who is selfish, who is unworthy! I have passed their test and in turn allowed us ALL to be worthy? Can you not see Luk? I have saved us from the next dawn-wave. It is coming soon, I know it because I am worthy. You know it too, because you are worthy." Oma said. Luk stood in silence. Akin saw his eyes dart to and fro in thought as he rose to a squatting position. Oma continued.

"You and I will survive the dawn-wave Luk. You and I are worthy." Oma turned to Akin. "Your anger will float you to the surface. Unworthy."

Akin charged the bow and the surprised Oma. His feral roar rang out across the black ocean. Akin crashed into Oma and the two men fell to the deck with an unsettling impact. Oma gasped as the air was driven from his lungs, Akin growled as he wrestled himself on top. Akin grasped the ragged cloth of Oma's shirt and pulled back a fist. Before he could bring his fist down it was halted by a vice-like grip.

"Enough!" Luk said loud enough for the Gods below to hear. Akin struggled in vain against Luk's grip before he was wrestled from atop the wheezing Oma. Luk stood ominously over the prone Akin who made no effort to rise.

"You are out of control Akin! What are you thinking?" Luk said, spittle flying from his lips to his patchy beard. Oma gasped and coughed as he rolled unto his hands and knees, Gods' flesh still dripping from his arms.

"Did you hear him?" Akin said breathing hard. Luk's stare bore a hole through Akin and then swung to Oma.

"Y-you," Oma said gasping, "you dare question me on matters of the Gods?" Oma rose gingerly and pointed a stained finger at Akin. "You raise your hand to me as I spoke the Gods' truth? You have sealed your fate Akin."

"So have you."

"And what fate would that be? That I have told an unworthy a truth they could not hear?" Oma said, eyes fierce with fervor.

"You will meet the Gods this night," Akin roared as he rose. Luk stepped between the two men.

"NO MORE!" Luk said. His face mirrored the red of the fading sky under the harsh white deck lights. Oma began, but Luk cut him off.

"Akin will not step onto my vessel again." Luk said. Akin's heart stabbed with pain and his vision was again blurred by welling tears.

"L-Luk."

"Akin." Luk's voice was weighted with regret. "Just...stop."

"Yes, listen to Luk. Stop now and accept your damnation." Oma spat.

Sound fell away as Akin's vision tunnelled onto Oma. Akin did not feel Luk's clawing hands as he flew past him, his elbow sinking into Luk's throat or his fingers grip Oma's neck. Akin barely heard Luk's splutters or Oma's gasping promises of damnation as the two men fell backwards into the bow. The only things Akin knew were his rapid breathing and his berserk heart beat. Then he felt the Gods' flesh from the open barrel spill across his face and heard the prone Oma's grasps become a bubbling gurgle.

Drowned by the Gods' own flesh Akin thought. The barrel opened by Oma lay on its side near the two wrestling men. Akin could see the Gods' flesh already flowing back into the sea.

"No." Akin thought before something exploded up from underneath him. Sharp pain blossomed into Akin's shoulder. Oma's slick arm now held the knife that was planted into Akin's flesh. Pale red blood rushed across the surface of the Gods' flesh slick deck, never mixing with it. Akin roared in pain and release his grip on the submerged Oma's throat. As Akin rolled he saw Oma's arm wilding slashing the air with his crude ritual knife, his face still obscured by the Gods' flesh, blinding Oma to the world. Through the pain Akin glimpsed Luk rush to Oma's aid.

Akin saw it before it happened, but could not scream. Oma's wild slashing had abruptly stopped. His knife halted by Luk's neck. The blind Oma retreated the blade and stabbed down again, and again. Luk dropped without a sound.

"Luk!" Akin said clutching his arm in pain. The bone white Gods' flesh running and clumping on the deck shone red with blood. This time however, Akin found no pause for beauty in the sight. Oma pushed the still body of Luk from him, slipping in Gods' flesh as he scrambled upright. He dropped his knife and frantically cleared his eyes.

"Luk! Akin is a mad man! He has doomed himself! I cannot guide him to the dept-" Oma stopped as his vision cleared. His bloodshot eyes saw the face down body. His eye widened, he jumped back in horror.

"No! No! NO!" Oma said pulling his last wisps of hair. Akin roared and tried to rise, but his lacerated shoulder would not let him.

"I was deceived!" Oma said glancing between the ocean and Luk's lifeless body. "Akin the unworthy guided my hand! I was deceived! I was deceived!"

Akin's retort was wordless rage. He rose, but slipped on the deck. The impact made his shoulder scream and his thoughts swim.

"You killed him Akin! You and your unworthy hate! His death is your punishment!" Oma said. He had regathered his bloodied knife and pointed it at Akin. "Pray the Gods never find you."

"I'll kill-" Akin began before he was cut off.

The ocean roiled about the vessel. Luk's body and the emptied barrels slid about the deck. Akin and Oma fell prone. The harsh lights on the deck flickered and then died with a burst of sparks. The ancient reactor-heart whined in protest and clunked silent. Smoke coiled from between the welded seams of its outer-casing. Ribbons of red light spiralled up from the deep and stabbed into the black sky. As they did, the light scattered and the sky became the canvas of impossible reds as it had before. The deck was bright as day under the red light, shadows and blood shared the same hue. The entire vessel lurched to the side as waves crashed against it. Like an island rising from the depths, a God breached the surface. The horizon was filled with the island-size bulk of the God as its ridged plates the size of mountains stood above the waves. The red light that danced in the sky leaked from between the God's colossal blackened plates. Though illuminated, the God's body resembled nothing more than an island of black rock, devoid of familiar features.

Oma said stammered, "I-I was right. They test us!"

Akin looked to the unfathomable size of the God and felt the blood left in his body run cold. Oma somehow regained his footing amongst the spilt Gods' flesh and rolling waves. He spread his arms wide.

"I welcome your dawn-wave Great One! Let me prove my worthiness! Cast your wave upon me and find me still standing!" His voice was strained to its limit. Akin scrambling to his feet, groaning in pain. Oma heard his rise and deftly regathered his knife.

"Are you so committed to damnation that you would attempt to kill me the God's presence?" Oma said. His knuckles popped as he squeezed the handle of his knife harder. Akin eyed the God on the horizon and then stared at Oma's glistening face which was set in determination under the ruby sky.

"You said it yourself, I am already damned. What do I have to loose?" Akin said. He took an uneasy step forward. Oma shifted his footing and squarely faced the advancing Akin.

"A dawn-wave is coming Oma. Whether you are worthy or not, your life ends here."

Oma looked to the horizon and its Godly visitor. His face flashed with fear. Akin charged, almost losing his footing and still clutching his stabbed shoulder. Oma yelped, dropping his knife and sprawled for the vessel's side. Before Akin could reach him, Oma cast himself into the waves using the hatch he had laid the dead to rest through. Akin slumped heavily on the rail and watched Oma in the roiling, red hue ocean.

"Great One I am prepared! Send your dawn-wave and save your servant from the damnation of Akin!" Oma said, spluttering as salt water filled his mouth. Akin felt dizzy, and his body leaden. His shoulder still poured blood to the deck and pain clouded his mind. He watched Oma for an unknown time as the man swan towards the horizon, his cries for salvation becoming weaker. Akin turned and slid himself down to the deck. He saw Luk's body. His eyes filled with tears, his heart tore itself in two and a hopeless wail escaped his lips. Spittle dropped from his lips, mixing with the blood and Gods' flesh on the deck, as he dragged himself to Luk's side. He buried his face in the dead man's back and howled with loss.

By the time he raised his face again, the sky had changed. The brilliance of red was stabbed with the fierce yellow of the dawn. The sun was rising, it too was stained red with the God's own light. Akin's knew his time grew short. Akin turned to the horizon and squinted at the sun's red radiance. The behemoth silhouette of the God cast a shadow which stretched beyond sight. Akin wiped his eyes and mouth. He knew he did not have long before the God returned to the stars, taking those Oma laid to rest and wiping out all those unworthy in its wake. Summoning strength he did not have, Akin rose and limped to the barrel his fight with Oma had spilled. He rolled it towards Luk and steeled himself for what came next. Screaming through the pain, he gently guided Luk's body into the empty barrel. Gasping from the effort he pulled the barrel upright and slumped over its top. Vision fading, Akin fumbled for the barrel's lip and partially sealed it.

It has to sink Akin thought as fell beside it, unable to rise and lost in his pain and sorrow. Warmth spread over him. But the warmth was not the sun's doing. It was sharp, stinging, stabbing. The taste of metal exploded into Akin's mouth and his ears rang. He looked to the God's colossal form and saw the light leaking from its body burn brighter. It pulsed as well, much like a heart beat.

"No," Akin said whimpering. "Not yet, not yet." He looked to the horizon and his fear was confirmed. The God's light grew brighter and brighter and its pulses faster and faster. The vessel rocked and the barrel with Luk inside threatened to fall. Akin screamed and dragged himself to his feet. As he did, the God's light pulsed brighter than before. The solid ripple of crimson light rolled across the ocean and scattered into the sky. As it passed through the vessel and Akin he screamed. His vision become bursts of colour, his skin stung and blistered and he vomited. The metal of the deck and barrel was hot to touch and the spilt Gods' flesh steamed as if boiled. Fumbling, he pushed with the last of his strength against the barrel. He could not be sure of his aim, but he hoped he would find the deck's loading gap. Another step and another step. The second step was met with another pulse of light from the God. Akin arched his back and howled as he felt the skin of his back split and bleed. He vomited again, but this time it tasted overwhelming of blood. Akin opened his eyes but saw only mockeries of colour. He felt his tears fall down his blistered cheeks.

"I'm sorry." Akin said as he took another step. "I'm sorry. I'm sorry. I'msorryI'msorryI'msorry." Akin felt the barrel tilt forward and he let go. He hit the deck and pain bellowed in his chest. Though his ears rang, he heard the barrel splash into the water and smiled.

Another pulse of light passed over Akin and the vessel. The last motes of colour in his vision danced. His ears screamed. His skin roared with pain as heat threatened to roast him alive. The taste of blood returned as he vomited again.

"A-aceppt, Luk," Akin mouth's said but his ears could not hear. "He is worthier than me."

Akin breathed in, the air was so hot it burnt his lungs.

Akin forced his eyes open and looked to the horizon. All he saw was a corona of red light shoot upwards faster than sight could truly follow. A roar shook the world, though Akin felt only its rumble through the deck. Heat like he had never known hit him as his vision died with an explosion of half-real colour. The God's red corona as it shot towards the stars burnt into his mind as the last image he ever saw. He felt the vessel roll too far to right itself. For a moment he lifted from the rusting deck and felt weightless. Blind and deaf, Akin hit the water. It was the temperature of blood. The last of the burning air left his chest and Akin sank just below the surface.

But he did not sink. Panic filled his mind as Akin thrashed blindly in the water towards his best estimation of down. I'm unworthy I'm unworthy I'm unworthy he thought. He felt his face brake the surface of the boiling water and against his will he reflexively gasped a breath of searing hot air. Akin guessed he was crying, but his tears were lost to the ocean as he floated on his back. I am damned he thought and stopped his thrashing.

Akin's limp arm hit something hard. His dying mind barely registered the contact. The ship hasn't sunk Akin thought. He moved his arm and felt the hard object move under his failing strength. He lashed out again and felt a rounded edge and the unmistakable shape of a half-closed barrel clamp. Luk's barrel! Akin's mouth coughed but his ears again could not hear. He then felt the barrel slip in his grip. He felt it begin to slip down. It's still sinking! Akin though with shock and held the half-closed clamp with the last of his strength. He felt his burning skin sink beneath the waves, his nose and mouth were filled with hot salt water. He felt himself falling deeper and deeper. You waited for me Luk. You knew I was worthy. Akin's mind lazily thought as the last of his breath left his bleeding lips in a stream of bubbles. Akin's hand could no longer hold the barrel, he let go and was left alone in the hot salt water. But it did not last. Before his mind faded, Akin felt his burning skin soothed by a gentle cooling touch. He felt himself wrapped in a comforting embrace of cold water. Cold pressure wrapped him like an infant in a blanket. With the red corona burnt into his mind's eye and touch of Luk's barrel in his memory his pain was soothed. Akin smiled.

Worthy, he thought. Then knew no more.

The Wedding Gown
By Leigh-Anne Robinson

1990

Lyndi sat hypnotized by a ruby droplet as it waltzed along her index finger to an unheard melody before dropping off the end like someone falling off a cliff. It spun anti-clockwise, as if it were turning back time. Back to that night six months ago when Tazmin burst into her room.

"He proposed. Lyndi, I'm engaged!" Tazmin flashed her left hand in front of Lyndi's face to display the glinting diamond ring. "I'm going to be Mrs Jonathon Ward, and I want you be my Maid of Honour." Lyndi wanted the verbal diarrhoea to stop. "Oh, and I know your Gran taught you everything there is to know about sewing, so I would love for you to make my wedding gown," Tazmin gushed.

"Taz, I love you dearly, like a sister even, but its friggin' three o'clock in the morning." Lyndi wanted to share in her friend's happiness but the news pierced her heart. "Please, just let me go back to sleep." She rolled over and buried her face into one of her pillows. Lyndi squeezed her eyes shut trying to stop the tears from flowing as Tazmin closed the door behind her.

But Lyndi couldn't sleep. Thoughts of Jonathon played through her head. She remembered how both she and Tazmin would chat about the gorgeous guy in their first anatomy class, how his deep soulful eyes were like rockpools. They had giggled like schoolgirls over the thought of checking out his anatomy, purely for study purposes. In the end, Taz had gathered enough courage to ask him to join them to study. It was usual for the study sessions to run late into the night and sometimes it was just easier for Jonathon to sleep on their lounge. And yet the next morning he still looked amazing as he stood in their small kitchen with a pot of coffee, cooking up a batch of pancakes. Except that night, when we all had too much to drink in celebration of passing grades then decided to give Jonathon a haircut while he slept.

Lyndi glanced over to the handcrafted wooden keepsake chest on her desk. Her grandmother had stored an assortment of buttons in it. It now housed a different collection. Amongst other things, Lyndi kept the lock of Jonathon's blonde hair taken that night, tied with a tiny elastic band and narrow blue ribbon. She was sure if anyone ever saw it they would think it was saved from a child's first haircut, but she was the sole person that knew the truth of the contents hidden within.

She had an uncontrollable urge to stroke the silky threads of hair, she slid from under her covers and tip-toed across the room. The pokerwork flowers burnt into the cedar chest were rough in her hand. She withdrew the tiny silver key from its hidden drawer, and after giving it a little wiggle the lock clicked open. A little thrill of excitement coursed through her as she caressed the hair.

She noticed the chewed-up pen and with trembling fingers ran it over her lips. The indentations that were made by Jonathon's teeth felt rough against her delicate lips causing the tiny hairs on her neck to stand on end, it gave her a thrill.

I guess it's the closest I'll ever get to kissing him.

Lyndi hated herself for the feelings she had for her best friend's boyfriend. In fact, she did everything possible to keep her emotions in check; it was exhausting but she knew it would tear Tazmin's heart and then their friendship apart if her friend ever suspected. Lyndi hated the way she secretly followed Jonathon, just so she could accidently run into him and suggest they go for a coffee. She had even studied up on some of his favourite topics so they would be able to have a meaningful conversation with him, not just the usual small talk they were used to. But most of all she hated the jealousy that kept percolating beneath the surface, threatening to boil over, and to dissolve her sugary sweet facade.

It's so unfair. What does Tazmin have that I don't? We like all the same things. Why can't he feel for me the way he feels for her? Can't he see how much I love him? Lyndi brushed a tear away. Tazmin could have any guy she wanted, why did she have to choose him? Lyndi thought.

Lyndi had a sinking feeling in the pit of her stomach, part of her didn't want to make the gown, the other part felt ashamed for having her crazy mixed-up emotions. She wanted to be a part of her best friend's excitement like any best friend should, it's just she would be happier if Tazmin's special day was with someone other than Jonathon.

The bead of scarlet completed its freefall and splattered along the edge of ivory silk that lay across Lyndi's lap. Lyndi watched the fibres absorb the blood like it was drinking in a glass of claret. She remembered the words of her grandmother:

It is a bad omen for a seamstress to prick her finger and stain a wedding dress with blood, it means the bride will die young.

At the time Lyndi had thought the superstition was silly, and she didn't believe it. But now it seemed like a good omen; if something accidently happened to Tazmin then Jonathon would turn to me for comfort. It seemed to be the perfect solution. Another drop of blood should be enough, Lyndi thought as she sterilized her sewing needle in the flame of the lighter they used for candles. Her palms became clammy with sweat and her hands began to tremble with nervousness. Lyndi wiped her hands on the front of her shirt. She cursed through gritted teeth with forced restraint, then with a swift jab the needle pierced her fingertip. A tiny bead of blood formed on the surface of her skin, and she smeared it across a raw edge of bodice, covered it with cream lace then hid it in the fold of the seam. Just to be sure.

Lyndi felt fake, like she had been wearing a mask for far too long and she wasn't quite sure which face was hers anymore. Lyndi recalled a day from high school.

> It was the first day of a new school year. She could still feel the cold floor as she cowered in the bathroom while a group of girls rummaged through the personal belongings in her bag. This humiliation had been a usual occurrence since the beginning of high school. She had always hoped that each year would be different from the previous one, and in a way, it was, each year was worse. Now the torment had escalated to new heights.
>
> The biting pain of the girl's nails as they gouged into the flesh of her jaw forcing her mouth open. They were manicured to perfection. Lyndi watched wide-eyed while another girl took a dead mouse from a plastic zip lock bag, swinging it back and forth by its tail as she closed the gap between them. The rest of the gathered entourage laughed almost mechanically, like a malfunctioning robotic clown.
>
> Then the daughter of the new principal Mrs Johnson, entered the bathroom.
>
> At first, Lyndi thought the girl would join in with the others, but she did the unimaginable, she gave each of the girls a look that was a clear warning, grabbed Lyndi's bag, helped Lyndi to her feet, then wrapping an arm around Lyndi's shoulder, lead her from the room.
>
> "Hey, I'm Tazmin," the new girl introduced herself with a wide smile. "Oh crap, I forgot to pee!" The laugh that erupted from her was contagious, and Lyndi never wanted to be immunized against it. This was the day she had been praying for, this was the day she finally had a friend.

A wave of guilt washed over Lyndi. *How can I want harm to come to my friend,* but the answer was clear: *Jonathon Ward.*

Lyndi and Tazmin had been sitting in the Limo for almost an hour, after getting stuck behind a funeral procession. Lyndi walked between the pews towards the minister in her sleeveless midnight blue chiffon cocktail dress. She couldn't help feel the colour was appropriate; it was dark enough to remind her of a woman in mourning, and although she wore a smile she couldn't have felt bluer. The crossover bodice would have been suited to a more voluptuous woman however, she was severely lacking in the bust department. The rhinestone encrusted comb tangled in her dark auburn hair dug mercilessly into her head and Lyndi was sure she would have permanent dints in her scalp.

She smiled at Jonathon who looked dashing in his debonair suit. It was easy to imagine he was waiting for her, if only for a moment; then his face ignited as his gaze fell on Tazmin. Lyndi tried to convince herself that there was still hope for him to see her for who she was. They had not said their vows - the minister had not yet pronounced them husband and wife.

Tazmin reached the altar and handed over her bouquet. Lyndi watched them enter their own little bubble, like she had hundreds of times before. She had lost, but hopefully not for long.

The remainder of the day passed in a blur. The signing of the marriage certificate, the photos, and then the reception.

Lyndi stood up to make her speech, but by now she had consumed way too much alcohol and not enough food, her head felt like it was spinning out of control. Her legs were unable to hold her, and she crashed to the floor.

"I have to throw up." Lyndi announced scrambling in what she hoped was the direction of the bathroom.

The following morning, Lyndi stood at the back of the crowd to wave off the happy couple as they headed to the airport in their taxi. The throb of her head had given way to the ache in her heart. Back at home, Lyndi began to pull down the celebratory decorations. A bitter reminder that Jonathon had not chosen her. It was somewhat satisfying to stab a pin into the white and indigo balloons that were scattered around the room. She jabbed at them like they were voodoo dolls, each pop giving her more and more pleasure. She was interrupted by her mobile's ringtone.

"Oh Lyndi, come quick. I'm at the hospital. There's been an accident. I can't face this without you." Lyndi recognised the voice of Tazmin's mother on the other end.

"Okay, I'll be right there." She hung up.

Man. That didn't take as long as I thought it would. Her lips twisted into a slight smile. Soon Jonathon will be crying on my shoulder, and then, in time he will realize he loves me. Lyndi grabbed her purse and went to the hospital, a little glow of happiness sparked into life. I must not seem too happy or everyone will think I'm heartless.

Tazmin's mother threw her arms around her when she entered the emergency department.

"Oh Lyndi, it's horrible. They don't think she is going to make it."

"What happened?"

"No one seems to know."

Lyndi looked around. "Where is Jonathon?" Panic started to rise in her voice.

Tazmin's mother sobbed into her handkerchief, "He died in the ambulance."

"Mrs Johnson?" A man in hospital scrubs approached them. Tazmin's mother nodded hopefully then saw the look in the man's eyes and wailed.

Three days later Lyndi sat in the second row of pews wearing the midnight blue cocktail dress. *At least I got more than one use out of it I guess.*

"They will be united forever in Paradise," the minister said, closing his sermon.

Lyndi did not notice the people around her shuffling out of the church. All she could do was stare at the identical coffins before the altar, the way the shine of the dark wood reflected the glow from the candles surrounding them, like a candlelit dinner for two. *Damn even their funeral is romantic.* She couldn't help feeling that she had died as well.

"You can't blame yourself." Startled, Lyndi turned around, coming face to face with the almost perfect replica of the man she loved.

She gasped, hesitant to reach out to touch him. "Jonathon? Is that you?"

"Um, no, sorry." The man took a step back, "I'm Jason. Jonathon was my cousin. Our fathers are identical twins, so I guess that's why we kind of look the same."

"Yeah, that's an understatement." Lyndi looked him up and down, somewhat disappointed that Jonathon hadn't found a way back to her.

"Say, do you need a lift to the wake?" Jason pointed his thumb over his shoulder towards the door.

"Um, okay. Just give me a few minutes." Lyndi waited for the man to leave then wandered to the coffins. She touched the tips of her index and middle finger to her lips then caressed the mahogany lid of one of the caskets. "I love you, Jonathon, I always will. I'm so sorry it happened like this." She wiped a stray teardrop from her cheek. Lyndi turned and walked away grabbing her purse off the pew as she left.

That night Lyndi and Jason found themselves sharing a bottle or two of Whisky, and before too long they were sharing a bed. One night of cold comfort created the child Lyndi could never have with Jonathon.

1995

Lyndi's arms swung about her head in frantic circles as she slept. The same nightmare had been plaguing her for weeks. The buzzing droned on around her as the bees swarmed. No matter where she ran, the bees were surrounding her. Lyndi seemed to feel each of their stingers pierce her skin. Her flesh became red welts, the welts became blisters which in turn became infected scabs oozing pus.

Lyndi could feel her heart racing as she switched on her bedside lamp. She inspected her arms for any sign of wounds. A few deep breaths later Lyndi's pulse began to return to normal. *This is ridiculous. Why on earth am I dreaming about bees?* Lyndi went into the kitchen and poured herself a shot of whisky, she didn't bother to add ice.

"Mummy? Did you have a bad dream?" came a small voice from down the hall.

"Go back to bed, Joanna."

"I heard you scream -"

"Did you not hear me?" Lyndi's voice was full of warning.

Lyndi listened to the tiny feet of her five-year-old daughter pad down the corridor, then there was a soft click as the door latch slipped into its notch. Lyndi raised her glass in a silent salute to the heavens then shot the burning amber liquid down her throat. She gasped and coughed, then the warmth crept into every cell of her body. She began to relax. *Another drink, before I climb back into bed.*

A week or so later Lyndi read in the paper about some woman who died of anaphylaxis shock on her wedding day. The paper reported that the couple were attacked by a swarm of bees whilst having their bridal photos. Bees. What a coincidence.

There was a small image of the couple sharing a cocktail accompanying the article. *I guess it was taken whilst they were on holiday,* Lyndi thought. On closer inspection, a small note was beside the glass with the words 'Marry Me'. *They look like they could have been happy,* Lyndi thought.

"Joanna are you ready for school yet?"

"Is Daddy picking me up for the weekend?"

"Nope, he cancelled again!"

A loud disappointed grunt came from behind a closed door.

I couldn't agree more kiddo. I couldn't agree more.

2000

It was about the tenth night in a row that Lyndi woke gasping for oxygen. She struggled to get enough air. It felt like someone was sitting on her chest, crushing her. Lyndi's shaky hand reached for her Ventolin on the table beside her bed, her fingers brushed against the pokerwork keepsake chest that now sat under her lamp. She didn't open it as much as she used to, still, it was a comfort to know it was there.

She placed her inhaler into her mouth then sucked the contents into her lungs. She looked at the amber lights displaying the time, three thirty-seven. *It has to be later than that.* Lyndi shuffled to the bathroom to rinse the excess Ventolin out of her mouth. The swirling water across her tongue made her realise how parched she was. After spitting the liquid out, she reached into the cabinet on the wall above the sink. She withdrew a bottle of vodka she had hidden behind a box of tampons.

"Mum, are you alright?" Joanna, now ten, asked from the hall.

"Yes, I just had another little asthma attack, okay." Lyndi drank the clear fluid and steadied herself against the sink.

"But I need to pee," came her daughters whine, this time the voice was just outside the door.

"Okay, I'll be out in a minute." Lyndi could hear Joanna shuffling from one foot to the other in urgency, so slipped the tiny bottle into the bin and hid it under scrunched up tissues. Then she flushed the toilet and turned on the tap for a few moments.

I'm acting like a teenager trying not to get busted with booze or cigarettes. The realisation dawned on her.

One night, about a week later, Lyndi was listening to the news while cooking dinner. She heard about a woman who passed away at her wedding reception due to an asthma attack.

Oh, how tragic. She glanced at the television to get more information. There on the screen was a head and shoulders picture of the woman.

"Oh, my God!" Lyndi stated.

"What is it? What's wrong?" Joanna popped her eyes over the top of the book she was reading.

"That scalloped sweetheart neckline is identical to a dress I once made."

"Pretty. What's for dinner?"

"Cheesy topped fish fingers," Lyndi replied somewhat distracted.

"I bet I could have pizza if I was at Dad's."

"Well as usual he cancelled, so you're not at dad's."

2005

Lyndi's head throbbed again. The doctor had sent her for tests, but as yet there was no real reason for the onslaught of migraines that had plagued her over the last week and a half. She popped two ibuprofen tablets from their blister pack and swallowed them down with a large gulp of whisky straight from the bottle. She grabbed an ice-pack from the freezer and although it was lunchtime, headed back to the quiet of her room. Every step made the contents of her stomach ebb and flow. It made her think of a ship on an ocean and she worried that the stormy sea within would soon make its journey to the surface. She lay on the cool sheets and closed her eyes against the burning that blurred her vision. Lyndi covered her head with a pillow to ward off the bright light streaming through the curtains.

The sensation of falling woke Lyndi with a jolt. She heard movement in the lounge.

"Joanna, is that you?"

"Yeah. You left the front door wide open, anyone could have got in, but I suppose we don't have anything worth stealing."

"I had a migraine– "Lyndi tried to explain.

Joanna poked her head into Lyndi's room. "Well maybe if you didn't drink so much you wouldn't have so many hangovers."

"Migraine. It was a migraine, you know, blurred vision and everything.–"

"Still sounds like a hangover to me. Anyway, I've got homework." With that Joanna went to her room. The slamming of the door made Lyndi flinch.

Nothing's worse than a fifteen-year-old with a chip on her shoulder the size of New Zealand, and an attitude to match. Lyndi thought. Maybe if Jason had taken more of an interest in her she wouldn't be so bad. But at least her grades are good.

Lyndi switched on the radio "Here's an oldie but a goodie," announced the DJ, as Ben E King started to sing *Stand by Me*.

Lyndi reached for the pokerwork box on the bedside table. Jonathon would understand. She let her thoughts drift off.

At five o'clock the news began, most of it was humdrum, but something caught Lyndi's attention. The tragic story of a bride who tripped down a flight of stairs; apparently, she hit her head on the wooden banister and died on the way to hospital. The news made Lyndi feel uneasy, as if she was somehow to blame for the accident.

That's impossible. But still the thoughts nagged at her subconscious.

2010

Lyndi shivered, if felt as though someone had walked over her grave. It happened again, causing an involuntary jerk of the head. The muscles in her legs tightened as they started to tremble. She had expected the usual side effects of detox as she worked through the twelve-step program, but the full body shakes were starting to become a hindrance. Lyndi lay down in the recovery position until the seizure had passed.

I wish Joanna was here to look after me, but she has her own life to live now.

Joanna now twenty, had moved into a flat with her boyfriend Gregory, whom she'd met whilst doing a placement at the school where he was teaching. It had not taken long for them to become friends and within eight months they were a couple. Although Lyndi was happy for her daughter it meant she had no one to support her through the difficult times when the temptation to drink was foremost in her mind. Joanna had warned her that she would not be allowed to see any grandkids if she continued drinking. It had been enough for Lyndi to recognise that she was an alcoholic and that she needed help.

Lyndi turned on her laptop. She had found a decent support group on Facebook, and wanted to let them know she was struggling and wanted advice about the seizures. The first thing that popped up in her news feed however was about a lady who had suffered an epileptic seizure whilst signing the register, lost consciousness and stopped breathing. Lyndi clicked on the post where a full-length photo of the gown was displayed. Lyndi's mouth fell open.

I don't believe it, this must be some sick joke or something. The sweetheart neckline scalloped around the edge, the lace covered bodice and the silk skirt, glared at Lyndi from the screen. Lyndi swallowed hard and licked at her parched lips. *I wish I had left at least one small bottle hidden away for emergencies.*

2015

Weeks went by. Night after night, Lyndi woke in a sweat, plagued by a recurring nightmare. All she remembered was the heat of the fire and the ear-piercing, agonized screams.

Weeks turned into months and the nightmares became more vivid. Through the flames and smoke, she thought she could catch glimpses of someone in a wedding gown, arms flailing. She did not recognize the woman, but she seemed familiar just the same. Lyndi had the feeling she should know her but couldn't remember where from, like when someone's name is on the tip of your tongue and you just can't get it out.

It has been about twenty-six years since I sat in this church, Lyndi thought as she sat in the front pew, surrounded by family and friends. The opening chords of the 'Bridal Chorus' began and everyone stood to watch as the flower girls sprinkled heart-shaped confetti over the maroon carpet.

Then her only child entered the chapel unushered. *Just one more thing that Jason couldn't be bothered with, where his daughter was concerned.*

Joanna had insisted that no one would see her dress until she stood in front of the minister with Gregory by her side. All Lyndi knew was that Gregory's mother had purchased the gown second hand and Joanna loved it. Draped in a white riding cloak Joanna made her way down the aisle. The cloak's hood served as a veil, shrouding her face. The faux fur trimming skimmed along the carpet seeming to hover without effort, but the static it created caused some of the confetti to stick to the hem of the cape. At the altar, Gregory removed the hood from Joanna's head, undid the ties that held the cloak in place, and pulled it from her shoulders. Everyone gasped in awe - all except Lyndi. She gasped in horror, colour draining from her face. Standing before her was her beloved daughter in the cursed wedding gown.

Lyndi was desperate to stop Joanna from saying her vows, but no words would form in her mouth.

What would I say? How could I stop it without Joanna hating me? At least if I stop the wedding, Joanna will not die. Lyndi bit at her lip, knotting her fingers together as she waited for the priest to ask if anyone objected. But as Joanna and Gregory had written their own vows, the chance never came.

Lyndi pulled at Joanna's arm in an attempt to stop her daughter getting into the car. In the slight struggle Lyndi did not notice that the shoulder strap to her bag had caught on the child safety lock, moving it into the 'safe' zone.

Gregory shifted closer to Joanna, without realising it, his knee pushed in the cigarette lighter. Family and loved ones waved their support. The bride and groom waved back at the crowd with wide smiles. They were unaware that the lighter had ejected, landing in the folds of Joanna's gown and was slowly starting to scorch the fibres. Then tiny flickers of flame crept upwards. Lyndi could hear her daughter's screams as she franticly attempted to unlock the door. Then the dress was engulfed in flames. Then, after all these years, Lyndi recognized the woman from her nightmares. She watched unable to move as her daughter burned. After what seemed like an eternity, there was silence.

Lyndi sat in an ambulance being treated for shock. The acrid smell of charred flesh permeated the air. *Oh Jonathon, what have I done?* Her stomached heaved, then, without warning the front of her new dress caught the coffee and toast she had for breakfast.

The paramedic passed her a sick-bag and a box of tissues. When the vomiting had subsided, he covered Lyndi's nose and mouth with an oxygen mask. "It's alright, just take slow deep breaths."

But every breath hurt more than the one preceding it.

"I should have stopped it."

"That wouldn't have helped, the preliminary investigations indicate there was a fault in the car's locking mechanism, that's why they couldn't get out."

Lyndi curled into the foetal position and rocked to and fro, just like she rocked Joanna to sleep as a baby.

Later that evening Lyndi lay in a hospital bed after taking her dose of sedatives. They had helped to calm her and about half an hour later she was feeling drowsy. Lyndi shut her eyes for mere moments, but before long was in a deep tormented sleep.

Lyndi felt like her skin was melting, she was convinced she could feel it sliding off her face the sensation was unbearable. Lyndi woke screaming, but no sound escaped her lips. She tried to reach the button for the lamp, but her body would not move. Lyndi tried to stretch out her fingers, but the nurses alert button was out of reach. The numbness in her left arm gave her pins and needles in her fingers. She started to panic, as the stroke caused her heart to beat one last time; she and the wedding gown were gone.

Harbour of Death

By Annie DeSouza

The icy winter air, cut deep into my lungs as I struggled to keep my stumpy fingers warm. Blowing on them with what was left of my semi-warm breath, brought no relief. Before me was the evidence of rivers gone by; canyons crudely chiselled with blunt tools. Staring out over the morning horizon, the sun etched its way through the puffy clouds. I felt so small, insignificant, and unimportant against this phenomenon of life. Yet so many wasted this precious gift and *I* was responsible for taking so many. As the years matured, cruelty became my default.

Alone and desolate, absorbing the red glow of the sun. I watched as it cast its rays over the Grand Canyon. The realisation came. I didn't deserve to be there with no witnesses to my regret. My life up until that point, had been all about death. That was me - Shaun Drew hired hitman. So many years had been spent killing and butchering. It came easy and my reward was high. So many lives, were taken, humans and animals alike. Such power was felt as their memories and their fire slipped away. Some existences were magnificent. Yet, in that single moment when a gun was held to their heads, they were reduced in every aspect of dignity. But my enjoyment was slowly turning to repentance.

Some got angry, but most cried like little bitches. I once had the CEO of a major bank, pissing in his boots pleading, begging for his life. He was almost allowed to leave until he began to grovel like the snivelling bastard he really was. Making small talk is a waste of time and oxygen. So I pulled the trigger, not even blinking as a single clean shot went through his forehead. He jerked backwards before falling. The ground behind him was a mess splattered with bits of brain, flesh and oozing blood. His body fell with a thud, and all I could think of, was how the fat shit deserved to die.

Everyone and everything had a price. There was no shame in taking a life for me. My consciousness did struggle with women and children, so those jobs were declined. Call me old fashioned, but I couldn't do what 'Johnny no fingers' did especially to women. Tired- tired of death became my thoughts. Ten years of carnage and I was worth over ten million dollars for my services. No wife no kids no conscience. I restored the balance in society. Representing innocent people who had been cheated in some way, was my preference. Unfortunately they could not afford me. So the rich and powerful dominated my business. Enslaved and trapped by my own greed of more. More money, more power, more death. Clarity began to hit my consciousness. My eyes absorbed a melancholy moment observing creation. It's as though Mother Nature was whispering to me; stop.

And then I saw him. Cloaked in black wings shimmering a touch of jade green. Light darted across his back, strong, heavy and with nebulous dark eyes. His perfect thick beak pointing towards me like I was a naughty child. He had been watching me the whole time, judging, sentencing and awaiting my execution. He sat perched on a cold metal railing obscuring the perfect picture shot. Good thing I wasn't taking a photograph, I thought. My ears burning hot and my neck paralysed. Fear and dread wafted over me in waves but my confusion couldn't work out why. He was only a crow. Legends believed that a single crow was an omen for bad luck. Harbouring negative feelings of doom. But the Native American Indians believed that it meant good luck. My beliefs polarised. I moved closer thinking he would move away. After all I was the supreme species, the top of the food chain and I was a trained killer. He shuffled left to right rearranging his weight from one claw to the other. That's when I noticed a missing foot replaced with a stump. Across the right of his beak was a deep scar as though he had been swiped with a blade. Curiously, it felt like we shared a similar story, that somehow we were connected in our bloody histories. I too had a scar across the right of my face from a blade.

It happened a few years previously when fist fighting with a gang member who I was hired to kill. He had caught me by surprise- no guns only this one large hunting knife hacking at my body. I remember the blade slicing my cheek open tweaking the end of my nose. As the knife swayed back and forth, the intricate markings of the bone handle carved its own memory into my mind. How fascinating. The handle resembled similar markings to a book my mother had given to me decades before. Whilst deep in thought about the patterns my body fell into autopilot. I managed to grab his wrist and turn the knife into his body and it was driven hard into his chest. I'll never forget the all too familiar look on the Hispanic's face. His mouth fell open dripping blood, a sweaty brow and eyes that whispered the same final words - oh shit! I removed the knife and wiped the blade clean on his shirt before inspecting the markings on the handle. I knew it! The patterns were identical. That knife was destined to be mine. Years on that very same blade had ended forty-eight lives, the same number of years I had been alive for.

Back on the Canyon to my surprise, the crow stayed there taunting me into a stand-off. Stepping closer- still he did not move. Does this bird not know how dangerous I am? My confusing thoughts were racing in my fatigued mind. Then with no warning he stretched out both wings, flapped a little and then casually flew to the ground. He then continued to hop away. I flinched. How curious was my action, it confused me. Never had I shown anxiousness or nervousness. Yet that crow made me feel uncomfortable. Was my gut instinct right or wrong? Was my feathered enemy an omen a bad omen, harbouring death? It was only a bird, nothing more nothing less I told myself.

My leathery skin absorbed the tepid warmth of the morning sun. No more thought was given to my winged companion. The final job was around the corner. Retirement was imminent. I could taste the freedom. This final hit had a large payout. Money wasn't needed but there was a desire to have a final farewell, a ceremony of my parting. Deep in the canyon was the hit and his wife riding mules. But I was travelling on foot, which was tricky. Temperatures at ground level were sub zero and ice made the rocks slippery. On entering my car to head further along the road, the crow was found sitting on the bonnet to get warm, I presumed. He sat there peering straight at my soulless surprise. My pounding heart softened as I found myself searching for food to give to him. It's as though I was searching for retribution. Nestled between the gear stick and handbrake was a two-biscuit packet. Compliments of my motel. Crushing the contents and sprinkling some on the bonnet, the crow tilted his head to one side and watched my movements. He edged forwards to peck at the delights left for him with no caution. `

A sense of urgency drained from my schedule, after all I had the whole day to kill. The crow finished eating- stared at me as though he was almost smiling and then flew away. A wave of calmness swept over me and for once- I was at peace. My feathered friend had restored my faith in life. His small action of friendliness replaced the pining for normality. One more kill- hell I'll do her in as well if she gets cocky I thought. Okay, two kills and I'm done forever. Can't leave witnesses. Content with that thought. I planned to do the killings first while it was a comfortable brisk temperature. Then hike out of the valley back to civilisation as the day warmed up.

An hour later found myself clambering over rocks as I descended into the canyon. No one was around but my given instructions were that my hit had camped a little further ahead. My only concern, was that it echoed; every rock falling, cough and sneeze, even my breathing sounded loud. If there was a scuffle or scream, it would be heard. How was I going to keep them quiet? There was no access to my L42 Enfield sniper rifle. I was going to have to do it the old-fashioned way; with my bare hands and my trusted bone handle hunting knife. Being splattered in other people's blood, still makes me squirm. There is always the worry about catching some disease but more so, is the smell left on me. Believe it or not different people have quite unique blood smells. Once dried out it can be disgusting. It's as though I can smell their life story. Filled with inadequacies, missed opportunities and perverted idiosyncrasies, seen only by themselves. That's where my disposable plastic rain poncho came in handy on that occasion. Not the trendiest attire but functional.

The otherwise flawless blue sky was interrupted by billowing grey and white smoke in the distance. Only the city slicker would be stupid enough to light a fire for all to see. It had to be my target. I crawled over more rocks to get a clear view of them. He was a tall man in good physical shape and his wife, at least ten years his junior. They looked like they would be hard to kill. He was well built but I was confident that my previous experience, was going to make this double execution hopefully quick. His wife was attractive in a showgirl way. What a shame but I had to leave no witnesses.

Stopping shy of the horizon, I hid behind some rocks and cactus. The shadow cast offered some added cover as I tried not to get pricked. But feeling clumsy, like it was my first-time stalking- my actions were childish. In fact my first ever kill was hit and miss.

In those days I earned an honest living working in New York City for a pension insurance company. Boring, yes...long hours...yes; chance to sleep with my boss; absolutely! I was a young buck of twenty-one years old with everything to prove especially the size of my dick. That's one thing God had blessed me with and I knew how to use it. My boss, was a forty something woman named Kristie. She was married with two kids and a boring husband. She spent her whole working day flirting with me until I finally banged her on her desk. Her family pictures watched us with disgust. Since that day she did nothing but over pay me and demand more sex.

I had finished one of 'our sessions' and had entered Penn Station. The champagne was repeating in my throat and then came the urge to spew. Cupping my mouth and looking around for somewhere discreet to chuck. Nowhere was found, in a crowded subway so I spewed in my hand. The vomit leaked between my fingers and the smell made me wretch some more. So, there I was, puke in one hand, sweat pouring off me and low and behold some random hobo had struck me hard across the back of my head. The memory of falling forwards, regurgitated champagne flying in the air and my assailant standing over me, was hacked into my memory. As I lay there on my side, a boot swung towards me straight into my face. My nose exploded and the pain was excruciating like my skull had been split wide open. Despite the horror, all I could focus on was my airborne puke descending in slow motion as it splattered my attacker. He let out a little girl scream, that's when I knew *I had this*. Tackling his leg made him fall. The man was dressed in old layers of dirty clothes and stunk of piss, oh and my insides.

I don't know what it is about New York City but no one cares; about anything or anyone. On one street, a baby could be born and dumped outside a restaurant and on the next, a brutal stabbing. No one came to stop us or help me. People walked on by. In fact the passageway became vacant. Alone with no one to stop me, I pinned the man down and began to punch him hard across the face. The sensation draining from my drunk fists. He put up a bit of a fight but then he went limp. Thinking he passed out- I wasn't going to take the risk of him coming after me. I grabbed a tuft of his wiry hair as though he was about to be scalped. Slamming his head onto the concrete floor felt powerful. Then the thud noise became a squelch sound. He was dead. There was no going back. Rage had taken over. Feeling violated, my revenge was satisfied. I was surprised- it felt good, liberating. Was I supposed to feel that good after killing someone?

Well after that night I became a changed person, hunting for opportunities to kill. I wanted to explore my skills but more so, the exploration of my mind is what interested me. That's when Roderigo Dominic- a retired assassin walked into my life. He put my talents to good use. Gone was my pension job paying measly twenty- five thousand dollars a year and bang I started my new job at two hundred and twenty thousand dollars a hit. Off course the hits were mainly the rich and famous. The only downside was missing my sessions with Kristie. I remember being very clumsy in the early days. Noisy and blood was splattered everywhere. There was evidence of fingerprints and DNA left around, not to mention the murder weapon on several occasions. Thank heavens for Roderigo who sorted out my careless blunders.

Hiding behind the cactus back in the Grand Canyon felt like I was twenty-one again. Bumbling along dropping rocks and sliding straight into cactus spikes. My hand tried to stop the advance but who does that? Me of course. Yelping out in pain, my palm, speared with spikes, I snapped my other hand over my mouth. The spikes penetrated my flesh and I couldn't believe what a dick move I had made. The hit and his wife were going to notice the yelping. In my grand moment of stupidity there beside me, smiling again; was the crow.

My attention was divided between watching my feathered friend laugh at me with surprised eyes and the hit and his wife looking around in my direction. I ducked further behind the cactus getting more spikes pierced into my body. My hand snapped back over my mouth again muffling my own voice as I winced from yet more pain. Feeling uncomfortable, my body twisted like it was possessed by a demon. They patrolled their camp then they soon settled after about five minutes later. Pulling out the spikes embedded in my throbbing hand was like pulling out teeth. All the while the crow watched me with amusement.

'Not funny!' I grunted, 'don't look at me all doom and gloom.' But the crow perched on a rock and stared. His hunchback protruding with wings dipped to the earth. It was as though I was being tested. Tested for my final performance. My hand was burning with pain and it began to swell. After thirty minutes of physical and psychological torture, I edged forwards keeping low. The crow as my only company hopped down with me. He seemed to enjoy the fact that I was in agony and he would not go away, despite my futile attempts to shoo him. Panic set in as my chances were looking bleak. Being on foot meant I had to get to them quick before they mounted their mules. Throughout my ordeal, the crow followed me offering no help or even empathy only ridicule.

Finally getting to a swimming hole, near the Havasu Falls was the man bathing. He must've been one of those adrenalin seekers since the water temperature would have been a brisk twenty-two degrees Celsius all year round. The woman was back up over a ridge cooking breakfast well out of sight. The man was diving underwater unaware that his life was about to be gone. When he resurfaced near the edge I grabbed his hair and before he had a chance to say anything, his throat was slit. My blade wasn't as sharp as it usually was and he gurgled a noise as blood filled his throat. I ran the well-used metal several times across his neck as he in desperation clung to life. Flaps of flesh floated from my successful cuts but his will to live was strong as his arms thrashed around. I decided to hold him down underwater to silence him. He splashed in a frenzy like piranha's feeding and I hoped to god that the woman hadn't heard the water fizzing, from his choking.

After a couple of minutes, he was dead. Pulling his limp body out of the water was easier than I thought. Although, dragging to hide it behind some rocks proved problematic as the rocky ground kept grabbing him slowing my movements. Don't know why I bothered, there was blood everywhere-in the water, on the bank and a clear trail to where he was hidden. The crow hopped onto the body and wasted no time in striking his eyes. Several hard blows and the little nugget popped out, ligaments still attached. The crow seemed happy with his prize and soon went to work on the other eye. My stomach turned with disgust and fear. On one hand we were partners in crime, yet on the other, he was my grim reaper. Were my eyes also expendable? It would only be a matter of time until the woman saw the blood-stained swimming hole and the lack of her husband. I approached her to gain the element of surprise. She sat by a fire pit drinking coffee. Relief was close. These were my final murders. On nearing, the crow hopped close to her. The mules were tied to a tree and they began to shuffle in fear- running into each other, dust flying. She screamed and started to throw rocks at the crow. When she saw me, she ran in my direction for protection.

'Get rid of it!' she exclaimed, 'I hate crows.'

There was no, who are you and what are you doing here? I wrapped her frail body in my arms and said, 'Don't worry, he'll soon get bored. He may be hungry.' Even though I knew he had minutes before eaten her dead husbands' eye balls. 'I'm Shaun, you can call me ranger Shaun. Thought I'd check on you folks. Do you have a permit for camping?' I asked in an authorative manner hoping she would fall for my confidence.

'Oh erm; yes, we do somewhere,' she spoke with a nervous voice as she picked up various bags in search of the permit. 'My husband will know where it is he's having a swim and will be back soon.'

'No problem, I'll wait.' I was already planning how best to end her life, when my crow friend decided to appear again. This time he had a bit of blood dripping flesh in his beak, from the fresh kill stuffed behind the rocks. My heart pounded hard, as I could not believe, that he was blowing my cover.

'Eww, what is that?' she asked scrunching up her nose.

I diverted the conversation elsewhere, 'There's a dead lizard a little way back,' nodding with my nose towards the opposite direction. She walked towards me and I did not want to exchange in any conversation. I wanted her gone. My feathered friend hopped closer which caused her to scream again. This made the mules break their ropes and gallop away. It sounded like someone was murdering her, yet I hadn't even started yet. Oh shut up! I thought, you dumb bitch. My opportunity came quick as she ran towards me again. She was desperate to be rescued. But instead I drove my knife into the top of her skull. Holding it steady, whilst hammering it in deeper using my opposite fist, she dropped to her knees. I drove the blade further by pushing it into her tender head listening to it crunch and vacuum blood. Stepping back, I watched her die. Her eyes lifted towards me blood oozing down her pretty face. There was no noise only a look of bewilderment. Sitting in the dirt, forearms resting on my knees watching her movements- this kill was symbolic to me. A closed chapter, the end of the book. It left me wondering, what was she thinking in her final moments? Was it your life flashing before your eyes, was it peaceful or painful. She was innocent, but she was married to a bad man and she was a witness. Tiny ants swarmed around the pool of blood collecting on the ground. Her precious life was slipping away. Her eyes searched for me looking for comfort, as though it was someone else that drove the blade into her skull. She finally fell forward, lifeless. I paused for a good five minutes with a sense of relief. My first kill was exhilarating but my last, saddened me. Not from regret or empathy but from the realisation that I was good for nothing else. She had to die otherwise she would've involved the cops. At least that way, both were dead with no witnesses. My contemplation and serenity was interrupted by the crow who sat on her back pecking and twisting her flesh from the base of her neck.

'Stop that,' I said trying to shoo him away, but he kept coming back. After a frustrating few minutes of my perpetual hand fanning, I finally turned her over. The crow stared at me in appreciation then pecked at one eye. He had some difficulty trying to pop it out. My attention went to raiding their camp which took me a good ten minutes to get rid of all identification. On returning to her body, the crow was still there desperate for her delicacies. He hopped towards me twisting his head from side to side and then hopped back to the woman's body. It's as though he was signalling to me.

'Really? You want me to dig her eyes out?' It seemed so. The crow kept swooping towards my head, harassing me until finally, in disbelief, the thought was entertained. 'Alright, alright. Fine, I'll do it. But you leave me alone after this.' The knife was hard to pull out of her skull but once released, I proceeded to cut around one of her eye balls. All the time the crow looked from her eye to me in anticipation. The ligaments were tough like thick elastic bands holding on. Finally severing the last string, made the eyeball pop out in the air and roll along the dirt. The crow swooped down to catch it before returning for the other. The process repeated. What a sick and twisted bastard I had become. It was as though my services as a hired hit man were still needed by my accomplice. The crow as my new boss. I was doomed-perhaps he was an omen indeed. Not to hurt me, only to keep me killing. Trapped, with no retirement. But my connection with that creature had me questioning my purpose.

I thought my life couldn't become more complicated, when it took a sharp ninety- degree turn. My cloaked friend began to morph into something big. A black smoke swirled around it, engulfing both of us, making me feel dizzy and sick. Once the mini twister was gone, standing in front of me, was a creature. He wore a long black hooded cape on a human frame, but had the head of a bird, the crow. His feet exposed. One had talons the other was a complete stump. He was holding a wooden staff, its shape, twisted and knurled. At the top, was a metal claw that held an eyeball. Ligaments draped through the claw and the eye darted in several directions trying to focus. Then it stopped when it saw me and the once green eye turned blood red then black.

The ground shook as the creature limped towards me. Was this an illusion, had I lost my mind I wondered? It picked up the knife and inspected the markings then pointed it at me. Petrified and unable to move, the scene playing out before me made me gasp, this was real. I was afraid for once in my life. As the creature approached, it pulled out a small notebook that looked identical to the one my mother had given me years before. It opened the pages and stopped at one. The book was then flipped to face me and it used the knife to point at the blank page.

I struggled to see but soon enough, the page lit up as though an invisible pen was writing in blood; a word. It said Shaun and then the book burnt up into ash. What did it mean? The creature with no hesitation ripped out the eyeball that was resting in the staff. It threw it to the floor and rushed towards me holding the knife under my bottom eyelid. It all happened so fast. With the beak facing me, eyes blinking like an alien, it paused waiting for a response from me. The understanding came about the meaning of my life. Destined for doom from the way I lived, to the way I killed. The notebook was my first warning as a small child and then the knife as a young man. And now older, the crow. My chance for salvation was staring at me. All that needed to be done, was lose my dignity, to plead for my life, to beg forgiveness and redemption but I was a killer. No empathy. So I smiled at the creature. In one swift action, it sliced and tugged my left eyeball out. There was no pain, only the sound of it popping out. I cradled my bleeding wound as it dug in deep into the other eye.

The blood oozed down my face, warm and sticky against the cold air. My hands were wet from feeling the empty sockets, yet somehow my sight was untouched. Looking around I saw myself kneeling, dark pits from where my eyes once were. On the floor I could see one of them rolling. The creature placed its stump over it and pressed down. Brown jelly popped from the sides as the eye collapsed under the pressure.

Next there was a black mist and then I was somehow in the streets of London watching a man carve up a woman. Then, back in New York watching a gang of thugs brutally bash an old man to death. Russia took me to an abattoir and these horrendous journeys continued, over and over. I witnessed the most terrible atrocities and with no eyelid or the ability to turn, the horrors became immortal. The crow stayed with me everywhere, that's when the conclusion came, that I was the eyeball in the staff. My only redemption; was to not empathise, to stay a killer, cold and apathetic.

Writings on the Wall
By Michelle Mullins

Hudson City, the City of the Isles, a haven for metahumans and the last stronghold of the British Empire in North America. The slings and arrows of history and fortune has left the territory perched on the southern coast of the American colossus since the 17th century. With winter coming, with its very slight cooldown, the tourist season was slowing.

It had been quiet for the last few months, with little metahuman activity, at least that drew untoward attention. The many churches and faiths in the town held their feasts and holy days and such. The business and market districts hummed with activity, albeit at a slower pace. For those at Zhang's Herbal Shop, things were moving back to something approaching normal, considering the usual things going on. Having an owner who was one of the leading lights in the local supernatural community did have its ups and downs. Maiyu and Kilala, students of said owner, one Zhang Guo, also known as Sensei, were back to their studies, minding the store and their private investigation business.

Early Tuesday morning, Maiyu was organising things in the house behind the storefront. A fit, short haired brunette of Japanese extraction, with pink dyed streaks in her hair, Maiyu was unexpectedly busy. She was collecting research materials, getting notebooks and such, and calling various friends and contacts. Earlier, in the subterranean, and magically grown gardens, lab, and the training areas there, Sensei had given Maiyu her marching orders. Maiyu preferred to get cases herself, but when the Sensei commanded, you obeyed. So now she was finishing up a phone call to Little Sister, cyborg, tech genius and surveillance expert.

'Sophie, it would really help if I could have those cameras today.' A muted voice replied. 'No, I don't want you to have it set up as a holographic display, or with attached biometric sensors.' Another mutter. 'You want to hack the police and local CCTV? Ah, no thank you.' You had to be cautious with Little Sister. She got enthusiastic. One time she attempted to assist Maiyu with a robot, when said robot identified a passing feline as a deadly threat. One burned out warehouse and a traumatised cat later, had taught Maiyu a valuable lesson in dealing with the tech genius. The cat, her shapeshifted, sometime friend Kilala, had not been amused.

'Well, of course you can watch. And yes, if we get in trouble you can help. No, not with fire support. No death rays.' A final mutter. 'Ok, see you.' With a sigh, she hung up and considered her next move. A snack?

Walking past the kitchen door, Maiyu noticed her house mate Kilala draped over a chair, and decided to get that ball rolling. 'Hey, Kilala do you still have some of that magical paint remover?'

Kilala stretched on chair, without taking her eyes off the book she was reading. 'Oh, yeah. It was easier to make a big batch. Why?' She replied, her tall, lean frame draped in a way to make Maiyu's back hurt. Her long dark hair was messily tied back, matching the lose black clothes she was wearing.

'I was just talking to Sensei. He said he would run the store today.' Three, two, one.

'Ok fair enough... Wait, what?' She seemed confused.

'There have been some idiots leaving creepy graffiti around a store, on Dillon St. Probably trying to intimidate the owners. They hired us to go and have a look.'

'Wait, wait. Us? When was this situation an 'us' situation?' Book forgotten, Kilala focused on Maiyu.

'Sensei wants us to go and have a look at some, possibly magical, graffiti. Most likely a bunch of punks trying to frighten people.' She said offhandedly, moving to the fridge, and looking in.

Kilala's eyes narrowed, obviously trying to decide if Maiyu was lying. It had happened before.

'Come on, it'll be nothing, just going and swatting down some idiot kids.' Maiyu took out cold cuts and bread, and started making herself a sandwich. Being height challenged, she pulled out a small stool so she could reach into the upper cupboards for mustard.

'Wow. Now we know it's going to be something like a fallen god or mad sorcerer after saying that,' Kilala said, deadpan.

'You are a massive pessimist, you know.'

'I prefer to consider myself a realist.'

'Then you should come and help me then shouldn't you, if certain doom is fated,' Maiyu pointed out cheerfully. 'I've arranged tech support.'

'Oh, goodie. I love tech support. It went so well, last time.'

Maiyu smirked. 'Sophie has promised to be on her best behaviour. Just cameras and overwatch.'

Kilala glared 'I really hate you, you know that, right? This will all end in tears.' She drained the rest of her drink before standing.

Maiyu finished her sandwich. 'Well, think of how you can say I told you so.'

The argument getting Kilala in the car had taken another few minutes but soon enough they were on their way. Technically, the vehicle was the store car but Maiyu was the only one that had a car license. Kilala usually rode her motorbike, or jumped across rooftops. After a few long minutes of silence Kilala spoke. 'So, what exactly are we doing?'

'Well graffiti has been turning up around a convenience store.' Maiyu waved in the air vaguely as she drove. 'Apparently, it's strange symbols and diagrams.'

'They think it's magic?' Kilala said. 'Nothing has happened, I guess.'

'Pretty much, except for a disturbed shop owner and his staff. It was all in chalk, so they have been cleaning it up. But it's redone each night. The police haven't noticed anything in their drives bys.'

'If they have been dealing with it with no consequence, why is Sensei having us look at it.' Kilala sounded grumpy, fixedly staring out the window.

'The last time they did it in paint. The owner, at that point, decided to get someone else to look at it just in case.' Maiyu flicked her phone on with one hand, activated the map app.

'Yay,' Kilala sighed, 'Well at least the paint stripper might get some use, and I suppose we are being paid for this.'

Maiyu hummed in agreement focusing on the directions from her phone. She also watched Kilala fidget out of the corner of her eye. The taller woman's gaze restlessly followed things outside the window, fingers tapping on her legs. Maiyu wondered if Kilala had always been this way or if her resident cat demon was the cause.

Maiyu's powers came from her own demonic heritage, a throwback to a Kitsune ancestor, as much part of her as her skin or hair, whereas Kilala's came from an uneasy balance with her demon 'guest'. Odd that it was Kilala, who had started out as wholly human, was the one people noticed as not quite normal. It disturbed people, which made Kilala self-conscious. She wasn't a people person, whereas Maiyu was. Kitsune were trickster spirits, after all. Fitting in was part of their skillset.

Soon, they made it to Wraight Way, a suburb on the edge of the industrial district. It was early, but even so there was a small crowd looking at the mishmash of symbols around the store. The symbols were painted neatly in red, with only a few words in the same language. Maiyu recognised Kanji, Elder Furthrak, and even a few words in English. A name, Robert Fairfield was repeated several times. Maiyu looked over at her companion to see her reaction, as they had both paused to look at the wall.

'What?' Maiyu asked in response to Kilala's raised eyebrows.

'That was done by idiot teenagers?' she said gesturing to the graffiti.

'Look, none of it makes sense, its gibberish. Bullshit. The ones who wrote this are worse than amateurs.' Maiyu trailed off. There was a lot of stuff painted, and even though the languages were slapped together, they had an obvious theme. Fear, ill fortune and death. She rallied. 'Let's go. We won't find out anything standing here.'

'Red writing, a bit inauspicious.' Maiyu moved closer to the writing, examining the individual letters.

'Oh, come on, why would you think that?' The shorter woman replied, then paused realising the reference. 'People don't write names on gravestones in red here and even if they did, it's just a superstition.'

'It's a bad omen. These words have a common purpose. They want this Robert Fairfield…'

'The owner' Maiyu supplied.

'Ok, the owner, either dead or wishing he was. This is his symbolic gravestone. And it is written in red. This is a very bad juju. Just saying.' She stepped back. 'I mean we are just living in a city famed for its magic and superheroes, and you are saying that maybe that finding a wall covered in strange symbols painted in red isn't just a bit worrying?'

Maiyu refused to dignify that with a response, causing Kilala to snort.

'Well, I'll have a look at this, before we clean up. You'll talk to the owner?'

'That was the plan,' Maiyu said, 'you need anything for that paint remover?'

'Bucket of water... maybe two considering the amount. A stiff broom or brushes for scrubbing.'

Maiyu nodded, walking into the store to find the owner.

It only took a few moments to find the owner, a tallish white man.

'Ms. Chiba?'

'Yes, Mr. Fairfield. Pleased to meet you,' Maiyu said, offering her hand out to shake.

'Sorry to bother you about this, but it's very weird and I am going to start losing customers.'

'We are happy to help, I just need to ask a few questions, then we will see if we can get to the bottom of this.'

'Of course, of course.'

'So, when did this start?' Maiyu asked, taking out a pen and notebook.

'Six days ago. It was just chalk then, nothing too much. To be honest I was just glad it was easy to get rid of, even if it was kind of creepy. Most graffiti isn't easy to get rid of after all, but more turned up every night and now they have started painting the stuff. Cleaning it up, when they come back and do it again so quickly just isn't practicable anymore.'

'I see,' Maiyu agreed, 'So you have no idea who would be doing this? No threats or strange behaviour?'

'Ha, it would be difficult to say on the second and nothing credible to the first. Although...' he paused, uncertain.

'Anything at all could be useful, even if it seems silly.'

'About a month ago these two kids came in. Teenagers yeah? They looked looked pretty strung out, not all there, like they were on something. One asked me if I was going to pay for my sins. Well I told them to get out and after a moment they did. Very strange.'

That was one way of putting it, Maiyu thought. 'We are planning on watching the store overnight, and we may see who is responsible. Do you remember what they look like? Might make it easier to identify them.'

'The one that didn't talk was all bundled up,' he said with a frown, 'hoodie and stuff. They had grey eyes, but other than that I am not sure. I couldn't even tell if it was a boy or a girl. Really thin, dark hair I think, pale skin, but kinda sick looking you know?'

'Okay then, and the other?'

'Young man, looked like he used to be an athlete. Musclely you know, but he looked really out of it. Didn't really look at me, jittery. Brown hair and eyes, good looking I guess, a jock type, you know?'

'Ok,' Maiyu said finishing taking notes. 'The idea is for me and my colleague to clean up outside, first. We will need some buckets of water and a broom or scrubbing brushes.'

'Oh, of course.'

'After that we will go and get a few things ready, then tonight we will watch the store and see if we can find out who is doing this. We will clean up any stuff that turns up so you will have no problems tomorrow.'

'Excellent.' He smiled in some relief. 'I'll go organise that for you.'

Some minutes later, with the application of water and magical cleaner, the outside of the store was probably as clean as it had ever been and Maiyu and Kilala were back in the car.

'Nothing much strange from what Mr. Fairfield's said, some drugged out kids is the worse he can think of. So, the idiot kid idea seems like is what is happening.'

'There was something odd there though,' the other woman pointed out.

'That could have just been anything, a passing magician, for all we know. And even you said that the symbols were just random bits and pieces,'

'That first part sounds like rationalisation to me.'

'There is no reason to think it is anything but some kids trying to freak people out,' said firmly.

'Pretty organised kids,' Kilala said crossing her arms and leaning back into the car seat.

'Why complicate things? This is just a simple ID job.'

'Ok, that is just bad luck there. Everyone knows to never say that... it is going to be cultists now or a magical drug ring or unspeakable creatures from beyond trying to make a gateway into our world to eat our faces.'

'Really? That's ridiculous, and you have already said that already' Maiyu said incredulously.

'I thought we were both being ridiculous,' Kilala replied, 'Seriously if you are so confidant, how about a bet? Say twenty bucks.'

Maiyu just stared at her house-mate.

'And I want you to admit I was right, that it was more than just some idiot teens.'

'What do I get when I win,' she shot back.

'The same.'

'Ugh, fine.' Part of Maiyu was aware she was being pushed into this. 'When I win you had better not quibble over it.

'Back at you, ' Kilala said with a smug look on her face as Maiyu gunned the engine.

It was slightly before eight when they set back out for the store. Kilala had insisted on taking her bike, but as they were planning on parking a few blocks away anyway, Maiyu hadn't insisted on the car. Walking to the store they looked for good look camera spots. Arriving, the store was just closing, and the pair got to work.

They started attaching the cameras from Little Sister to walls and objects, making sure the store and major paths leading to it were covered by their cybernetic eyes. A quick call to little sister made sure the uplink was working. That done Maiyu found a place to watch the store and began carefully weaving an illusion to conceal her and her companion. After that all they could do was wait.

The occasional person passed by until almost twelve, but it was sometime after that before anything happened. Maiyu felt the hairs on the back of her neck rise, a sudden shiver shuddering up her spine as a surprisingly large group of people came up the store. They passed her and Kilala by without a glance. Nearly all the people moved with a grotesque jerkiness, like someone was pulling at their joints to get them to move. The exception was near the middle of the pack, bundled in layers of clothes and a ragged coat that swirled around their knees, rather inappropriate for the climate. The figure's head moved restlessly and as it turned to look in the hidden pair's direction Maiyu could see the wide grey eyes pulsing with a ghostly light. The group arrayed itself outside the convenience store, the bundled figure left at the back of the group.

'Go and mark this place!' The leader said throwing out a hand. The voice was female, answering one of Maiyu's questions. The woman paced back and forth as the group lurched forward and began to paint symbols on the store.

'I am going to take a closer look,' Maiyu's companion quietly announced.

'Wait, what are you...' she started to respond as the air around the other woman rippled, leaving a large black cat there instead. The cat jumped forward, the fluff on her body and forked tail flattening with the speed. Maiyu leaned back letting out a breath from between clenched teeth. *Reckless moggy! This is why you get attacked by robots.*

The short brunette watched the dark form of the Kilala cat move around the edges of the group as they continued to paint. Some tension fell from Maiyu's shoulders as they paid no attention to the feline, and a few minutes later Kilala came back to their hidden corner.

'There are sixteen,' she said changing back, though her eyes still flickered green. Maiyu nodded.

'Let's hope we get good looks at them,' she replied quietly, still focusing on the bizarre scene in front of them.

It was a good hour and a half before the group finished. Turning away from their handiwork the woman said, 'back to my sanctum.' In a group movement like a poorly done puppet show, they turned and walked almost in unison back the way they came. They left, leaving the hidden pair looking at a store once again covered in layers of painted symbols.

'Well that was creepy,' Kilala said, her voice almost bored. She stood from her crouch and stretched. She looked at the now repainted store wall. 'We should start cleaning that up, so we can get some sleep at some point.'

The next morning, they were both working in the herbal store. Maiyu watched her house-mate taking down earthenware and glass jars from the tops of shelves.

'How long did Sophie say she needed to identify the people in the video,' Kilala asked, carefully stepping down the ladder carrying several sealed jars.

'Should be this afternoon she said,' Maiyu squinted at the labels on the jars Kilala put on the shop counter. They were old enough to be labelled in Japanese rather than English. Considering the writer, their centuries old Sensei, it wasn't uncommon for recorded characters neither she nor Kilala could read.

Maiyu looked up as the bell above the door rang.

'Welcome to ...,' she cut herself off as she focused on the people entering the shop. The odd jerkiness of their movements set off internal alarm bells. Flicking her eyes over to Kilala, Maiyu noticed her intense stare.

'You will no longer interfere with the Haunt,' one said in a toneless voice, pointing and firing a small gun, but Maiyu was already moving, ducking behind the counter. A sharp cry from a male voice was masked by the grinding of stone as the store defences activated. Two muted whumphs sounded, one after another as beams of pale blue light hit two of the intruders as Maiyu glanced around the edge of the counter. They both fell to the floor joining their companion, taken out by Kilala, who now crouched over his prone form.

The sound of grinding stone started again, the two remaining intruders scattering in jerky fashion, like puppets pulled by impatient hands. One stepped around the counter, his movement adding force to a savage uppercut from Maiyu's fist. Dropping back into a crouch and massaging her knuckles, she heard the statue blast again. Five down. She was pretty sure that was how many had entered the shore. Carefully Maiyu looked past the counter and she began to stand before hearing a click and a gasp of pain behind her. Whirling, she saw the man she had punched, his right hand being crushed against his gun by Sensei. With a quick movement, the gunman was rendered unconscious.

'Really, Maiyu, you should pay more attention. 'he said chidingly, 'Who knows what could have happened if I had not come in just then. I shall plan some lessons on combat awareness.'

Maiyu felt her face heat as embarrassment overtook her, internally scolding herself for getting distracted.

'Well that answers the question of what you saw last night for certain,' Sensei mused looking at the fallen forms in the store.

'Some sort of mind control?' guessed Kilala, flexing her hands, trying to get rid of the claws she had sprouted.

'Yes,' Sensei said, 'Maiyu please get my kit from the backroom and Kilala call the police.'

'Shouldn't we leave this to the police, especially if we are calling them ourselves,' Maiyu asked quietly.

'The police are limited in their responses for situations like this. These people don't deserve to be killed because someone is controlling them. And to find the person controlling them we are going to need some blood from these poor people before the police get here.'

Maiyu nodded quickly going into the back room of the shop, and grabbed Sensei's kit before returning.

Dealing with the police took a good few hours, but soon Maiyu and Kilala were moving. The spell Sensei had created, and the information Little Sister got to them, led them to a warehouse in one of the industrial districts. The building was dilapidated, peeling paint and flickering lights, but there were people inside. Both young detectives scaled the fire escape on the outside, and entered from the roof. Soon they were crouched on a catwalk, above the main floor.

The warehouse was mostly empty and rundown, bathed in fitful electric lighting. The ground floor had a few boxes on one side, upon which could be seen several tins of paint. The floors and walls were covered is a crazed mish mash of words and symbols, scribbled in red. There was a chill in the air, and smelled like dust. On the office level, they could see a computer's monitor on.

Maiyu whispered 'they still have the power on? Odd.' She attached a camera to the catwalk, to cover the floor below. Part of the deal with Little Sister.

'Watch,' Kilala said quietly, eyes intent on the figures visible below. Most, around a dozen, were statue still while a single figure paced and ranted. The moving figure was shrouded in layers of clothing, obscuring form and face but Maiyu recognised the voice of the woman leading the people at the store.

'...darkness all around, consume us all...gates to the darkness below but no one ever sees...'

The figure continued to speak, weaving her way through the unmoving figures, waving her hands. Maiyu let out a long breath, considering the situation.

'You think you can take out the thralls?' She asked, looking at Kilala.

'Yeah, so long as you can take down Ms. Chatty down there,' the other woman looked eager, lines of green bleeding into grey eyes, body in tense lines, but waited for Maiyu's agreement.

'I'll wait here,' she continued, eyes locked below, 'You kick things off with this Haunt and I'll keep everyone else occupied.'

Nodding Maiyu slipped over the side of the catwalk, dropping to the floor into a convenient shadow. She continued to hear snippets of words from the still muttering sorceress. 'unknown forces... gates beyond... evil infecting...' Maiyu did her best to tune it out. What to do? Maiyu internally shrugged. It was somewhat against her nature, but sometimes the direct approach was best. She moved out of the shadows, walking right up to the heavily clad figure, without being noticed until she cleared her throat.

'Excuse me.' She said politely. 'You aren't very observant, are you?' Maiyu couldn't help commenting, the look of shock in the eyes of the swaddled figure was priceless. Haunt, stunned, was as still as the rest of the room.

'How dare...' her words were cut off by a feline scream, even the controlled people jerked to look over at Kilala in surprise. She was crouching over a now fallen figure and the entire room was shocked silent. That was broken as the dark-haired woman slammed a kick into a nearby thrall with bone shaking force.

'Deal with her,' Haunt shouted and the rest of the people moved into action, an army of marionettes lurching towards Kilala before turning back to face Maiyu.

The glaring woman threw a hand out, blue black energy flickering towards Maiyu. Dodging to the side, she felt a chill go up her spine, goose bumps rippling up her arms. Concentrating, Maiyu created a blur around herself, hazy images obscuring her position as she watched her opponent continued to throw blast after blast of skin crawling energy. A sharp cry from the brawl behind her made her flinch, and Maiyu found a blast coming straight for her. Crossing her hands over her chest she created a shield against the attack. Sweat appeared on Maiyu's face, the shield creaking and chills shivering up her spin as little bits of the bruise like energy bleed around the shield.

As the energy stopped Maiyu quickly threw out an illusion trying to distract her opponent so she could move further back. To her surprise Haunt flailed at the illusion, easily letting Maiyu move back, where her eyes narrowed. She flicked another illusion straight at Haunt and there was no resistance at all, her opponent flicking her head to the side in surprise before focusing back.

No defences, Maiyu thought, *maybe that isn't strange, this is all raw power and focus, no training. Takes about a second to wind up her blast.* Maiyu could see getting the time to build up an attack that could take the other woman down was difficult. Straight forward attacks like that were not her strength. *No defences, all attack. But if I try to directly physically attack her, I will be wearing one of those blasts.* She then recalled her sensei saying, 'If facing a strong attack, seek first to avoid it, and if that is not possible, seek to redirect it' *Yes, that should work.* Deciding on a plan, she watched for an opportunity. Haunt, shrieking curses and lost in her fury, sent blast after blast at her deceptive opponent.

Maiyu feigned that she was staggered by a near miss and, sensing an opening, Haunt pulled both hands back and focused an intense beam of light swallowing energy on her enemy. Maiyu threw up a shield, with a subtle variation. *I must make a good show of this.* This shield seemed incomplete, and started to buckle under the force of the continuous strikes, stretching apart like molten glass. It barely held, but the black magic built in strength, seeping around the shield, seeking weakness. Maiyu's senses in faded to darkness, pain radiating down her arms as if the bones were melting and warping. *A little longer. Now!* With a shout, she pushed at her magic, activated the effect she had prepared. Her shield snapped taut, and the power of the attacks backfired, straight back at Haunt.

The energy crackled black around the gaunt woman. With no defences, she took the full blast, and she threw her head back with a shriek before collapsing, curling upon herself. The sounds of fighting nearby cut off at the same moment. Looking over Maiyu saw all the other people had fallen, not even a groan coming from them, Kilala standing in the middle of the group, knuckles swollen and split. Smiling, she walked over, favouring her side a bit, eye swollen and lip bleeding.

'You ok?' Maiyu asked.

'Bruises,' was the reply, Kilala looked down at Haunt, 'damn I almost feel bad.' Black energy still discharged and curled from her still form. Amazingly, Haunt was still speaking.

Maiyu blinked confused for a second, then knelt down beside the curled-up figure of the fallen sorceress. With some effort, she could hear what Haunt was saying.

'No, I don't want to go into the darkness... it writhes...'

'Yeah,' Maiyu said grimacing, 'Looks like there is a good reason she got the powers she did. Control through fear.' She shook her head, before looking around.

'Check all of them to make sure none of them are too badly injured, I'll secure her, no reason to take any chances,' Maiyu said, feeling tired, 'I'll call the police as we leave.'

As they exited Maiyu dialled the emergency line on her cell phone. Focusing for a moment she waited for the call to be picked up and when she spoke a male voice came from her throat. Quickly weaving a story of a gang fight and injured people, and a crazy super powered individual, she gave the address and hung up. They continued out quickly and ended up standing at Maiyu's car. Holding her bike helmet under her arm Kilala put her hand under Maiyu's nose.

'The hell?' Maiyu asked squinted cross-eyed down at the proffered hand.

'I won, pay up,' Kilala said blandly and as Maiyu opened her mouth continued, 'and no saying that it wasn't bigger than you said it would. The store was attacked and we ended up dealing with a crazy woman with mind control powers. And it's your fault. You tempted fate, and here we are.'

Silence as Maiyu looked at the other woman incredulously, before muttering and reaching into her pocket for her wallet and handed the money over to Kilala. Who closed her hand around the money but continued to look at the shorter woman with raised eyebrows.

'Oh, for fucks... ok you were right and I was wrong. Your pre-cognitive abilities are beyond mine.'

Maiyu got into her car trying not to hear the sniggers behind her.

Later in the week, Maiyu and Kilala were summoned down into the gardens. Looking up as they entered, he began to speak.

'When you engaged this Haunt, most successfully I might add, you did take steps to be discreet, yes?

Both nodded in assent.

'Then, can you explain this?' Drawing their attention to a laptop with a paused video on its screen, he waited as they watched the short clip. Leaning over Sensei played the video. It showed the fight in the warehouse. Though low resolution it was surprisingly easy to follow. Except for the faces of both Maiyu and Kilala, which were obscured, blurred to unrecognisable blobs.

A neat piece of editing, Maiyu mused, goddamn it Sophie!

'Well,' she started to explain, 'Sophie kinda wanted to see what was going on so...'

'I see,' Sensei said, tapping his lips in thought, 'and you didn't think to ask what she wanted with such footage.'

'No, Sensei,' Maiyu said in a muted voice.

'I see,' he repeated, 'you are most lucky that Little Sister had some forethought in this matter. I doubt anything will happen in regards to this.'

There was a slight lessening of the tension in the air.

'From the law at least,' he said turning back to the video. The tension pinged back up, 'I believe we can learn much from this video. Shall we begin?'

When the Clocks Stop Dead
By Michael Huddlestone

Time is my faceless enemy; it must be written before it is too late. It has only been a few hours but already I find the fog of uncertainty clouding my memories. How long will it be before the fog takes me over completely? How long will I be able to remember? What happened tonight I must never forget.

Early memories of the night are little more than brief flashes swirling in the haze. Some are only sounds, like the ticking of the old grandfather clock echoing in the hallway. Its rhythmic beating heart slowed before it stopped. Other memories are visions; the sight of the old clock face, its second hand no longer moving. I raised my watch and compared the old clock's time to mine. They were in sync, right down to their second hand which pointed upward to the twelve. Stopped dead.

The last flash is the sensation of confusion mingled with fear and panic. The haze clears and I can see the open road laid out before me. I can feel it still pulling at me now as I write, consuming the memories of the night even as I struggle to keep my grasp on them. They slip through my fingers out into the fog.

I sat in the driver's seat, the gloom of the night shadowed the scenery from view. Headlights revealed the road ahead. My hands moved on the steering wheel as I allowed myself to be piloted by an unseen force towards a location I didn't know. I watched the speedometer, its needle moved up and down. Dropping as we entered bends, rising as we sped up along the straight roads. The dashboard clock did not tick over. Its numbers read the same every time I looked at it.

A faint tapping sound came from behind me, Dean, my ten-year-old son sat in the back seat. I watched him in the rear-view mirror. His emerald green eyes flickered, catching the moonlight. He looked as bewildered as I felt. Still, there was a sense of excitement and anticipation in the air of what lay before us. Silence remained. Throughout the entire journey, not a single word was spoken. It was as if we were monks on a pilgrimage to a holy landmark.

I remember being alone on the road at first. As the drive continued other cars began to join us in our unplanned journey. Our single pair of headlights became a convoy of lights. Like a funeral procession traveling in the night. Time was an illusion, gripped by the night. Its fingers holding fast to hours, minutes and seconds, refusing to let them go, but for what reason?

With each kilometre travelled I felt our destination approaching. The increasing tempo of Dean's tapping on the window told me he felt it too. Headlights revealed dense forest on each side of the winding road. It was a stark contrast to the wide rural farms that greeted us earlier. The echoing hum of car engines was the increasing tempo to the song's crescendo of our journey's end.

A strange sensation fell over me as we turned around the final bend in the road, we had arrived. The forest gave way to an enormous clearing, the size of a football field. Dean's tapping had become the fast beat of the drum. I drove to the far end of the field, turned off the headlights and the ignition. Dean stopped tapping.

A rush of cool air welcomed me as I opened the door. The procession followed my lead and as I watched, each car parked as if the field was a well-mapped car park. Each vehicle, in turn, turned off their ignition and lights. Their passengers emerged from the vehicles. Shadows grew. They reached out from the thicket until the clearing fell into darkness once more. While we were many, not a single sound heard, no-one dared speak. We watched and waited.

The night erupted into light as torches lit one by one along the left and the right side of the edges of the clearing. Each torch lit at timed intervals. Flames lashing upwards to the sky before simmering down to a small amber glow. In the end, the line of torches came together lighting a way through the undergrowth. Dean took my hand and we began to walk. As we drew near, other torches ignited. Their flames revealed an old cobblestone path through the undergrowth. The crowd gathered at the start of the path.

I felt a sense of unity as the crowd converged, moving with a hive-like mind. The crowd numbered in their hundreds. Men, women, children, old and young. A mix of strangers all sharing the same experience with the same expression that I had seen on Dean earlier. Bewilderment mixed with excited anticipation. The crowd moved like a snake along the path. Branches of the guarding trees hung low, my head almost not able to pass under them. It was as though the trees had grown from the earth to make this tunnel. Just for us. Just for this night.

At last, we arrived. The natural light of the torches gave way to modern flashing neon coloured lights. My eyes welled with pain, burnt by their brightness. As it subsided I discovered where it was our mysterious journey had led us.

The erratic notes of electronic music boomed from large speakers. The beat radiated up into my legs. Intertwined with the music came noise of other sounds. The echo of grinding of cogs. The mechanical hissing of hydraulics, and the low hum of motors as they turned chains and pulleys. The thundering roar of metal wheels on rickety rail tracks rattled overhead nearby.

Looking past the iron bars of the gate, the cobblestone path continued on. It weaved past sideshow rides, hot food vans and into a dark shadowy void. Beyond the path and amusements, I saw the faint glimmer of the moon reflecting on the water of a lake. It was only then I knew exactly where we were. We were stood at the entrance of the abandoned amusement park. I cannot remember what the name of it was, or exactly why it had been abandoned. All I can recall is that the park stood along the side of Lake Hampton, and abandoned shortly after opening. The kids at school used to tell ghosts stories about the place when I was young. I never believed in any of the stories but I know the place existed. There I was standing at its very gates. A park no longer abandoned with its ghosts, instead, a place brought to life but I fear, still haunted by the past.

The crowd paused at the closed iron gates, awaiting the park to bid us enter. The night air chilled me to the bone, I pulled Dean close to keep him warm. He wore a pair of action hero pyjamas with a black hooded jumper over the top. Unlike Dean, I was still in my day clothes. Dark denim jeans, a white and maroon quarter length sleeve tee shirt and unzipped jumper. Despite the jumper, the breeze cut through me like a knife. The wind was not natural, but something altogether different. Hairs on the back of my neck stood on end, I discovered I was powerless to turn and leave.

The grinding metal-on-metal sound took over the night. The large iron gates creaked open on their own accord. We all held our stance, the open park lay before us yet we awaited an invisible invitation to enter the grounds. Then I was gripped by the same feeling that I had experienced in the car. I had the sensation of being drawn in through the gate and I could not resist. I gripped Dean's hand tight and together we took our first steps into the park. The others followed. A horde of bewildered people entered the park. The hive-like mind took control, we stayed close to one other, all drawn in the same direction. A place deep in the dark shadowy void.

We passed through the line unmanned food vendors and player-less sideshow games. Moving ever forward along the cobblestone path. A large structure emerged from the shadows. My heart began to race again, we were close. As we approached, the neon lights disappeared behind us. Instead replaced with the natural warm light of newly lit torches. The dark structure towered high above us. The crowd split, passing into doorways in the stone building. I stepped out from the tunnels, my hand and cheeks stung as bitter cold kissed us welcome. We stood in a large clearing, the moonlight reflected on the water only a hundred meters away. I turned and saw that it was indeed like a colosseum with rows of plastic seating lining the stepped levels. The building almost surrounded the shoreline in the shape of a crescent moon. Large stone walls continued from the edges of the Colosseum until reaching the shoreline, a boundary between the arena and the park. All seating faced the vacant land that stood between it and the black waters of the lake. It was like a stage for some specific event. Flames danced along the placid water's edge, tongues of fire licking upwards in the night.

I stood lost in the motion of the black water, Dean pulled on my arm, my attention turned back towards rows of seating. I followed him as he led me up to the stone stairway. We ascended a flight of stairs before we turned to the right, two empty seats sat side by side. For the moment, the journey was over, we now waited to discover why we had been summoned. The torches grew dim.

Showtime.

'Ladies and gentlemen. Boys and girls,' a man's voice spoke. A deep rich tone that echoed from the shadows at the centre of the stage, where the light of the flames could not reach. I heard his voice long before I saw him. As he spoke the torches grew stronger and the shadows slowly crept into the night.

'Tonight, you have the honour to witness something kept secret from the world.' As the light grew, I began to see his vague outline standing in the centre of the Colosseum's arena, in front of the lapping edges of the lake.

'A battle which knows no beginning.' He paused, 'An unspoken feud which knows no end.' Through the shadows, I saw the outline of a top hat and long coat. The light's intensity grew. The figure stepped closer into the light, colour broke through the gloom. He wore high black leather boots with laces tied to the top, his black pants tucked in. Dressed in a long white dinner jacket and a crimson red vest which flashed a black buttoned shirt. He stepped closer to the seated crowd. His white skin glistened behind a black and white checked cravat tied around his bare neck. His shirt unbuttoned at the top with the collars turned up. Shadows from his black top hat shielded his face from sight. It had a satin band with a large red and black image on the front broach that shimmered in the light. I could not make out what it was. He was a haunting ringmaster and his audience was enthralled.

'*He* was taken as a child from this very place,' He stepped closer, pacing along the stage. 'Kept as their slave, groomed for battle on a single night of each year. His only crime...' The hairs on the back of my neck quivered as I waited for him to continue.

'Curiosity.' He gestured, 'a child's curiosity.' Goosebumps ran to crawl up my skin as I listened, thinking of my own son Dean. I gripped his hand tight. A quick glance at Dean's saw his emerald eyes fixated on the man. He didn't notice the skin of his hands turning white under my grip. I loosened my hold on his hand. A single thought took over my mind, my gaze shifted back to the ringmaster for answers.

Who were they?

Boots kicked up tiny swirls of dust as he paced from side to side, he spoke as if talking to each audience member. He approached our side of the complex. With the shadows thrown up by the torches and the mist that approached from the lake that swirled around him, I still could not see his face.

'*They*' he held the word, 'are a race as old as time.'

Had he taken my question from my mind?

'They live under the still surface of this lake, under the calm of all lakes. Existing far below where you, the land dwellers, will ever go. Far down in the depths where a culture of might and magic reign. You will have never seen them before, and will never see again.'

He turned, his back facing us, hands raised to the sky. 'Tonight, he will fight their champion for his freedom. Win and he will walk from here free.' He paused, his voice dropping to a more sombre tone 'Lose and he will stay their captive.' In his right hand, he held a black cane with a round silver handle.

'Prepare...' The ringmaster paused building intensity before continuing. '... to bear witness!' His voice boomed throughout the Colosseum. Torches surrounding the stage erupted with intensity illuminating the entire stage.

No words yet had escaped my lips, I was too enthralled and quite speechless. The sound of clapping echoed like rain. It grew with volume and intensity into a thunderous downpour. Others around me were clapping. Dean was slow clapping, and as my eyes fell to my hands, found that I too was applauding this grand introduction. The ringmaster, still his back towards us, took off his top hat. The white skin of his bald head glimmered in the light. It was as he turned I understood why I had not seen his face earlier. He had none. White flesh clung to the bone, moulded to give shadows where his eyes and nose should have been. His mouth was strips of torn flesh. A gasp was all that my lips could muster. The palms of my hands continued to beat against the other, their clapping guided by a mind of their own.

He returned his top hat to its place and stood still absorbing the crowd's ecstatic applause. With a large noise, he exploded into thousands of shadows, shooting out in every direction. The ground lay bare. The torches dimmed. A gong sounded in the distant. One strike. Two strike. Three strike. Then nothing but the echo of the last strike.

The final sound ricocheted off the colosseum's stone pillars. Each echo, softer than its predecessor, faded out across the lake and into the night. The silence unnerved me. We watched. We waited. The moonlight cast an almost black and white wash over the landscape with the faint hint of colour able to be seen thanks to in the dim glow of the torches. A loud splash broke the silence. I could see only the disturbance in the water, the broken moon's reflection on its surface.

Had something been thrown into the lake? I saw something hurtling through the air towards us. I grabbed Dean from beside me and shielded him with my own body. I closed my eyes and braced for impact.

It did not come. A wet thud sounded nearby instead. The moonlight revealed a body lying motionless on the stone steps. A tall, bearded man, water gleamed from his shaved head and bare chest. The crowd was silent, every bystander looked toward the still body. I held Dean back as he tried to get a better look. I watched for the man's chest to rise, a sign of life. Seconds seemed like minutes, still no movement. He wore only a pair black trousers greyed with age and torn at the knees. Leather bands cuffed his wrists and ankles. His muscular physique was noticeable, large biceps and ripped abdomen. In life, he would have been a formidable foe to even the most prized fighter. I rose and moved closer, I kept Dean behind me, blocking his view. As I approached the number scars on his body became noticeable. So many scars, so much pain. I found myself deep in speculation on the cause of each wound. Age was hard to determine. His long beard masked a majority of his face, signs of battle disguised the rest. If I had to guess, based on his appearance he would have been in his late twenties to mid-thirties. Though I still wouldn't wager on it.

Still no breath. A dark crimson pool began to seep out from beneath his shaved head. My question answered. Dead. I felt Dean behind me trying to get past to see. I turned to Dean and shielded his eyes from the sight. No child should ever have to see a dead body. I knelt in front of Dean. His eyes met mine. At first, they wavered, trying to look at what lay behind me.

'Don't look Dean.' It was the first words I had spoken in hours since this whole pilgrimage began. My voice was rough against my throat as I spoke. Dean didn't speak but his eyes remained on mine and acknowledged my request.

The buzz of the crowd sounded behind me. Their attention turned away from the dead body, back to the water. I turned, stood up, and tried to get a better view. Moving in the shadows something was rising from the still waters. It cast a silhouette against the light of the moon reflected off the lake. Water lapped against whatever it was. I heard a wet gurgling sound. It would sound, then stop, then sound again at set intervals.

It breathes. The torches that lit the stage grew in intensity, light swept over the new entrant. The crowd gasped in horror as a scream pierced the night.

It stood over seven feet tall judging from the nearby stone archway. It swayed as it stood, surveying the crowd. This was the creature from the black lagoon in every sense. Its dark green-brown skin shimmered with the reflection of the torches. Lake water dripped from its body. Scales covered its skin, each overlapping another. It had the muscular physique of a man, but its face, oh god its face, I pray one day to forget. It had large eyes, offset on each side of the creature's face like that of a fish, yet still quite humanoid. A long thin bone separated its eyes. It ran from a high needle-like point at the top and back of its head, all the way down to a lip-less mouth revealing sharp pointed teeth. Where the ears would be on a man, the creature had fin-like barbs flowing from the sides backwards. They swayed as the creature walked with a graceful flow. Moving like that of reeds swaying in the water as the current swept by.

Its arms rippled with well-built muscles. They bulged from its large round shoulders running down to its forearms. Fanned out fins ran along the back of its forearms. Each lined with sharp spines separating the fin's webbing, able to flex at will. I watched as they spread out then fall flat against the creature's arms. What caught my attention lay in the middle of its sculptured chest; a large bright yellow stone. At first, I thought my eyes were playing tricks on me, I saw fire, it burned deep within the stone. I stared at it, mesmerised by its life.

A second scream brought me back to the reality. The creature advanced towards the spectators, towards us. Dean gripped my hand as I did his, our bodies were frozen unable to move. To the right of us came movement, from where the dead body lay. I glanced down at the body of the man, he remained still. His eyes flashed open, I stumbled backwards. His eyes were a grey colour I had never seen before. He was alive.

But how?

The crimson pool was nowhere to be seen. He stared straight ahead, looking at the starry heavens above us. His right arm shot up, hand gripping on to the stair's railing. As I watched the muscles in his body tensed, as he pulled himself up. He rose to his full stature, he looked even taller than he had lying down. A giant of a man. His gaze swept the grounds before he fixated on the creature as it approached.

I was watching the standoff between the two foes when I noticed something about the man I hadn't earlier. His beard was flowing. It hung in the air as if it was smoke in the breeze or seaweed in the ocean. It had a life of its own. I slumped to my seat, my eyes transfixed on him as he descended the stairs, one step at a time. The realisation sank in. We indeed were witness to a secret buried deep within the stories of myths and legends. If what is happening to me now as I write this account is happening to the others, no wonder it has never been known.

My fingers ache, the pen continues to scratch at the paper leaving an ink trail in its wake. I struggle to keep going, I want to go back and read what I have written, but time is of the essence. I pause my thoughts, searching my memories. I find only emptiness, I have no recollection how I got to the colosseum. Only the sight of it before following the others into its dark tunnels. My mind is starting to feel like the dark emptiness of those tunnels. I pause but for a moment, clutching on to the memories as they fall like sand between my fingers. I must continue before my memories are lost. As his father, I can never be allowed to forget.

The man descended the final steps to the arena. He stood on the last step, motionless as the creature moved forward with caution. It swayed as it walked as if preparing for any attack. Inch by inch, I saw the man's beard grow before my eyes. The hair parted, binding together in strands like thick tentacles. These tentacles descended his body as if they were searching for something. They wound around a chair, gripping it tight. An ear-piercing shriek stung my ears, a battle cry from the creature. It charged towards the man. He held still.

Closer. Holding.

Closer, the man did not move a muscle. It was but a few yards away when the chair, torn from the grandstand, hurtled towards the charging beast.

What had my eyes seen?

His beard had torn the chair away from the stand and launched it at the beast with precision. The projectile colliding with its chest, propelling the creature backwards. The chair shattered into pieces of steel and plastic, debris rained down to the ground. A cry of pain resonated through the arena, overtaken by the cheering of the crowd. Injured, the creature lifted itself up and rested on its forearm. Its eyes focused on its opponent, cautious of his next attack. It gripped at its chest with its free webbed hand, ensuring that the stone was still intact.

Was the stone a vulnerability? Was that the creature's heart?

The man ran to the remnants of the chair scooping up two of pieces of steel leg piping. He took a fighter's stance as he brandished the weapons as batons. His beard once again moved, shortening, tying itself until formed that of the single plait. He was ready for the battle.

The creature rose, its hand felt across its chest, pulling a piece of debris lodged in the skin near fire stone. Blood trickled down from the wound. It tossed the piece to the ground it and let out another deafening war cry and ran towards its prey. The man followed suit. This was the commencement of two fighter war, a war which we have had the honour of being forced to watch. I say forced, as I found myself unable to look away.

Did I even try? The memories are unclear. I watched. I cheered.

Blow for blow, the two duelled around the arena. The man had his batons. The creature had discovered an old harpoon and carried it like a staff. Many attacks were hindered by defensive moves and counter attacks. Wounds were made as weapons sliced flesh, punches connected with ribs, kicks contacted bone. This dance of death held a strange mesmerising beauty as the fighters battled.

The creature broke the blow-for-blow deadlock with a counter move which captured the man off guard. The man hurtled across the arena with such a force that the aged stone wall he collided with crumbled. It smashed an entrance back to the amusement park. The creature charged towards its unconscious opponent. It approached and leapt high into the air confident of the final death blow. The harpoon shimmered in mid-air, held high above the creature's head with both hands aimed at the chest of the fallen. Time slowed as I watched for the finale of this battle. It was premature. He rolled away in time, sending the creature crashing into the stone rubble at full force. Its unshielded face collided with broken stone. The ground shook with the impact.

Standing, he grabbed the creature by the leg, throwing him across the arena with an inhuman strength I have never seen before. It clawed at the ground as it slid towards the lake, it stopped as the water lapped at its feet. The man turned and ran through the newly formed opening, escaping to a new battlefield.

Minutes passed as the creature lay there, the rise and fall of its chest slowed in tempo as it recovered its breath. It pushed itself up back onto its feet. Blood trickled down the side of its scaled face. Rage engulfed its expression as it increased its pace from a walk into a hunter's pursuit. It grabbed the fallen harpoon as it passed without missing beat, leaving the arena through the same shattered wall. The hunt was on. The crowd spilt from their seats. I grabbed Dean's hand and joined the wave of people as they flowed through the rocky opening.

Outside the colosseum, we followed the frantic sounds cracking of steel and shattering wood, finding the creature on the large carousel. It searched for his prey, tearing the crafted horses from their steel pillars. We surrounded him. We stood close enough to watch him, yet still at distance, none brave enough to step closer. The shadows beneath the carousel appeared to move, stretching out along the ground into the light.

A Snake? I questioned as it slithered into the neon light but it had a coarse texture like rope. It dawned on me as it wrapped itself around the creature's legs. The beard. A pair of silver grey eyes shone like cat's eyes from the shadows moments before the creature's legs were wrenched out from under it. The creature fell, colliding with a half-smashed horse. A faint spray of crimson splashed along the side one of the remaining white painted horses nearby. It screamed as it slammed onto the carousel floor. A broken steel pillar caught it by the shoulder. The grey eyes disappeared into the shadows, his tentacle-like beard followed. The crowd cheered, I heard my own voice amongst the chorus. I even heard Dean's tender voice scream out for his champion. I turned toward him as he stood by my side, guilt plagued me that his innocence was being taken by this night.

The creature groaned as it attempted to lift itself from the carousel floor. My eyes returned to the scene, guilt for Dean's lost innocence no longer had its hold on me. A hush swept through the onlookers. It rose half way before it stumbled forward collapsing over the edge of the carousel floor. It hung there, half on, half off. It fell to the ground under the weight of its own body. A puff of dust swept up as the creature's face collided with the dirt.

This was unexpected for the creature, having dominated the early stages of the battle. The tables had turned and caught it off guard. The crowd cautiously began to ease forward before they again retreated as the creature groggily arose to its knees. It balanced itself with one arm, palm to the ground. Its head slumped and swayed. I half expected it to fall again to the ground, instead, it stood up. A forward lunge before eventually it steadied its footing. A single breath escaped my lips in a quiet gasp as the creature lifted its head, its eyes rolled in its head, struggling to focus. A mass of skin and flesh hung from the side of its cheek, stained with blood that fell to the dirt. The white of its jagged teeth and exposed cheekbone glimmered amongst the scarlet liquid that stained all it touched. Its eyes found focus and scanned the crowd. Whoever eyes it met stumbled backwards to the safety of the masses. It stopped as its gaze met my own.

It held mine with a forceful, knowing intent. I held it, unable to move of my own volition. My breath caught fast in my chest, unable to be free. The murmur of the crowds and music of the park passed away, replaced by the rapid beat of my heart inside my ears.

A shimmer caught my attention. Behind the creature, to the right of the carousel behind the crowds, approaching fast. Our stare broke as a severed wooden horse head collided with the creature's head. Dazed for a moment the creature then spun around, hissing at its hidden attacker. Its eyes darted from left to right. The crowd all stepped back in unison. The carousel's lights flickered and its music erupted into life as it slowly began its melodious spin. The horses that remained began to steadily rise and fall with the beat. The creature limped cautiously forward then to the side, its nervous gaze searched for its ghost-like opponent. It didn't know where to look. I didn't know where to look. As the large amusement ride turned, I wondered if the bearded man was even there or whether it was yet another misdirection.

My answer came soon enough as the man leapt through the dark night sky the creature's own harpoon in hand. He must have taken it from where it landed while we watched the creature after his last attack. As he fell he howled, a battle cry that drowned out all other noise. He had hidden on the roof of the carousel, waiting for the perfect moment to strike. The creature looked up too late to defend itself. He was already on top of it, bringing the harpoon down onto the creatures already disfigured face. The sheer force of the blow broke the harpoon in half. The half with the harpoon head fell to the ground while he gripped tightly to the remaining wooden staff. He hit it again and again, each blow brought with it a new bloody wound, each brought a cry of pain from the crippled beast. The creature struggled to hold its stance. As it fell the man shot out his left hand, gripping it by the shoulder, his hold drawing blood. The man was merciless. His grey eyes flickered with a crazed filled rage that burned deep inside. Each blow fuelling the insanity that coursed through him. With each blow came a squelching sound of wood on flesh that made my stomach churn. I thought once again of Dean's lost innocence, but the thoughts were soon lost again to the brutal spectacle. A spray of blood expelled with each impact. Crimson droplets descended to the ground staining the earth as the staff was brought backwards only to be hurtled forward again. Blow after blow, time and time again.

The man dropped the broken staff to the ground, its blood-stained shaft was just as mangled as the beast from the sheer brutality of the rampage. He released his grip on the creature, it slumped down in a bloody heap to the ground. Its only movement was the rise and fall of its chest as it struggled with every breath. The bearded man stumbled backwards before he limped over towards the other piece of the broken harpoon. He picked it, his breath was short and erratic. He gripped the harpoon with both hands, thrusting the broken end deep into the earth. When he let it go and it remained upright, its steelhead pointing to the heavens. I knew what he was going to do, it filled me with an excitement I had not felt before, a mix of anticipation and disgust. My stomach churned again as I looked down at Dean, madness gripped him. I tried to pull him close, to shield his eyes from what was to happen. Dean swatted at my hands and pushed away from me. I had no choice but to stand back and let him watch it happen.

The man returned to the fallen, he leant down, gripping an arm and a leg of the creature. With a roar, the man hoisted the creature above his head. He staggered towards the mounted harpoon, a dead weight hovered above his head. The crowd erupted with cheers, all eyes were locked on him, we all waited for the final blow. He paused. The crowd fell silent. His muscles swelled under the weight. Blood and sweat ran from the creature, down his arms, forming river-like patterns as the mix spilt down his chest.

A cool breeze flowed from the lake as he lined up the harpoon, its point shimmered with a myriad of colours, reflecting the surrounding neon lights. In the final moments, even the amusement park's music fell silent, paused for what felt a lifetime. I took one last look at my son who stood out of reach. His last strand of innocence about to be taken. My heart sank. My eyes were pulled back to the man as if it couldn't happen without my gaze.

With a victorious roar, the man brought the creature down upon the harpoon tip. An inhuman blood-curdling scream exploded in the night, I gripped my ears as I felt them begin to bleed. The spear pierced the creature's body, impaling it. The battle was over. The fire stone within the creature's chest shattered. A single flame burnt high towards the heaven before it went dead, the shards falling to the ground. The man stumbled backwards, swayed as he stood in place. We watched on as the leather cuffs around his wrists and ankles fell to the floor by an unseen force. He looked down and saw his bare wrists, his eyes fell to the broken leather reminders of his captivity. I wasn't sure what he would do or what would happen next. By his expression I don't think he did either. His grey eyes scanned the crowd. I noticed glimpses of confusion beginning to set in as if he wasn't sure what had just happened.

The man took one last look at his fallen opponent before he pulled his gaze away from the bloody stained mass towards the entrance to the park. Slowly, he began to walk towards it as if called by a voice far away. With each step, he straightened, his head held high. A victor's walk. As he neared the crowd separated allowing him to the past. At first, it was a single clap, followed by another, soon the entire audience was clapping, their champion walked with pride towards freedom.

As I stood applauding, I felt as though the sensation that had kept me so engaged in the battle was lifting from me. It was time to go. I dreaded seeing the face of my Dean after all he had seen. I reached blindly for Dean's hand to lead him to the car, nothing returned my grasp. I turned and looked where he once stood. He wasn't there. My eyes darted from side to side. He was gone. My heart felt like it stopped and plunged deep into the pit of my stomach. The crowd were taking their leave. I surveyed the multitude of nameless faces, Dean was not there.

'Dean!' I yelled. No reply. Thoughts of how he may have got caught in the crowd surge only eased my panic slightly, I had yet to feel my heart beat again.

'Dean!' I screamed his name again. The crowd were oblivious to my screams, still locked in a trance as they departed the amusement park. I pushed past those nearby as I frantically searched for my son. Thoughts how I should have made him stay close flooded my mind, how I should have forced him to not watch.

The wave of people passed. I fell back from the masses, my steps stopped dead as I spun hoping for a familiar figure. Nothing. I trailed the rest of the crowd as they made their way to the front gates, leaving the carousel behind me. I pulled at my hair, my mind screamed at me.

What have you done?

With a final glance behind, before I ran back to the crowd to search for him outside, my gaze swept across the empty carnival. They finally fell on moving shadows. Three creatures appeared ahead of me, walking near to the colosseum, their fallen comrade carried between them. They were heading back to the lake. Ahead of them were two more, they also were carrying something. A large shape, a bag, it squirmed, something fought to get out.

'Oh, my god… Dean!' I screamed as I ran towards them. Panic made me run faster than I ever had before. With each stride, the shock of impact shot up my shins as they ached. Closer. Closer. I was gaining on them, but they were almost at the broken wall. Before I could reach them, the creatures disappeared back into the colosseum carrying Dean.

I launched myself through the remnants of the broken wall, cutting my hand on the jiggered edges as I pushed past. I searched the vacant arena for any trace of my son, only to be met with the sight of rippled reflection of the moon, shimmering on the lake. He was gone. My son was gone. Taken by them.

I stood there in shock, for how long I cannot remember as the clouds of fog continue to settle in my mind. All I remember is that I heard the faint tick of my watch, felt the tiny vibration on my wrist. The second hand moved before stopping again. It was no longer paused, yet still, it moved ever so slowly.

Was time beginning to return to normal? The sky began to fade in light shades of the night as morning approached. My feet were guided, being led by that unseen force that also called out to the champion. With each step, the pain that pulled at my heart and turned my stomach eased as if I was being drugged. The memory of my son being taken was still vivid, yet I felt nothing.

I passed through the front gate on the way back to my car, none of the others were nearby yet I did not feel alone. I sensed someone else was there. I turned, on my left was a young boy, no older than ten, sat with his back against the stone gate pillar his head was bowed buried in his pulled-up knees. I knelt beside the young boy.

'Are you alone' he nodded without raising his head.

'Do you need a lift home?' The young boy raised his eyes to mine. I gasped. As I understood all that occurred. Everything was connected. Grey eyes stared back at me, not sharing my newfound knowledge, instead, confusion was impressed across his now young face.

'Come with me, I'll take you home' He rose to his feet and as we walked I asked one final question, 'What is your name?' There was a pause before the child finally spoke.

'Dean.'

Sleep is overtaking me now. I sit here still writing, the pen falters, its ink trail stalling. My hand aches with pain, yet I know not why. I stare at the words on the page, not reading them instead I battle with my own mind. I struggle to write these final words.

Why did I begin to write? When did I start? I have no recollection of this at all. Work will have to wait as I don't feel myself. My eyelids are heavy as I stare blankly at the paper. My heart beats steadily in my chest, beating almost in time with the ticking of the grandfather clock down the hallway that echoes faintly. It is a welcomed sound as if reminds me that life continues despite the confusion that currently is swamping at my mind. Looking around my study where I now sit, I see two feet on the lounge arm nearby, my son Dean is asleep. A strange confusion sweeps over me as I look at him though. It is as if I am looking at a child I only just met, yet the photos on the wall confirm that he is my child. On my desk, there is a photo of Dean and I at an amusement park earlier in the year, a lake glimmering behind us. We are both smiling, a happy day. Dean has always made me smile. He has a sense about him, a soul older than his years. I find myself staring at the photo, his grey eyes stare back at me. Eyes that seem to bear witness to something, something long passed and hidden. A secret. Maybe one day when I read exactly what I have written in the early hours of this morning I will understand but for now, I sleep.

Broken Home
By Kate Grenenger

A crash of porcelain came aloud from the downstairs kitchen. A woman gasps in fear, her sobs choked and silenced by the sound of her own drowned apologies. A thump rattles dust from the deepest crevices of the house as grey clouds with distant rumbles gather above the small two story home before it erupts into chaos. Lidia cowers in the corner of her dully lit bedroom, watching the clouds cast shadows on the polished timber floorboards, before wavering over onto the large white rug caught between her white metal bed, and the only way of escape, the closed door.

"Damn It Bridget!" Another muffled thump and a scream erupts under the crack of the door where the only light source invaded her darkness. Lidia had ran, a memory of her footsteps pounding against hollow stairs. Her breath quickens as she whispers to herself.

"It's ok, It's ok." Her blonde hair clouded her vision as it piles in her lap rocking back and forth. Caught in the corner of her lavender-grey bedroom, the beach styled louvers of her white wardrobe dig deep into the side of her spine, though her pain did not matter right now. She was waiting it out, frozen in fear with her knees tucked up to her chest whilst she watched the walls she called home fall down around her. A fist plastered through the dry wall down below, almost like taking a single straw out of a hay-house. Lidia chokes on a squeal and forces her head down further wondering just how many hits it could take before the entire house collapsed inwards, killing them all.

"I told you a thousand times! I told you—" Her fathers voice bellows. He was always like this when he came home, whiskey hung on every breath, and if she clenched her eyes hard enough perhaps she would not see the twinge of hate in his eyes when he looked at her.

"How could you?" A broken plea, just audible through the walls, echoing through the crack in the door. She looks up, cheeks salted and arms tingling in a cold heat where she had clung so tightly to her knees. Her white crochet cardigan now sunken into the darkness behind her, her tanned three quarter jeans just standing out in the fading sunset. Lidia looks at the long body mirror, her reflection staring back at her. Blonde rib-length hair, braided roughly down the left side, tucked up over her ear and her fringe just covering the bruise beneath her left eye. She was a mess, red cheeks, tired eyes, mascara smeared leaving black patches of soaked misery. Lidia couldn't stand it when they fought, when his fist met the walls and caused destruction, when he tore this house apart with his words and bare hands. Sniffling wetly she glances over to the black cat sitting on top of her sanded oak dresser, tail counting down the seconds before the next blow of bone against plaster. His yellow eyes look at her, piercing, sharp and unrelenting.

"Here puss-puss .." Lidia whispered, clicking her middle finger and thumb together with an extended arm towards the small animal as her mothers muffled cries wail through the house once more. A soft meow and the resentment to move itself is all Lidia receives from the cat. Leaning forward on her ankles, her left hand grips the rail of her double bed, she stands, intending to make a move towards the creature in an attempt to gain comfort. She steps forward, the cat jerking its head at the movement, eyes widening sharply in a definite objection. He did not want her love today. Taking another step towards the creature, her foot crunches on a shard of glass. Lidia hisses, pain spiking in the ball of her foot, mouth gapped wide as she twists her knee up to grab the base of her ankle. A small trickle of blood dribbles its way down the middle of her sole, but thankfully no glass had made a home beneath her broken skin. She was quick to piece the puzzle together, remembering the perfume bottle she had knocked over practicing her senior high prom routine last Friday night - just in case she had the honour of being asked to dance, though what chances did she have. Lidia softly lowers her heal to the ground, careful to not jar her foot any further, before preparing to step towards the cat. A soft protested meow and an extended jaw of teeth caught the glimmer of the grey sky, its tail tapping faster against the oak drawers as if warning her. Chester was good for that, being a black cat it was in his blood to be superstitious.

"Oh stop it." Lidia sniffles before the cat hisses back at her. The latches on the bay windows give way in a rusted screech, the curtains blown inwards with a sudden breeze, snapping Lidia's head towards the racket. The breeze blows the crevices of the dark wooden floorboards in a soft whistle as she watches the cloud of twisted dust and dirt roll across the room to rest in the skirting panel of the wardrobe. Frowning softly, Lidia wipes away the tear tracks that had dried upon her cheeks as the world comes to a silent end.

"You can be happy you know."

A soft, tender voice of a thirteen year old girl murmured in the silence, immediately twisting Lidia's head to the long body mirror at the end of her wardrobe door. Her reflection, not like herself, sat cowered on the ground, hugging her knees to her chest, hiding her blonde hair, much like she had just a moment before. Lidia's thoughts began to run as she stood frozen, unable to move, listening to the sound of her own heart pounding like a marching drum in her ears. Slowly lifting its head, the reflection allows itself to look up at Lidia, eyes crimson red and swirling in a smokey haze. A sharp inhale in and Lidia prepares to scream at the top of her lungs — No this wasn't happening.

"They won't hear you here."

"Our father who aren't in heaven—" Lidia slams her eyes closed and begins to ramble in fear, clutching at the golden cross wrapped around her neck.

"He won't hear you either." Fresh tears threaten to fall under the glimmer of the grey afternoon light.

"Careful now." The girl warns, voice soft and tender as the cat hisses in protest of their new guest, his back arching in spikes of ruffled black fur. His back leg throws a red-leather bound book from the drawers, before taking off under the bed in a cluttered thump. The book now lay open and bridged with crumpled pages and bent edges. Lidia glances towards the baseball bat resting against the end post of her bed, eyes shifting back at the mirror before returning her gaze to the bat.

"You don't have to suffer you know. All this.." It pauses, eyes unyielding to break their gaze as they swirl in crimson horror. "I can make it all go away." Lidia shifts back slightly, left hand tucked behind her back, glancing at the door as she fumbles for the bat. A metal rattle against the white metal frame told her she had found it. The cold chill of metal on skin provided her a comfort, knowing that she held the upper power. Wrapping her fingers around it she lifts the head from the floor in solid preparation —

"Do you really want to risk it?" It warns, eyes darting between Lidia's skinny legs, watching the bat twitch in time with her racing pulse.

"Risk what?" Lidia plays cooly, desperately trying to still the shaking of her hand in an attempt to silence the metal bat from colliding with other objects.

"Your happiness." It stated clearly, it's eyes unwilling to leave hers as a chill runs down her body, leaving her breath coming out in a cold fogged pant. The blonde hairs on her arms begin to rise on the islands of goose pimples as if warning her.

"You're not real." Lidia snaps, face breaking up in emotion, eyes threatening to burst at the streams as her mother wails in the background under another thunderous punch of the walls. Dust falls from the ceiling as she looks up watching it as if it were snow, though this was the falling of misery and nothing more.

"I'm everything you wanted your life to be."

"No." A simple answer formed the words in her throat, as she swung the weighted weapon around her right side and into the mirrored glass, shattering the centre. Her mother cries and begs her father to stop once more in the wake of her destruction. The house shakes again, dust falling from the crevices of the timber sledged cathedral ceiling before the world falls silent. The reflection no other than herself.

Lidia crouches down before the mirror. Her reflection multiplied in random broken shards as she looks closer, her nose an inch from the shattered remains. Blue eyes cast there glance back at her and for a moment she breathed a sigh of relief. She glances away, eyes dashing to meet the two green eyes smouldering beneath the bed, watching closely but never moving, never leaving. Chester knew, he always knew. A soft breath whispers against the hairs on her neck. Lidia snaps her head back to the mirror. Red eyes multiply through the broken reflection. Lidia squeals, jolting back and falling on bare glass, legs scattering through the clinking of crystallised shards before a pale blue hand shoots outwards grabbing her by the left ankle, pulling her back. Shards of glass slice her back and thighs in thin streaks of pain. Chester groans on a harsh meow followed by a sharp hiss, his teeth bare in the light, tail pounding down the final seconds. The girl's black hair showered out, wet, tangled and unkept as Lidia watched her ankle disappear through the blackness of the mirror.

"Mum!" She screamed, making it clear she was still here. The spirit drags Lidia torso deep before yanking her into the darkness, shattered glass falling like snow before razor sharp teeth and glowing red eyes bare down on her face. Lidia screams loud enough to hear, but no one came running to her aid to save her from the darkness that had swallowed her whole.

Leaves prickle against her back as Lidia lies still. Beneath the shade of the cool old oak tree branches sway in the wind as she glances around. Two, dark dots centre her vision and as she tries to blink them away she realises she cannot blink. A small child laughs in the distance, her happiness muffling Lidia's fear, leaving her to only feel the warmth of the afternoon sun as it bares down on the cold purple sky.

"Lidia, come on now." A male's voice murmured, soft and caring. "It's getting cold." Wait was that her fathers voice calling to her? She tried to open her mouth to reply, only she could not.

"Coming Daddy, just let me get Peaches." Warm hands grip her right side beneath her armpits as her head lulls back like a swing falling backwards in slow motion. She felt the height as leaves tumbled away in her absence. The blonde girl giggles, hair falling in her face as she is lifted higher in her fathers sudden embrace. Lidia's arms were lifeless and her head ungodly light, she wanted to scream as she tried to focus through the bouncing vibration of the surrounding world as her materialised cheek is pressed between the little girl and her father, their hearts beating against either side of her head.

Autumn reds, and dusted blue skies become wooden panelled walls as the fly-screen door came to a tender close. It's dark, wooden door soon shutting the world outside as the brass pin lock slid in place in a rustled scrape. The earth lowered, and the ceiling heightened, as the girls black polished ballerina shoes hit the floor in a soft clunk and one heart beat departed, leaving her cheek feeling oddly cold.

"Run along now Lidia." The small child with eyes sky blue looked up at her father, kind, caring and full of love. A father that looked like, well, her own. His head neatly shaven and stubble encasing his jaw, sweeping down to his neck before escaping on smoothed skin into his neatly buttoned, white chefs shirt. "Dinner will soon be ready." He spoke evenly, as if there was nothing in the world that was bothering him. His eyes were rid of the black bags that she knew so easily. Through buttoned eyes, Lidia attempts to piece the pieces together as if they were some kind of broken puzzle in need of fixing — That was before he twirls out of her vision in a twister of ash and her head bounces loosely to the skipping beat of her keeper. Surely if she were real, her neck would snap off, but today she felt no pain. The white door she knew so well bypassed her head as it slipped shut and the silence began to ring.

"Let's put you down." The little girl spoke as she positioned her rag doll at the end of her bed, propped up against the wall. The mirror that she swore she had smashed stands whole beside the last louver of her Hampton styled closet. Lidia looks at the little girl face on, her button eyes unmoving, her limbs now still as she realised she is looking at a seven year old version of herself. "Don't move, I'll be right back." The little girl announces with her hands held out in front of her, pulsing as if nearly sure Lidia was going to run away, or fall off the bed. Lidia remembers when she used to care for her belongings, now she lives in the fear of losing everything she once held onto. The small child twists and runs across the white mat, darting out the door, and leaving it ajar at the slightest. A relief tingled through Lidia's body as she began to feel the weight of her bones return to her. She glances down to the black and white checkered dress covering her body, to the black and white stitched ballet shoes enclosing her feet. There's red wool fraying her vision in what can only be described as her hair. Lidia turns her head to the side, dismissing the orders of the small child, hearing the distinct tug of stitches and stuffing as she captures her reflection in the mirror. A small doll, perched at the end of a perfectly made bed, sheets ironed in a way she was not use to. Deciding to test the truth of the mirror, she lifts a fingerless hand and waves at her reflection, her head lolling to her left shoulder, her stitched mouth lifts in a soft smile as she finally realises, she was alive.

"It's not real kid." Comes a raspy voice from down below, beneath the mattress and as her button eyes stare at the reflection in the mirror, a blue furred hand snakes itself out from between the bars of the white metal bed frame- her bed frame. Her mouth tries to part, but Lidia is soon aware it can not.

"I know you can't talk, so let me tell you what you need to do." He pauses as he hears thundering footsteps running down the stairs at the call of her mothers voice. "You need to run." But it all seemed so perfect, her dad acknowledged her, played with her, everything looked picture perfect — "It's not all it seems. Your family" He sighs as he leans his tattered head against a post in the middle of the bed end and quite frankly she couldn't work out what he was —"Your real family is missing you." She feels a small stitch unwind in her heart at the thought of them.

"At Midnight, this portal will open and you will have a choice. You'll have 10 minutes. You can stay, or you can go." He pauses as she watches the small creature grip the white iron bars and pull himself over into the white slip of afternoon light, skidding beneath the bed. He was a bear, a tattered blue bear no bigger than the child's small hand - his fur showing no other signs other than pure love. His brown glass eyes glistened in the suns dying purple gaze as he muttered. "You go, and you return back to your normal life. You stay and you turn into her. You get to watch yourself grow up, be happy, your parents stay together …and this house stays alive. The grass is greener here, the tree's forever have leaves and they will always love you." If she had actual eyes she did not doubt that her tears would be non-existent. It was everything she ever —

"The choice is yours kid." — wanted. The little girl's footsteps shadow beneath the crack of the door on the outside as Lidia drops back into position at the creak of its hinges. A small hand sneaks around the white wooden door before emerging with a bright smile.

"You did it!" She bounced, as if she knew so well of her little conversation with the bear beneath her bed. The plastic pink teapot she held clattered against the door as she slipped the latch closed. She knelt at the white play table in the centre of the room, carefully plonking the purple flowered teapot in the middle, water splashing out the spout before the little girl pounced onto the bed and hauled Lidia lifelessly down to thin air. Lidia's legs dangle briefly before she is perched in a pale blue plastic chair, her eyes in line with the harsh edge of the rounded plastic table.

"There we are …Would you like some tea Miss Peaches?" The little girl questioned, kneeling on the rough tainted white carpet rug with a smile as bright as the sun. Its light capturing the gap in her teeth that Lidia remembered having before the days of dental wires and rubber bands. A white small teacup imprinted with a yellow daisy in the centre is pressed against Lidia's stitched smile before a drop of water seeps though the material and she laps internally for more. For a moment she wonders her decision as the child removes the cup and casts her eyes back to pouring herself a drink. Lidia cast a quick glance to the blue bear twisting beneath the bed, his eyes glassy and tinted maroon in the suns dying rest. He gives her an attempted thumbs up before she returns to her mannequin-like posture. She only then notices, watching how happy the child-like version of herself is, that she was somehow caught between a nightmare and a lost dream.

An hour passed and Lidia had sat watching the child scribble on an old drawing pad in coloured crayons of yellow, green, bright blues and purples. It was a drawing of her family. Her mother, drawn as a pink stick figure with a belly triangle dress, her father, blue with purple pants and an orange shirt, whilst she drew herself in orange and pink with blue shoes and yellow hair being hoisted up between the two by her arms. They all had smiles etched on there faces. Behind her the grass was green and the sun was hoisted high on the top right corner of the page burning bright in a twisted swirl of orange and yellow. It was perfect; the perfect life, the perfect family. She felt a love she had never felt as the smell of a roast dinner wafts beneath the door. The kind cooked in oil, with vegetables roasted in the fatty remains.

"Lidia, dinner!" Her mother called, before the girl jumped, grabbing her rag dolls arm once more, knocking her head against the table carelessly before hurrying out the door. The stairs came unexpected as her mind raced to try and keep up. She glances around the corner as her escort slowed down in declined preparation, capturing a solid glance at the bear as he scoots back into the shadows. Her head jostles in a scurried zigzag motion as her keepers polished shoes skip down the dark timber staircase, its skirting left staggering in her vision of never ending patterns. She is hauled into the kitchen and left swaying by one arm, her body turning ever so gently. The little girl pulls her chair back just as her mother puts the roast on the table.

"Looks beautiful sweetie." Her father remarks, giving her mother a gentle kiss on the cheek.

"Thank you honey." And she was genuinely happy. Lidia crawls into her chair, placing her doll on the spare seat beside her as she listens to her family say grace. They were thankful, and they were happy.

At night when the sun was at rest, they tucked her in with her rag doll by her side and a kiss on the head. It was pretty special, to feel that kind of love when you weren't even real. The lights went out and the moonlight filled the room with the occasional tussle of the purple curtain drapes. The little girl lay with her back against the doll and Lidia wondered if the life she had here was really worth staying. Her five hours were coming to a close and she knew her decision needed to be made.

The moon stood tall in the sky, it's luminance ricocheting off the black button of her right eye as the child rolled over tenderly, pushing the small doll down the side of the bed. The crumpled sheets consuming her like quicksand in a desert as she comes alive to catch herself on padded hands and hard dusted floors before standing tall. The wooden slates were padded between swirls of metal springs and the floor was cut angled between the moonlight and the darkness. She needed to choose one side, but for now she walked over to the tattered bear, resting her fingerless hand on his shoulder before he whispers.

"Almost time kid." He doesn't look at her, instead he stares ahead at the musty pink wall clock sitting on top of her chest of drawers, resting against the wal,l ticking away in the ringing of the silence. It's time reading ten to twelve — "What will it be?" Lidia looks at the two of them in the mirror, before walking out into the open space of the bedroom, her left foot backing into the white plastic post of the play table as she stares at the restful child. Everything was perfect here. They loved her, they played with her and they loved each other, but her real mother needed her. Lidia walks back beneath the bed to look at the bear as he hands her a pale yellow sticky note, folded and stuck together with the helping of a few stray pieces of mattered blue fluff.

"Don't open it until you get back." He warns, voice stern as he refuses to part his grip on the paper until she nods. The bottom corner of the mirror cracks and bleeds a beaming light blue. "Now go kid, before it's too late." She nods at him before her hands grip the cold bars of the bed frame and she steps up onto the bar off the ground like a sailer on a boat, parting for greater seas. Her mind screams at her to stay, to save herself from the nightmare on the other side of the mirror, but she couldn't live with herself if she left her mother to suffer alone. Lidia jumps down and lightly walks over to the mirror, her button eyes and fluffy red hair reflecting who she truly was, fake. She crouches down, her tender arms removing the shard of cracked glass before the light comes pouring out to flood the corner of her room she knew so well. Lidia presses her left leg into the mirror, watching it disappear in slow, eager anticipation, before she ducks under the triangular glass archway, disappearing into the light.

Lidia emerges through the darkness, her hands landing on the remnants of shattered glass, cutting her palms and staining the floor in smeared shades of red. Her stomach tears in pings of sharp pain, pieces of broken glass fall to the floor as she returns to the darkness of her room, pulling herself free from the mirror's hold. The note she holds, is still in her left hand as she stands and looks at herself once more. She was human, she had ten fingers, a mouth to smile with and a heartbeat she could feel. Lidia folds the note in her hands contemplating the words that lay behind the folded piece. Could a bear even write, and if it could what would it say? Lidia dismisses her fears and unfolds the sticky note, listening as it catches on the remains of his mattered fluff before glancing at the note in utter confusion. It was blank. That was before the letters began to place themselves one inked letter at a time on the page.

> *"Tattered gowns and broken crowns, what had taken you down?*
> *A fathers hate, a twisted fate, that you refused to let drown.*
> *The perfect life, free of knives wasn't enough to make you stay.*
> *Take these shards, bury them in the yard on the return of your*
> *seventh day."*

Lidia glances around, realising her room had not changed at all. It was still dark, dim and mostly in grey. Her mother still cried in her room. She stepped outside, her hand hesitant to twist the brass handle and open her world to her mothers exposed wails. Her eyes meet the darkened hallway. Her feet stalked slowly down the hall. The picture frames that once hung straight on the walls, now hung slanted, or worse scattered on the floor. The clouded sun had casted a grey shadow throughout the house, though that didn't bother her, for there was never any colour in this house. Her mother sobs from the last door on the right as Lidia pauses at the top of the staircase, her sadness tearing her heart apart once again. She knew it would take more than a safety pin to pin the pieces of her brokenness back together now. Slowly, she walks down the stairs as hands protrude from the walls, almost as if they were made of pale blue latex. Desperate to get out, their voices whispering in echoed murmur as they follow her down.

"*You did this. Listen to her. It's. All. On. You.*" Tears sting her eyes as they laugh chaotically in demonic distances.

On the seventh day, Lidia returns from school, sweeps the shards into an old creme tank top, careful not to miss a piece before knotting the top and stepping out into the hall. She walks the living room, her hand carefully guiding over the torn brown leather couch, almost in fear that it too would break apart under her touch. She slips into the kitchen hallway. There are holes in the walls, cracks and more shattered glass. The back door screeches on it's hinges as it swings softly, left ajar to reveal a stormy sky. Her mother howls aloud once more as Lidia stands before it, watching it sway invitingly, waiting for her to step outside. It wasn't hard for her to draw the conclusion that her father had once again walked out and left them alone. Though he would be back, he always came back, and that was the fear. Her left foot met the outside deck before the tank top yanks itself back and throws itself from her grip, shards of glass stabbing into the blank wall of their dining room. Her head snaps back as a gasp falls from her lips, her eyes capturing the words formed on the wall, *"It's all on you."* Her eyes barely had the time to read before they fell to the ground in a resounding shatter, and her mother appeared on the staircase.

"What's wrong?" She all but shrieked, her hands now trembling as she perched herself on the bottom step, fragile hands gripping the rail. She looked so broken, her hair tattered, unbrushed, and her eyes sunken and wrinkled behind bags of heartbreak.

"I broke the mirror. It's ok, I'll clean it up." Lidia began, forgetting how broken her own voice sounded. "You should go back to sleep." Her mother nods, pulling her white woollen nightgown tighter across her chest before taking herself up a few steps.

"Hey Mum," Lidia began, she stopped, glancing at her daughter "I love you." Lidia reminded. Her mothers smile tainted on her features to which she replies.

"I love you too." Before her feet carry her upstairs. Lidia sweeps the shards back into the top and takes them outside, this time with ease. Her feet patter down the wooden steps and walk the dusted spikes of their dying lawn as she stands beneath the shade of the twisted oak tree that had lost its leaves in the autumn months. Lidia drops to her knees, the lumpy shirt discarded by her side as she digs her hands through grass roots and dry soil. Her hands cast a hole as deep as half her forearm before she drags the shattered remains into the hole and begins to sweep the clump of dirt between her knees in and around, securing the hole and burying the evidence. Lidia runs inside, her feet pounding up the stairs before she stands at her mothers door, her hand hesitant, left hovering above the oil marked brass handle. Lidia sighs and twists the handle. Leaving the door ajar, she crawled into the bed and held her mother close, holding her through her broken sobs.

"You had your chance." Her voice mumbles into the pillow that had clogged her face and made it hard to hear her.

"What." Replied Lidia softly, lifting her head off her mother and allowing her to breathe.

"That mirror I gave you when you were seven ...She showed you a better life." Her mother sobbed through her explanation, the tears rushed down her face. "Why'd you come back?" It was a fair question, only a madman would throw away the perfect life for something so messy, so broken. Lidia had no words, no explanation. Her mother knew of the mirrored deals as if she too had made a decision once upon a time.

"My heart wanted to come home." The words left her lips before she could realise the full truth of her explanation to all her madness.

An hour passed and her mother had slipped into an exhausted slumber, her tears now still behind closed eyes as Lidia returned to her bedroom. Turning to close the door, she listens for the soft click before turning to look at her room. Everything was the same as it had been just seven days ago. The play table she once sat at, stood still in the middle of her white rug, the pink clock, still leant against the wall. Lidia walks over to the corner of her wardrobe and wedges herself around the mirror before turning and walking herself back into the corner she knew all to well in this world. She gasps, her eyes not believing what they were seeing. The mirror was made whole again as she stared at her reflection once more. Her left foot grazes against something fluffy beneath the bed. Her back met the white wall and she slides herself down to the floor, looking between the rails to see the dark blue curve of a stuffed hand resting against the metal rung. Her hand reaches out to snatch the small bear she had once spoken to before putting him in her lap, her eyes catching on the bundled note snagged to his mattered and dusted fur. His head lolls back lifelessly. Lidia can't stop the flow of tears, wedging her palms into her eyes in distress. Chester bounces back on top of her oak drawerss as she takes the final note from his hand and unfolds it. Twelve words stared back at her as her brain racked itself to make sense of it.

"You came to me in pieces, so I could make you whole."

It all made sense. Things weren't always perfect, but everything was repairable, even if it was through stitches, torn clothing and broken glass. This was her home.

Omens - A Haiku

Birds, bats and black cats
Portrait falling off the wall
Death is coming soon

- Leigh-Anne Robinson

About
Townsville Speculative Fiction

Established in early 2014, a small group of writers came together, emerging from the shadows of their own writing journeys all with a common interest.

Speculative Fiction

An umbrella genre given to collectively describe works in the genres of Science Fiction, Fantasy, Superhero Fiction, Science Fantasy, Horror, Supernatural Fiction, Utopian, Dystopian, Alternate History, Steam Punk, Apocalyptic and Post-Apocalyptic.

We discovered that by discussing ideas with like-minded writers we could flesh out their story and develop as writers. And so Townsville Speculative Fiction (TSF) was born. We are a writers group, who are a part of the Townsville Writers and Publishers Centre (TWPC).

We started out with only a handful of members, today in 2017 we currently have 20+ active members and meet on a fortnightly basis. If you can image it, we probably have someone who writes it. Most of us have manuscripts on the go, some have already self-published, and we all knock out short stories when inspiration hits.

Check us out on our website or Facebook to keep up to date with us strange individuals and our projects.

http://www.townsvillespecfiction.com

Other Anthologies by TSF

A SHORT STORY ANTHOLOGY

THE

TYPHON EXPANSE

TF

TOWNSVILLE SPECULATIVE FICTION

The Typhon Expanse

Welcome to the Future

For nearly a hundred and fifty years the Terran Union, born of the fires of nuclear terrorism and fear of the other, has expanded across space despite all opposition, all threats real or imagined. In the build up to cataclysmic war, the Typhon expanse, rich in resources and filled with enemies. becomes the staging ground for a conflict between civilizations.

This anthology's stories tell some of the tales of the Union in its relentless advance. Stories include:

- A survey captain's descent into madness, losing his soul to an alien horror *(The Echo of Nothing by Michael Huddlestone)*

- A young alien girl discovering that good intentions pave the way to hell *(The Alien Integration Act by Ash Rutherford)*

- An orphan turned assassin on a colony world finding her place *(To Be the Surgeon by Michelle Mullins)*

- An unexpected leader joins the fight for freedom on the red planet, and beyond. *(The Queen of Mars by Marc Murkin)*

- An oppressive corporation on an irradiated, barren world grinding its workers down, and the beginning of their heroic response. *(The Dawn of Change by Joelle Cronin)*

- The violent backlash on an orbital farming colony, in response to worldwide attacks on Earth *(Sunraysia by Chris Picone)*

- Intrigue and suspense on the day the apocalypse came calling. *(Ghosts of the Past by William Elliot)*

- A young hacker, pursued by a relentless gestapo-like police, seeking escape for her and her AI companion *(The Chase by Terry Mullins)*

- An AI, finding itself in the one human polity to defy the Union. *(Jelana by Stephen Ryan)*

And more in The Typhon Expanse.

About
Townsville Writers and Publishers Centre

The Townsville Writers & Publishers Centre is a not-for-profit organisation that promotes a north Queensland culture of writing.

The TWPC was established in 2011 to bring the same opportunites to regional north Queensland writers that already existed in captial cities. Since its conception, the TWPC has established a number of faciliated writers' groups which members are welcome to attend and learn from other like-minded writers.

The Centre also hosts a bumper calendar of events and resources in our region. Here are just of the events, services and information offered by the centre:

      Manuscript assessments and mentoring
      Connection to writing and publishing opportunities
      Access to the Australian Writers Market Place
      Shut & Write facilitated group writing sessions
      Writers Workshops
      Writers Retreats

The Centre also partners with Townsville City Council, CitiLibaries Townsville and Queensland Writers Centre to help shine a light of writers in North Queensland.

Our office is located in the middle of the creative hub at Riverway Arts Centre, Kirwan.

Find the TWPC on facebook or at www.twpc.org

About
TWPC Writers Groups

TWPC's facilitated writers groups cover a variety of different genre's and writing styles. Here is the list of our current Writers' Groups:

ROMANCE & COMMERCIAL FICTION – A group where romance writers and writers of Commercial fiction are more that welcome to share works and advice.

VERB WRITERS GROUP - For writers and poets who are interested in connecting with like-minded creatives, developing skills and receiving feedback.

TOWNSVILLE SPECULATIVE FICTION - This group dips into all genres of fantasy and fiction, and offers support and publishing opportunities.

KID'S LIT GROUP - For writers and illustrators of children's and middle grade books, this group offers support and opportunities to develop skills.

EMERGE WRITERS GROUP - An after school program offering educational workshops to those between 13 and 17 years of age.